Praise for Horowitz's Previous Novel, *The Book of Zev*

A spellbinding story of international intrigue, suspense, love, and survival. Prepare for sleepless nights.
– Larry D. Thompson, bestselling author of *The Insanity Plea*

Sometimes a woman's gotta do what a woman's gotta do. A sharp psychological thriller of high intellect about a woman making some hard choices for the right reasons to stop an international catastrophe.
– Omar Tyree, *New York Times* bestselling author of *The Traveler: Welcome to Dubai*

Marilyn Horowitz paints a rich picture of a lapsed Jew, angels, and people having miraculous abilities to survive, foretell, and sometimes alter the future. Her book plays at the borders of the normal and the supernormal, of lust and faith, while focusing on each character's struggles with his or her purpose in life.
– Dennis Shasha, coauthor of *Iraq's Last Jews*

A well-constructed story. The parts that describe Sarah's cooking are mouthwatering, you can almost hear Zev's mother's voice nagging at him and see his father's disapproving frown. It's a slow burn of a novel, dependable in its telling, and possessing a solid payout at the end.
– *San Francisco Book Review*

A New York City story, *The Book of Zev* by Marilyn Horowitz is a dark comedy and mystery featuring an earnest dropout from religious life who becomes a taxi driver
chef named Sarah who is angry at God a
wine. These two get entwined in an int

and with each other. The author, who teaches screenwriting at NYU, creates characters on the borders of Jewish life with uncommon abilities to predict the future, all the while grappling with questions of faith and purpose.

– *The Jewish Week*

This book grabbed from the very beginning ... and didn't let go until the very end! While most suspense novels might tell stories to shock & awe, Marilyn Horowitz tells stories to engage & enroll the reader into the possibilities of what her characters face.

– TR Garland

Wow! What a nail-biter! Just when you think you have what is happening figured out, you are thrown a new twist to the story. Marilyn Horowitz is a masterful weaver of the elements that make up a great tale: action, suspense, humor, romance, internal conflicts. Enjoy!

– P. Murphy

Bad Girl Pie

A Novel

Previous Titles

Word of the Day: Transform Your Writing in 15 Minutes a Day
ISBN-10: 1803415169

The Book of Zev
ISBN-10: 1940192781

How to Write a Screenplay in 10 Weeks
ISBN-10: 1466317515

The 4 Magic Questions of Screenwriting
ISBN-10: 1466315695

Sell Your Screenplay in 30 Days: Using New Media
by Marilyn Horowitz and Paula Landry
ISBN-10: 1542904625

How to Write a Screenplay Using the Horowitz System:
The High School Edition
ISBN-10: 0979908922

How to Write a Screenplay Using the Horowitz System:
The Middle School Edition
ISBN-10: 0979908930

Bad Girl Pie

A Novel

Marilyn Horowitz

ROUNDFIRE
BOOKS

London, UK
Washington, DC, USA

First published by Roundfire Books, 2025
Roundfire Books is an imprint of Collective Ink Ltd.,
Unit 11, Shepperton House, 89 Shepperton Road, London, N1 3DF
office@collectiveinkbooks.com
www.collectiveinkbooks.com
www.roundfire-books.com

For distributor details and how to order please visit the 'Ordering' section on our website.

Text copyright: Marilyn Horowitz 2024

ISBN: 978 1 80341 763 9
978 1 80341 799 8 (ebook)
Library of Congress Control Number: 2024932635

All rights reserved. Except for brief quotations in critical articles or reviews, no part of this book may be reproduced in any manner without prior written permission from the publishers.

The rights of Marilyn Horowitz as author have been asserted in accordance with the Copyright, Designs and Patents Act 1988.

A CIP catalogue record for this book is available from the British Library.

Design: Lapiz Digital Services

UK: Printed and bound by CPI Group (UK) Ltd, Croydon, CR0 4YY
Printed in North America by CPI GPS partners

We operate a distinctive and ethical publishing philosophy in all areas of our business, from our global network of authors to production and worldwide distribution.

Contents

Chapters 1–40	1–244
Tango Glossary	250
Appendix: Outline of *Just Dessert*	251
Dessert Recipes 1–11	257
About the Author	274

My deepest thanks: I couldn't have done it without you!

Robert Browne
Jafe Campbell
Aileen Crow
Paula Landry
Adam Nadler
Wayne Nelson
Martin Sherlock
Cathy Shikler
Carol Woien
and
The Creator and Those Who Watch Over Me

Chapter 1

I stopped talk therapy when Aunt Cindy fell and broke her hip last year. She's my mother's sister and my godmother. She's tall and slim, with stormy ocean eyes, and wears her silver hair in a flapper-style bob with bangs.

In the ambulance, I asked her, "What happened?"

She looked at me in disgust and said, "You're always so effing morbid. Just like your mother, may she rest in peace. If you want the gory details, go read the report. If I repeat it, I'm making it happen again."

After that, I stopped talking about my own past and asking people for details about their current tragedies. Soon, my tendency to create a worst-case scenario out of every event dwindled and I began to sleep more. But between me and myself, I clung to my story like it was a life preserver, because if I didn't, I'd lose my identity, such as it was.

Why we had to begin life in this format of birth had always baffled me. Where was the upside? Why not just be born later in the first place, maybe at eighteen, so that there was a better chance of not having to spend your adult life recovering from the scars of bartering pieces of your identity for survival? Everyone I worked with had been crushed in the battle to survive infancy and childhood, and spent the rest of their lives recovering from it. It was the human condition. I had faith in a larger force, but if He was most high, then whose stupid idea had that been?

As a child, I'd written down everything my parents said, so that when I was accused of something, I could go into my notebook and quote them verbatim. Both narcissists, they lied to protect their fantasy of being "good" parents, often at my expense.

I had a similar mistrust of my self-involved clients. I recorded them in case there was ever a dispute, and later molded their words into the perfect answers to my questions. My outline was the skeleton and muscles; their words supplied the flesh that covered the carcass.

It was now 4:00 a.m., and my Manhattan kitchen was warm and cozy. I was pulling my second all-nighter, fueled by Coke Zero and coffee. I wrote frantically at my large freestanding island covered in butcher block. My feet rested on a small sky-blue rug embroidered with a life-size Yorkshire terrier. My beloved Yorkie, the late Toro, was always with me in spirit. I caught sight of myself in the bottom of one of the shiny copper pots that hung from a cast-iron rack above me: pointy face, horn-rimmed cat-eye readers, and an oversize pink Food Channel sweat suit.

The island was surrounded by professional-quality appliances as I often had to verify recipes for the various celebrities I wrote cookbooks for. Outside my West Village window, a steely moon glinted off the dark winter waters of the Hudson River.

This epic was my tenth celebrity cookbook-memoir. My current client, Babette LeBlanc, a successful Creole actress, was a tall, voluptuous redhead with a booming voice and a keto-cooking show on the Food Channel. The face she presented to the public was slim and wholesome, but she'd put on weight and was concerned that they wouldn't renew the show since she was no longer a poster child for the food she was promoting. A book was the solution.

Babette's mind was a fractured mosaic cobbled together of snippets from her many award-winning performances. I'd studied her movies and could pick up which role she was playing each time I interviewed her. It was hard to get someone to be themselves when there was no self, but I don't like it easy. I'd created a complete, albeit imaginary, person for this

Chapter 1

cookbook-memoir; someone sane, supportive and admirable, a role model for women everywhere.

She had a raging ego that defended her persona with vigor. I'd fought hard to connect with the neglected, angry inner child who would do anything to get attention. Babette was like a fluffy cat who longed to be patted but, when you did, would hiss and bite. Luckily, she liked catnip, and a few glasses of Pinot Noir created an artificial consistency of personality that I could build a story around.

Babette was going through a bad breakup, and half of my work was letting her rant about her ratbag ex. No matter who was to blame, fat and forty was a scary place for any woman to be. We'd finally had a little talk over dinner at a Cajun restaurant on Greenwich Avenue. I waited until she'd finished the bottle of wine I'd ordered, then leaned forward and spoke when she took a breath between epithets.

"Okay, Babette, I get it. He's a jerk. However, the words you use make your future, so you get to choose which movie you want to be in. It's your narrative. Do you want to portray yourself as a victim or a victor?" She didn't get it, so I attempted an analogy.

"Are you a natural redhead?"

She looked at me scornfully. "No, *cher*, of course not."

"But you are a successful actress who is known for her beautiful red hair."

"So?"

"You made a choice about your hair color. Making a decision about who you want to be in your own life is no different. Redhead or blonde, everything is a choice." After I repeated the concept of personal agency ten or twenty times using different analogies, we parted. I was ready to quit the whole project.

The next morning, as I picked up the phone to resign, I got a Zoom invitation from Babette.

"*Bon matin*! I just hired me a new lawyer, *cher*, and got that hound on his back foot. I am ready to work."

That made me happy. I was furious with women who played the financial victim when breaking up. Effing men. But I digress.

Our collaboration went so well that Babette was inspired to actually read a book! It was a bestseller written by a woman who had traveled to discover new recipes between stops at various ashrams. Reading can be dangerous, make no mistake. Babette was so excited about understanding "choice" that she wanted to change our book. I had to talk her off of the ledge.

"You'll lose your audience."

"But I want to help people, *cher*. You know what a big heart I have."

I don't argue with self-appointed deities and offered a fake smile and an encouraging nod.

"Yes, but the author you admire is running a Ponzi scheme. It's a book about a woman who pretends to pursue enlightenment yet manages to stay blissfully asleep. She's using her reader to validate her own lack of awareness, and passing it off as wisdom. The book is a manual for how to justify being an unwitting victim." I made air quotes with my fingers as I said, "Unwitting."

Babette fluffed her hair proudly and thumped her chest with a red-tipped fist. "I am nobody's victim!"

"That was the point of the hair-color analogy. *Brava!*" I applauded.

"I can do better by sharing my recipes?"

"And losing those extra pounds. Maybe you can write a follow-up book on using dessert to lose weight."

"And alligators can fly. Ha, that's a good one, *cher*."

I typed the final line: "And all that I've learned has led me to appreciate my life. The End."

I took off the pair of Babette's green lizard spike heels I'd worn while writing her magnum opus. I was a Method writer, an actress with a pen. I submerged myself in the personality of the subject whose story I was writing. Wearing the subject's shoes was the doorway into his or her mind. As long as I wore them, I could tune into the owner's subconscious as I moved my fingers across the keyboard. The shoes stayed until I wrote the first draft. Afterward, I carefully bagged and tagged them and stored them on metal shoe racks in the coat closet near my front door. Ten pairs, one from the subject of each of my books. The closet was my morgue. I knew that I would spend the next two weeks pulling her shrapnel out of my brain.

I spell-checked the manuscript and was about to hit "send" when a wave of nausea washed over me. I ran to the bathroom, which seemed to belong to a different soul than the kitchen. Beige, with white tile, no photos or pictures. I didn't want to remember myself when I was in there. I threw up in the toilet, which more than once had been my partner in crime. Those days were long gone, but I still reacted this way when upset.

Projectile vomit mixed with tears. My guts clenched like an angry snake and I fought for breath. It's not easy to cry and barf at the same time, but as I said, I've never gone for easy.

After I cleaned up, I showered and ran spell-check again. As I sent the manuscript off to Suzanne Rotstein, my agent, she called me. Suzanne was a great agent and a dear friend. We talked every morning when I was on a project, which was most of the time.

"Hi, Suzanne."

"Are you trying to kill me?"

"I just sent it."

"You missed your deadline — again!"

"I'm sorry. What should I do?"

"I covered for you."

"Thank you."

"But it's got to stop. You have a problem. Maybe some therapy would help?"

"Maybe realistic deadlines would help?"

"Touché! So, what was this idea of getting skinny by eating dessert?"

"It was a joke. Babette thought it was pretty funny."

"I think it sounds pretty intriguing. What's the premise?"

"The premise for a bad joke?" I riffed, "You know that cliché: 'Life is short, eat dessert first'? By reframing what's important, you can learn to eat so-called fattening foods using portion control. Since you eat what you want first, you'll naturally eat less of everything else. That's actually how I became slim. And blah, blah, blah…"

Suzanne gasped. "Really? When were you…"

"… fat? Until my second year of college. I lost over twenty pounds."

"That's brilliant. Keep it to yourself. I could do something with that concept."

"I need a rest."

"No, you don't. You need to crank out another one for me."

"Why would I say yes?"

"You have a gift for managing difficult people."

"Ha. I get it. I'm a difficult subject. That doesn't mean I want to use my gift on myself."

"You owe me."

"Okay, but I'm not detoxed from Babette." I held my breath, waiting for the fireworks.

"Look, Dots, my ass is on the line here."

"I'll do a crappy job."

"Please. I'll get you a nice bonus," Suzanne wheedled.

It was hard to refuse when she was being nice, but I knew my limits. I changed the subject.

"So, Suzanne, how're you doing otherwise?"

Big tears flowed. "I can't believe Gus is gone."

"I'm so sorry."

"Seventeen years together. Now every day is torture."

Chapter 1

"I know. It's only been a few months. It'll get better with time."

A long pause, then in a quiet voice, she asked, "Please? I'll owe you."

I paused for a moment. "No, I'm sorry. I only want to give you my best."

"Fuck your best."

The line went dead. Suzanne had been recently widowed, and it hadn't improved her manners. Her philandering, abusive husband had spent the past year dying painfully from testicular cancer. It seemed karmically fair for him to have been destroyed by the weapon he used on the people who'd loved him.

Chapter 2

I dreamt that I was walking through the hallway of a mortuary that had steel doors with nameplates of the refrigerated corpses which lay inside. I saw my name on a door and opened it. My body lay on a gurney, but I had no face. I screamed and woke myself up, as a hollow voice shouted, "If you don't write your own book, you'll become a ghost!" It was as loud as someone yelling from across the room. The sunlight made the experience less terrifying, but when I heard imaginary voices in my dreams, they were red alerts. I had a flash of insight: I defined myself by what I did, not by who I was.

I hurriedly dressed and put on flat, ugly Australian sheepskin boots and went out into a glittering day that hurt my eyes. As I crossed Seventh Avenue and 20th Street, I saw a pretty coffee-colored woman wearing a T-shirt that read, "Don't look back, you're not going that way." She had no winter jacket, so I assumed she was homeless or stayed at the shelter on 14th Street. I offered her a five-dollar bill and asked if I could take her photo.

"Yeah, five times," she said as she snatched the bill from my hand. "Where do you want the pictures?"

I pointed to a restaurant on the corner, behind which you could see the river. She posed with great enthusiasm. I got a candid shot of her talking to me and pointing a finger with a big smile. I gave her a thumbs-up, and she curtsied.

I asked, "What's your name?"

"Dorothy."

"Me, too," I smiled.

She pointed at the shirt and smiled, too. "Get moving, namesake. You look like you're going the wrong way."

A cold finger touched my spine. She was right. I was putting off the inevitable. Time to visit my father, Norman. I took an Uber to his farmhouse in New Jersey.

Chapter 2

When I was twelve, Norman gave me a 20-gauge rifle as a birthday gift, then took me hunting. It was the same age his own father had taken him hunting, and my dad wanted to share this with me. I had beginner's luck and found myself in a position to kill a deer, but I'd refused. My father was furious and accused me of being a girl. I didn't get the irony of this until later. He then murdered the deer, and I had nightmares for weeks. I refused to eat any of my father's latest victim, even after Aunt Cindy explained that if the meat nourished me, then the deer's death hadn't been in vain. Thank goodness he hadn't kept the poor beast's head.

It was during this visit that I understood why I had yet to find lasting happiness with a man: in the cage that hung from the living-room ceiling, instead of Heloise and Hector, the emerald-green, orange and white lovebirds Annette, my late stepmother, had adored, Hector was alone.

My father didn't like animals unless he was hunting them. In fact, my birth parents had divorced partly because of my mother's propensity toward menagerie — in her case, three cats stuffed into a modest suburban home along with one child and a dog.

Ironically, my father's new place now had the same cluttered feeling. My stepmother, Annette, a ringer for my real mother, had crowded my father's house with hundreds of crystal cat figurines posed in every way you could imagine; the only rooms immune from this invasion were the living room and guest bathroom. My father had escaped my mother's insanity and live zoo only to replace it with this woman's craziness and a pet family of another kind. At least these didn't pee on the carpet or try to sleep on his head.

Annette, dark-haired and sultry until she'd put on weight, had spent a year in a mental hospital as a teenager. She'd been abused by her own father and the resulting spawn died in childbirth. My father's scorn for her was part of the initial attraction, but was also part of the reason she'd gotten early dementia, and why she'd committed suicide. Fragile at the best of times, she'd just run out of energy dealing with this hostile creature that was supposed to be her partner but acted like her enemy.

Liz, my mother, had also attempted suicide, but in the end had succumbed to natural causes. Annette succeeded just in time to miss my father's cancer drama. The cause of the illness in both women was the same: marriage to my father. I'd watched them both go crazy with disappointment and resentment. I was the lucky one. I suffered from depression and an eating disorder, but I'd never tried to off myself. My open wound was a crippling distrust of men. I hoped to heal myself through the mechanism of tango.

At one point, I even took medication for my depression. I got off the pills after a trip to Paris, where I had terrifying recurrent dreams of Nazi minions marching into the town square beneath our hotel and mowing everyone down. My boyfriend at the time was an actor-dancer, gifted at accents.

From the moment I confided my dreams, he spoke in an exaggerated German accent, which increased my panic. He found my discomfort funny.

The boyfriend also drank a lot and, after a seven-course meal with friends, taunted me by insisting that the Nazis were coming to get me. He goose-stepped around the hotel room until I told him to shut it! Then he called me a bitch and came at me, intending harm. My right hand magically formed itself into a fist, and I punched him squarely in the jaw, knocking him to the floor. He cracked his skull badly enough to need an X-ray, and the German accent stopped for the duration.

For those who enjoy physical comedy, I'm a four-foot, eleven-inch blonde dwarf with large breasts that seem to have been stolen from a porn star while they were drunk. The boyfriend was six feet and 210 pounds. He "forgave" me, and I stayed

Chapter 2

with him for the rest of the trip for the sex. Since familiarity breeds contempt, it was a perfect fit.

But back to the lovebird. It bears repeating — the lovebird. Singular. That's what I couldn't get over. There should have been two lovebirds in that cage. Since my last visit, my father's bed had been moved from the upstairs bedroom to the living room, and set up where the couch had once been. The cage was at the foot of his bed.

My father was wasting away from lung cancer, and had gotten worse since I'd last seen him. As he lay in bed, he looked like a concentration-camp survivor, no longer the loud, fat bully with football shoulders. His passion was hunting, and he alternated complaining endlessly about no longer being able to indulge in his favorite pastime, and repeating the stories of how he'd caught each of the stuffed, mounted deer heads that covered the living-room walls.

As I entered, he opened his eyes and said, "I thought you were going to wait until I was dead."

"I had to turn in a manuscript. I'm sorry. How're you feeling?"

"You couldn't pick up the phone?"

"Where's Jada?"

"She's shopping. At least someone cares about me."

Someone you pay, I thought, and found my way to a straight chair.

"What happened to Heloise?" I asked my father.

"Oh, she died. Now there's only Hector."

Hector gave me a forlorn look and hunkered down in a corner of his cage.

"When are you getting him a new mate?"

"I'm not," he snarled.

"Lovebirds need a mate or they die."

"Yes, now you've got it. I'm just waiting for it to die."

"Why not put him up for adoption?"

11

He gave me an evil grin. "Annette liked the birds, but now she's gone."

"I see, a little postmortem payback."

"You know me well."

"Too well," I responded. "And how're you planning to facilitate that goal?"

He caught my suspicious tone. He knew that I knew what he was capable of. The petty bastard. He smirked at me. "No, I'm not shooting him. He'll die of a broken heart soon enough."

I studied my prick father's smug face. He was pleased with himself. I realized in a flash that he despised everyone, including me. It was a painful moment.

"I'll take Hector, find him a home." I went to get a ladder to get the bird down from the ceiling. Norman kept my childhood rifle next to his bed, because it was all he could manage now. He pointed the rifle straight at Hector.

"You try anything, I'll shoot it with your little gun," he said.

"It's not loaded, Dad."

"Really?"

"C'mon, you said you wouldn't hurt him. Dad, put it down."

He shot at the glass front cabinet Annette had kept full of crystal figurines. The sound of breaking glass was deafening. The sunlight glinted on the explosion of shards and broken cat statues that covered the floor. Hector cowered in his cage, and Norman aimed the gun at the little creature.

"You thought you'd call my bluff. I'll blast him, so help me. Ha, the joke's on you!"

"I guess you'd rather be right than happy," I said as I reached and opened the front door.

"Damn right, you stupid cunt," he shouted, then lay back, exhausted, holding the rifle tightly.

"Give me the gun." I turned towards him as Jada, Dad's home aide, a tall, elegant Jamaican woman, came through the

Chapter 2

door carrying groceries, which she dropped at the sight of the carnage.

"Mi mumma! What in the hell happened here?" She looked at me accusingly. "What did you say to him?"

"Nothing. He wouldn't let me take Hector."

She spoke in a lilting Jamaican accent laced with disbelief. "You fought over the bird?"

I nodded. She nodded back, and stared nervously at the shattered breakfront.

Norman shouted, "Get the hell out, Blot."

Something snapped in me, and I literally saw a bloody fog settle over the room. The gun was aimed at me, but I was too mad to care.

I got in his face. "Are you planning to shoot me with my own gun?"

He cocked it with a murderous look in his eyes. I wasn't taking any chances and grabbed the barrel so hard that Norman fell out of bed. He wore a diaper, which erupted as he hit the floor, spewing smelly feces, which mixed with the stench of used gunpowder. Even so, he was still the hateful monster I'd grown up with.

"Jada, help me," he whined.

As she rushed to his side, Norman glared at me. I matched his look as I emptied the weapon. I pointed to where he'd had my initials engraved on the barrel.

"I believe this is mine."

"No. Give it back."

"No."

I stood near the doorway with the door open. The room stank. I dialed for a car while Jada cleaned up.

"Jada, please make sure Hector's fed and has water. I'm taking this, because he'll shoot at you next."

She nodded, because she knew I was right. "No problem, I'll make sure the bird is fed."

I gave her a twenty, and she tucked it away in her bra.

"Thank you, Jada. I'll see you tomorrow."

When I got home, I put the thing in the front closet, behind the shoe rack, the ammo nearby. The odor of his incontinence permeated my clothes and hair. I showered. When I'd helped Jada lift Norman back onto the bed, I'd touched his dirty diaper, and would never forget the slimy texture of his excrement.

I had to work at something. Babette's book was still short by one dessert. I hated cooking, and farmed out much of the food testing now that I was more successful, but tonight I needed to engage in some banal, mindless task. I would test this one myself. Over dinner, I'd once asked Babette if she had a comfort food, a polite way of asking why she had gotten portly.

Babette laughed and said, "Yes, *cher*, I call it 'the lousy lay.' I put everything sweet I have in the house, chop it up, add bourbon and whipped cream into a pie pan. Add a pinch of cayenne pepper so that bad boy bites you back. Bake at 350 degrees for 30 minutes and eat the whole thing." This concoction definitely needed a new name: Bad Girl Pie. Suzanne would love it.

I never kept anything sweet in the house, so I thumbed through the manuscript to see what her basic dessert recipes included. No wonder she kept adding pounds. The list included pecans, powdered sugar, chocolate and cream. I made a list and tried not to think about my dad.

"No," Cassandra, my truth-telling aspect, yelled in my mind, "DO NOT CALL HIM D.A.D. Call him Norman to keep your distance. Remember that remembering isn't an innocent act; it doubles the power of what has occurred, for good or for bad."

Jada called me after midnight to say that Norman was failing.

"Why call me after what happened today?"

"He asks for you, Miss Dots. He no want the others."

I grabbed an Uber. As I entered, the lights were off and Jada was dozing in a chair next to him. An ugly urine-colored moon

Chapter 2

lit the room. I felt that I was in a black-and-white episode of that old TV show, *The Twilight Zone.*

I sent Jada to bed and said nice things to Hector as I watched over my dad. It got to be 5:00 a.m. and I dozed.

My father moaned, and I leaped to my feet at the sound. His eyes were open, glinting at me like one of the animals he'd hunted. His chest heaved in spite of the oxygen feed; his eyes bulged in terror.

"Water, Blots," he whispered hoarsely. "For shit's sake, water."

I got him a glass with a straw and aimed it so that he could drink. He sucked hard at the straw and gripped my hand holding the glass. His breath was foul. He looked up at me.

"I love you," he whispered, and sipped the last of the water.

"More water?"

He shook his head. "Did you hear what I said?"

"Yes, but that's not going to get you into heaven."

His eyes pleaded with me.

I shook my head. "Sorry, I don't love you back. Hector was the last straw."

He closed his eyes and a tear slipped down his cheek.

"Forgive me then."

"No."

"A dying man's wish."

He almost had me, but my rage at him for trying to play me one last time saved me.

"No."

His eyes begged, but I shook my head. "I'm going to find Hector a home."

I went to get the ladder to take Hector's cage down, and when I returned, Norman had passed on. I felt nothing. At least he'd closed his own eyes.

When it got light, I called Suzanne.

"What's up? I stepped out of a meeting."

"At 7:00 a.m.? My father just died. Will you come to the funeral?"

"I'm so sorry, Dots, got clients in town, so I won't be able to attend the funeral."

"How can you say that? I don't know when it is yet."

Suzanne hurried on. "Okay, then let me know. I have great news! The publisher loves the manuscript! He said that Babette is an inspiration to all women and has a great voice."

Babette's voice? I should have gotten an Oscar for my written portrayal. I shuddered as I remembered the faceless body from my dream. I was wasting the only thing anyone ever had: my own time. On top of that, my supposed best friend wasn't coming to the funeral.

Wow.

I had supported Suzanne while Gus wasted away from cancer. When he died, she'd asked me to come to the funeral home to help wash and dress his remains. And of course, I'd attended her shiva every day of the seven days. I felt betrayed that I didn't matter enough to her for her to attend.

Suzanne said, "I'll send a huge wreath. Oh, and Babette wants her shoes back."

Fat chance.

I left Jada to deal with the funeral home, and took Hector.

Chapter 3

Natasha was my Russian dance pal, a timelessly beautiful therapist with perfect blonde Heidi braids. She had a thick accent, and I loved to listen to her talk. We attended tango events together, and when we went to a *milonga*, we both danced constantly because we attracted different leaders. She owned a pair of lovebirds, and had told me recently that her male bird had died.

I called her. "Hi, Natasha. Are you in session?"

"No, haven't started for the day. What's wrong? You sound terrible."

"My father just died. Hector, his lovebird, needs a home. Did you replace..." I couldn't remember her late lovebird's name.

"Sergei. No, why don't you come by?"

Natasha worked from home, and her Upper East Side apartment had black leather couches and African statues from a recent trip. She kept the lovebird cage in her office area, as the birds soothed her patients.

I stood in her doorway, holding Hector's cage. I'd used my coat to cover it and shivered in yesterday's sweat suit. As soon as she saw me, Natasha took a throw from her couch and wrapped it around my shoulders. We hugged.

"Come in, come in."

"Thank you." I offered her the cage. She took it and placed it on her desk.

"Thank you. Are you okay?"

"Numb."

"Of course you are. Death's so final. It's always a shock. Come sit down, and let's get Hector settled. I'll make tea."

"Yes. Thank you."

Natasha didn't ask anything further. She took the hood off Hector's cage and engaged with him until he calmed down. She made mint tea in a green mug and handed it to me. I drank some and began to warm up.

Within an hour, Hector had resumed his demeanor and was eyeing Anna, Natasha's pretty blue-and-white widow.

Natasha explained, "Lovebirds need time to bond. I will put Anna and Hector's cages nearby. If they preen for each other, then I'll try to put them together."

"Thank you."

"People don't realize that lovebirds can kill each other."

"Just like people."

She laughed and nodded. "It's the human condition. With lovebirds, the females can be very territorial. Hector's very sweet." As she crooned to him in Russian, Hector fluffed his feathers and settled.

"Thank you, Natasha. You're a good friend." She nodded.

"Anna has been sick at heart." Anna, who'd been collapsed in one corner of her cage, collected herself at the sight of Hector. She stood, smoothed her feathers, and gave a flirtatious twitch of her head.

Hector stared at Anna until she met his gaze. Hector had just given Anna the classic tango invitation to dance, the *cabaceo*. I couldn't believe my eyes. She primped and nodded in agreement. They were going to dance. I felt a sudden joy.

Natasha clapped her hands in delight.

"Did you see the *cabaceo* he gave her?" Natasha moved the cages together, and the two birds immediately connected through the bars.

"So romantic," Natasha crooned. Hector was home. I was happy.

Maybe cages could be adapted for human dating. It was so simple and direct.

Chapter 4

Annette's family made all of the arrangements, and I wasn't invited to weigh in on the details. In fact, I wasn't invited at all. I had two half-brothers, fraternal twins as the result of a series of fertility shots Annette took. They didn't like me, never had. Brad and Thad. Small and wiry like Annette, they had my father's eyes and hateful, supercilious attitude. It was Frank, my dad's lawyer and now my lawyer, who let me know when and where the funeral was. Frank, a perennial bachelor with Black Irish good looks who'd lived with his mother until she died, had drunkenly made a pass at me when I was sixteen at a family barbecue. I'd made a joke of it, letting him off the hook, and thus avoided being assaulted in my own bedroom. We were friends after that, and he always watched out for me.

I put on a flamboyant red dress, rented a small enough compact so that I could see over the windshield, and drove myself to the service. The funeral home was a white Victorian house set back from the road, flanked by tall, bare trees.

I parked and walked up the steps. Frank stood alone, smoking on the landing. He smiled and waved when he saw me. He whistled when he saw the dress under my coat.

"Interesting choice."

"Yeah. I'm planning to dance on his grave."

"No love lost there."

"Nonetheless, thanks for letting me know."

"Even so, you came." He threw his cigarette to the ground and stamped it out.

I followed him into a dim, discreetly carpeted area leading to two reception rooms. The place was packed, and Norman never looked better than he did in his open coffin. A disgusting custom. They'd pumped him full of formaldehyde and returned him to his bloated, condescending self. The undertaker had perfectly recreated the smirk that had been Norman's natural expression. He looked ready to open his eyes and start hurling insults. I walked over to the coffin, and reached out and touched my father's hand. It wasn't sentiment; I wanted to make sure he was really dead. Touching a corpse is not something you forget. There's a waxiness, and a feeling of kinesthetic repulsion because the thing you're touching is rotting, but then everything is. I turned, and my two stepbrothers flanked me.

Thad, the better-looking and kinder of the two, hugged me. I felt like checking my bag for my wallet. I was shocked to see real tears in his eyes.

"I'm so sorry. He was both of our dads."

Brad glared at me. I glared back. "Frank called me."

The two men exchanged guilty looks. I decided to push my luck.

"I'd like to say something." I looked at Brad, who was the leader. He'd grown a little belly and a mustache that framed his thin lips, making them look like one of those clams that doesn't open when you steam them. Brad and Thad exchanged a look.

Brad said, "Okay, but can you keep it short?"

I nodded, deadpan. "No other choice." Neither twin got the joke.

The service started, and then went on and on. I wondered if Brad would "forget" about me, so when he was done praising Norman, I stood up, took off my coat to allow the full effect of my scarlet frock to be felt, and sashayed toward the wooden podium in front of the open coffin. Brad introduced me as "Norman's daughter, Dorothy."

"Thank you. I'm the progeny from his first marriage. Norman was a better father to his sons than he was father or husband to me, my mother, and Annette." There was a shocked silence. "I was sad that he suffered so much, but it was commensurate to the suffering he inflicted on the women in his life. I believe the balance has been restored and his karmic debt repaid, so if

Chapter 4

there's a next life, I hope he'll arrive free to enjoy it. I'm here out of respect, but not out of love. Thank you."

There was an awkward pause, and then the priest closed with a blessing.

I left quickly and followed the convoy in my rented car to Annette's family burial plot. Norman's grave was next to Annette's. I felt sorry for her being stuck next to Norman for eternity. Suicide hadn't freed her after all.

At an appropriate moment, I was handed a shovel to throw a ritual bit of dirt onto the coffin as it was lowered. It seemed a redundant gesture. Dirt to dirt. I just hoped he'd stay dead.

On the way home, I called Suzanne and told her I wanted to take a break from ghostwriting and write my own book. She was pleased and told me that my book should be about how to lose weight by eating dessert, and to include recipes for pudding, pies, cakes, ice cream, and cookies.

"Are you making a joke at a time like this? It's in poor taste."

"I'm sorry. I thought an opportunity would make you feel better. This idea is a winner. I can get you a big advance and everything. Tell me a little more about the diet."

It had been a throwaway idea, like pubic-hair dye. My father was barely in the ground, and she wanted me to pitch. Okay.

"Part of the book is about how to listen to your body. It will always eat right for itself. Stop making up stories like 'I'm not fat, I have big bones.' I believe in a responsive universe where all of the evils were created by man, not God."

Suzanne sneered. "Forget the woo-woo stuff. Eating dessert and losing weight is a solid-gold idea. By the way, does it actually work?"

"Do you care?"

She laughed. "That's what I love about you, Dots. You're so sincere."

"What's your favorite dessert?"

"You know."

"Apple tart with vanilla ice cream."

"Yes! My mouth is watering. How long will it take you to put together a proposal?"

"I need a little time."

"Of course. I'll send you my recipe."

"You're a good friend, Suzy-Q. I'm going to dedicate the book to my father."

"Sorry I couldn't make the funeral. How're you doing?"

"I'm fine. I pre-mourned."

"Call me if you need to talk."

"Thanks."

I hung up. I felt dizzy. Suzanne had just created my future as a known writer because the concept fit her fantasy that desserts weren't fattening. Was there any real truth in the world other than natural events like the sun rising and the connection during a good tango?

I dropped off the car. I didn't want to go home. I went to La Boca, an Argentinean restaurant with a big cozy bar. The entrance was on the corner of Greenwich Avenue and 12th Street. It was the café I'd used as the background for my photos of the other Dorothy. The restaurant was named for the famous area in Buenos Aires where the tango was born. The poorest of the poor had lived there and only been able to buy the end bits of paint for their tin shanties, so the neighborhood was filled with these gaily colored huts. The façade of the restaurant had been painted to resemble the colorful houses. Inside, the walls were covered with family photos and garish paintings of the place.

La Boca didn't open until 11:30 a.m., but Fernando was behind the bar drinking coffee and loudly ordering supplies on the phone in Spanish when I came in. Jose, a busboy, slender with a weak chin and glasses, carried a steel serving bowl over to the bar. Fernando took off the cellophane covering, looked at the contents, and yelled, "No!"

Chapter 4

Fernando threw the bowl at Jose, who missed the catch. The metal tureen landed and bounced, scattering lemon wedges on the tile floor. From the doorway, I could see that the wedges were gray with mold.

"Sometimes you just cannot make lemonade."

He laughed loudly at his own joke, said a few more words into his phone and clicked it off. He was a tall, graying Argentinean dressed in a uniform of black cook's jacket and pants, black clogs and an unlit cigar. He wore a headset with a mike and was usually on the phone. His boyish face, with its upturned nose and cleft chin, was crowned by a pair of liquid brown eyes. He spoke in a syrupy baritone, which once heard was unforgettable and offered a clue to the unlived life of a singer that he had forgone to run this place started by his grandparents after Perón came to power.

Fernando had been a nine-and-a-half-pound "surprise" to his mother in her early forties, turning her into an invalid. She later died with Fernando's father in a plane crash as Fernando was preparing to perform in his first professional operatic role. He'd canceled his debut and took on the restaurant. Did he have regrets? He claimed not to, and made his place behind the bar his stage. Fernando favored anthems of all musical genres and was a great imitator. Today he was singing Elvis Presley. As he put a cup of coffee in front of me, he leaned in and sang the chorus from "My Blue Heaven": "You're the only star in my blue heaven, and you're shining just for me..." He ended with a flourish, and I applauded. Fernando looked me over and nodded approvingly at my red dress.

"Nice dress, Dots. Going to a funeral?"

"Coming from one, actually."

"I'm sorry. Forgive my ill-timed attempt at humor."

"No, it was the right thing at the right time. The past can be the past if I can just let it."

"Why wouldn't you?"

"If I let go of the past, I would have no identity."

"That's not true. You can create yourself anew every minute."

"Like I'm a virgin every time I take a shower."

Fernando laughed, "I'm stealing that idea. So, who died?"

I told him about Hector. I told him about Norman. I told him about the new book idea.

"What's your favorite dessert, Fernando?"

"My mother's flan." He looked out the window, and his eyes were wet. "I haven't thought of it in years, but I can taste it, as if I just took a bite. Creamy and sweet, with a hint of orange and vanilla bean. And dulce de leche."

"Of course. You miss her?"

"Every minute of every day. What was your father's favorite dessert?"

"Special cookies my mother made. Hunting cookies. He would take them with him when he went off to murder deer. They were like cookie jerky."

"Are you very sad?"

I shook my head.

"Tell me about him?"

"I don't want to speak ill of the dead — until I'm sure he's out of earshot."

"You're funny, Dots, but one good thing?"

"He loved my mother's bread pudding. With whipped cream."

I felt tears, but the past was gone. I wasn't going to look back. I'll cry over him when I'm dead, I told myself sternly. Outwardly, I shrugged, "He drank good scotch."

"Really? That's all?" Fernando looked sad. "And your mother?"

"Never touched sweets." Fernando looked even sadder.

"So, what is your favorite, Dots?"

"I hate dessert."

Chapter 5

Every day, I wrote as soon as I was awake, followed by a break to feed the birds by the river, followed by more writing. I could see my favorite birding bench from my window. It was empty when I left the house, but by the time I got there, Charles, a neighborhood poet and grandfather of three who lived in the shelter on 14th Street, was perched at one end writing in his notebook. He was the color of bittersweet chocolate, his white grizzled beard nearly hidden under the hood of his dark sweatshirt beneath a cracked leather jacket. He looked up as I sat down.

"They're waiting for you." He gestured to the birds who'd gathered as I arrived. "You have so many friends."

I thought about that, but came up blank. My relationship with the birds was transactional. How could they be friends? I scattered a mixture of seeds and breadcrumbs, then offered him the bag. He reached in, took a handful in his fist, opened it and blew on the mixture. We watched as they wafted in the air, then floated to the still snowy ground. We shared a smile.

"How do you do it, Charles? I mean, write so many poems?"

His smile vanished and he looked heavenward.

"They well up inside of my head and come out through my heart. I feel like something is speaking through me. I'm not political. I'm spiritual, but not religious. In prison, they called me a 'neutral.' That means that if you're not in a gang, or part of a clique, you're a neutral. You don't belong to nothing. I got to write. All I got is the truth underneath the truth."

I didn't have that. I wasn't part of anything except when I told myself lies about bad people who pretended to be good. That was the only way I could have a family. I felt my heart ball into a fist.

I distracted myself by admiring the sparrows. They were tough little birds who found a way to thrive during the long, cold winter. Henry was my favorite. He had an extra white mark on his face, and landed fearlessly on the back of the bench near to where I sat. He stared at me cheekily until I threw him a breadcrumb. He dived for it, caught it neatly and waited for the next. I scattered large seeds for the pigeons, and small ones for the sparrows.

Charles watched the exchange. He scribbled in his notebook some more, then stood up to read me what he'd written. His bass voice resonated like a Shakespearean actor delivering a monologue.

"In the afternoon sun after the morning,
the brown sparrow is fed.
The Creator made the sparrow and the sunshine.
The sparrow looks with love at his little earthbound angel
who scatters the seeds.
The Creator made her, and the poet watching too.
A sparrow's love
is a pathway
to the great beyond.
These birds are his favorites and his love
cradles the little creatures, the pretty birdfeeder and the world.
To be happy, trust that
there's always a trail of breadcrumbs leading us home."

He paused dramatically. "Bet you didn't know that."

"Know what?"

"When you're recognized by a sparrow, you're also being recognized by God."

"That's big. What do I get?"

"Maybe a passport to heaven. Bye, Dots. I got to go pay the water bill. Do you...?"

Chapter 5

I gave him some money and he left, whistling.

Henry came back and stared at me until I threw him more breadcrumbs, and he caught them as they landed. It was a game we both could win. I quoted Emily Dickinson at him as we played.

"Hope is the thing with feathers
That perches in the soul,
And sings the tune without the words,
And never stops at all,
And sweetest in the gale is heard;
And sore must be the storm
That could abash the little bird
That kept so many warm."

My phone rang. It was Suzanne. "What're you doing right now?"

"I'm feeding the birds."

"Pigeons?"

"Among others." I felt her shudder through the phone.

"Rats with wings."

I rolled my eyes. "Don't be such a snob. Think of them as fellow creatures."

"I do. I think of most people as rats without wings, or tails, but rats nonetheless."

I laughed. It was probably true.

"What's up?"

"Good news! Write your book proposal ASAP."

"What?"

"You have thirty days. I need a proposal, with recipes, sample chapters, and a chapter outline."

"Great. Why the urgency?"

"That's not your business, but I can almost guarantee you a sale. Remind me about the hook. What makes your approach unique?"

"Huh? Brain fart much?"

"Whatever."

"You forgot already? Eating dessert first will make you thin and sexy."

"Yeah, but how? Can you prove it? Which desserts when, how much of them and why? What are the best desserts to lose weight with? Apple tarts? Ice cream? Chocolate cake? Cookies? Do it by category. And I need recipes. A seven-day, fourteen-day and one-month food plan. Just guesstimate the calorie counts and measurement sizes. We can check your facts once I sell it. Don't get anal about those details or it'll be months. Be personal, that's what sells. I'm sending you a contract. Sign and get it back to me." She hung up.

I hadn't considered that I should be careful about asking for my dreams to come true. Now I had to deliver.

Once home, I wondered how to prepare myself to write about myself. I was a sworn forgetter of the past, so how did I get personal if there was no history? The only memories I wanted to keep were the ones involving my childhood dog, Toro. My memories of dessert needed to be stored in a padded loony-bin room. To succeed would require my greatest performance — the temporary acquisition of someone else's happy childhood.

I put on the pink sweat suit. I sat in front of my computer and rubbed my bare feet on Toro's rug. I put my big dictionary on my lap. If I closed my eyes, the weight reminded me of what it felt like to have the little guy on my lap. I imagined petting him and smelling his doggy breath as he licked my face. A sob escaped me and I shut it down. I opened my email. I googled recipes for diet desserts. I clicked back to my email and saw that Suzanne had sent the contract.

The doorbell rang. A mismatched pair of delivery guys who reminded me of Steinbeck's dynamic duo in *Of Mice and Men* stood in my doorway, bearing Suzanne's ill-omened postmortem offering. They both wore mold-green bomber

Chapter 5

jackets and matching baseball caps with the name of the funeral home inscribed in white italic script. The wreath, if you could call it that, was a huge circular arrangement made from white lilies and evergreen fronds.

The card read, "Condolences in your time of sorrow. Warmly, Suzanne." There I was, like Hamlet, trying to make sense of my father's death, and on cue Rosencrantz and Guildenstern arrived, a day late but with perfect comic timing.

"I guess all the world's a stage." I couldn't stop laughing.

Lennie, the big, tall oaf, sneered at my lack of funereal decorum and asked with a disapproving lisp, "Where do you want this, lady?"

"Let me get you the address." I wondered if there was a specific address within the cemetery. Did the dead receive mail?

"Nope, this is the address we was given." The little skinny one with the birthmark over his eyebrow scowled at me. "You want I should call my boss?"

I gave up. "Just set it here." I pointed to the front closet.

He glared at me as they tried to bring the monster frond through my doorway. After a struggle, they leaned it gently against the closet door and left. The room was redolent with the crisp scent of evergreen mixed with the cloying sweetness of the lilies. Now my apartment smelled like a funeral home. The party was over.

My father was dead. I felt as if a razor had slashed the four chambers of my heart. Norman would never see my book. Now he'd never love me. I could no longer pretend that I hadn't loved him. I felt those razor cuts bleed inside my body like the tears I couldn't shed. I signed the contract and sent it back without reading it. I was too bereft to care. If I'd ever felt alone, it was now. What was unique about my book anyway? I had nothing to say. There was no voice to capture. No face to remember. I was suddenly lost in this bad place inside of me, and there was only one thing to do — take a nap.

I dreamt that I was at a funeral, and I was both the one watching the dream and the one in the open coffin. Hector and Heloise perched at the edge. The song "These Boots Are Made for Walkin'" was sung as a funeral dirge played. I woke up, shaken.

Chapter 6

The first step when I began a new project was to find out how my client felt about their mother. I did this by asking what their mother's best dish had been and did they have a recipe? I couldn't go there with myself, as it broke the code of never repeating the past. Therefore, I needed to borrow someone else's relationship with their mother, preferably a good one. Fernando was the obvious choice.

Although flan wasn't intrinsically interesting, Fernando always found a twist on every dish. I texted him.

"Can we make your mother's flan?"

He texted back. "Come now."

Florencio, Fernando's elegant head bartender, was setting up the bar when I came in. He cut limes like a surgeon, with deftly delicate flourishes of the paring knife, which gleamed as it caught the sun.

"Hello, Dots." He waved. "Some fresh orange juice?"

"You're trying to get me drunk."

"And why not?" He winked. I took the glass and drank, then handed it back.

"May I ask you one question? You're a successful writer. My daughter, Anna, wants to be a writer. What do you think?"

"Ask her if there's anything else she wants to do. Anything."

He was dismayed. "I didn't expect that."

"I'm sorry. It's a tough life."

"Would you talk to her?"

"Of course. Where's Fernando?"

"He's cooking."

"Thank you."

I walked back into the kitchen, which was a charming mixture of old-fashioned brick and modern industrial appliances surrounding a freestanding island with a steel top. Two big pots of La Boca's famous chicken soup simmered on the big stove. Fernando was singing "Don't Cry for Me Argentina" as he chopped a large bunch of dill then dumped half of the fragrant green herb into each pot. He quickly cleaned up as he sang the crescendo. I applauded and he bowed.

"Hola, beauty!" He kissed me on both cheeks. "So, you want me to show you how to make Mama's flan. Is this for the new book?"

"Yes."

"You will say the name of the restaurant?"

"Of course. And call it Fernando's Flan."

"No, Maria's Flan. That was my mother's name."

"Of course. May I record this?"

He nodded. I pushed "record" on my phone.

"When did you first make a flan?"

"With my mother when I was a little boy. I remember that it was in the winter and I was home sick from school. I was maybe ten years. She didn't want to leave me at home, so she brought me here. It was on a Wednesday, when we make desserts." He pushed buttons on his phone and showed me a photograph of him cooking with his mother as a boy. The photo had been taken right where Fernando was standing when I entered, at the central island, the stove behind him. His mother was slender and wore her dark hair in a bob that reached her shoulders. She wore an apron with a graphic of the restaurant. Fernando was already tall, nearly his full height, and wore a matching apron. Maria had her arm around him, and he leaned against her with a giant smile. "You were tall for ten."

Grown-up Fernando wore the same tender smile as he turned on the oven.

"No, she was the same height as you. She would be so pleased that I am in a book! She would be so happy that you are writing your own book at last."

"Maybe one day you will write one, about the history of this restaurant and the family."

He laughed. "And one day you will sing opera!" He placed ten aluminum cups on the counter, took a container of brown liquid from the fridge and poured a layer on the bottom of each ramekin. "This is for the caramel glaze on top of the flan. I melt sugar and water together in such a way that it turns this color."

"Show me."

He poured sugar and water into a pan and set it on the stove. "The first time I made this it was a disaster! I still have a touch of carmelophobia because I did it wrong. I mixed the water and sugar in an iron skillet, like Mama told me, but it didn't turn an amber color. After four minutes, I was going to throw it out, but Mama said, 'Turn up the heat and keep mixing it until the crystals melt.' It seemed hopeless; the sugar was in clumps in the middle. But I turned up the stove and it worked. Whenever I am struggling, I think, how can I turn up the heat?"

"I love that. It's a philosophy for life, not just for cooking."

"Yes. Like the concept that eating a little dessert first reduces the bitterness of having to eat less overall."

No matter how sweet this flan turned out to be, it couldn't top feeling understood.

Fernando took a pot and placed it on the stove. He gathered ingredients as I wrote everything down.

"Why are you writing? It separates you from any experience. It's lucky that you can't tango and write at the same time. It will all be on the recording. Let me say what's here: eggs, milk, cream, sugar, orange zest, half a vanilla pod, and salt. This is how we make flan."

I watched as he poured in pints of milk and cream, added a cup of sugar, then turned the burner on a low flame. "Your mother looks so slim in that photo."

"She was always *elegante*."

"What was her secret?"

Fernando laughed. "Her secret? She had a big heart. Like me." He thumped his chest.

"Seriously, it's for the book. How did she stay so trim?"

Fernando looked down at himself and pinched the roll of fat on his belly. "As you can see, she never told me." He laughed again.

"I bet she did, and you didn't listen. And you are not fat."

"No, but I go up and down. It's emotional. When I feel good, I eat, and when I don't, I eat. Maybe your book will help me."

"Did she eat dessert?"

"Tasted, but I never saw her eat a whole one."

"Ha! You make my point for me. Thank you."

"Good. What's your secret, Dorothy?"

"I don't care about food."

"Not even mine?" He was offended.

"Your food is very special, but I meant globally. It made me fat as a kid. It was the enemy."

His eyes widened at the venom in my voice. "Is there a story behind all of that anger?"

"I try not to reanimate ugliness."

He nodded. "I understand. A little flan will soften that bitterness."

"What? Me, bitter?"

We laughed together, and I felt happy again. I watched as Fernando scraped an orange and added it to the simmering milk-sugar mix, then split a vanilla pod, scraped out the sticky essence and put that in as well. "My mother always used a whole pod, but I only use a part. Life is only half without her being here." His eyes watered, and I watched as a glittering tear touched by sunlight fell into the saucepan.

"Flan made with tears." I was choked up on his behalf. A shadowy image of my mother in a bathrobe stirring something on the stove, and me watching, praying that in her drunken state she wouldn't start a fire ... No! I sternly reminded myself

Chapter 6

not to think about the past. Once was enough. Stop! But like a swarm of mosquitos, memories overwhelmed me. When I was a teenager, my mother would often drink herself silly in the afternoon and pass out before Dad came home, so I cooked. Norman often insisted that we eat the meat of the deer he murdered, so there was always venison. A visceral recall of the smell made me gag. I hoped I wouldn't hurl and swallowed hard. Think of something good, I told myself. I remembered my relief on the day I got my acceptance to a college far enough away so that I could leave. I shook myself like a wet dog.

"You okay?"

I nodded. Fernando put eight yolks and two whole eggs in a steel bowl and expertly whisked them. He turned up the heat in the pan, and I watched as the chalky blend bubbled and then boiled.

"Now what?"

He took the pot off the stove and slowly poured the spiced milk and cream into the eggs as he blended them. "This will be our flan base," he explained as he poured the mixture into the waiting ramekins. He placed the cups in a baking dish, half-filled it with water and put it in the waiting oven. "Now we will bake them bain-marie at 350 degrees for 45 minutes and we can test the soup. Bain-marie is when you cook food in hot water in the oven, mostly custards and such."

The soup was good, and when the flan was done, Fernando let the pan cool, and then turned the cups upside down, sliding the cream-colored pudding topped with a layer of crispy caramel into white dessert bowls.

"How will you serve them?"

"With a squeeze of dulce de leche and a strawberry." He squeezed a dollop next to the pudding, sliced a strawberry, added it to the dish and presented it to me. I didn't want to touch it, but knew I had to. I took a small bite. I mentally counted back from ten as I felt my gorge rise. I'd gained control over my

35

weight by hypnotizing myself into associating sweets with dog poop. My beloved Yorkie, Toro, had been cursed with the most awful digestion. I swallowed with difficulty.

Fernando waited expectantly. "How is it?"

"Delicious, lovely." I handed it back. His face fell.

"You don't like it."

It never occurred to me that my approval mattered to anyone. "I just ate all of that soup. Will you pack it up for me so I can eat it later?"

He nodded, gave me the sweet boy smile, and placed the flan in a small container with a lid. "What do you do now?"

"I'll go home and type up my notes. I will send you the recipe as I understand it, and you will verify what I wrote."

We kissed on both cheeks, and he started his next dish. I made it to the restroom just in time to be able to turn on the water so no one could hear me retch.

Chapter 7

After ghostwriting celebrity memoir-cookbooks that had done well for their creators, I asked myself, If I were to "ghostwrite" my own story, how would that go? How was a memoir diet book different from a straight diet book? How did I work with someone to get the book written? There was a reason why each client had succeeded and why a book would further their careers. Find the shoes, find the voice. Fernando's mother had put the very strategy I invented to good use. Maybe I really was onto something. How many people really ate dessert first to keep their weight down?

Each of the celebs I worked with had a "hook," a reason why who they were made their approach unique. One had been a Russian gymnast, a former fatty who dieted herself into an Olympic silver medal by eating potatoes and borsht. Another was a former Marine lifer who used army rations to drop the extra weight he'd gained when he retired, plus an exercise regime from boot camp. Each of these people did something unique and brought their professional experience to their book.

What had I done? I could say I was a ghostwriter, but I couldn't legally share the name of anyone I'd written for.

Who could I be for this book? All I had was how I changed myself into the Approval Rat, a version of myself that everyone liked. But she couldn't write a book; she was too afraid of offending someone. This was also a secret I wasn't sure I wanted to share.

I began every new project with an interview. In order to get this one done, I was going to have to treat myself, the writer, as if I were one of my subjects. I regarded my clients with a mixture of disgust and jealousy, which fit perfectly with how I felt about myself.

Every writer's job is to write. I told my mind to shut up and let me work. I focused on the pitch: eating dessert first would help you lose weight.

Of course, I immediately froze, unable to write anything, and found myself watching a lot of YouTube videos of people dancing the tango. I felt as if I were slowly graying out of my own everyday life, and that if I didn't get to it, I would just shuffle off, a weary phantom, unfulfilled, unloved, and bored. I knew there were reasons why, no matter how good any diet was, they rarely worked over time. I discussed this with myself as if I were one of my clients using a posh British accent.

"So, Dorothy, what do you think the theme of your book is?"

I answered myself aloud, letting my true raspy voice be heard. "If the concept of dessert as a reward is good, then the whole way of looking at weight loss is wrong, as evidenced by how we language it: We humans don't want to lose anything! The very description guarantees failure!"

"What will you call this masterpiece?" I was enjoying this conscious splitting of myself, and was amused to see that I now felt the same exasperation towards myself that I did when dealing with any self-important celebrity.

"I'm not sure yet. I'm exploring a new way to address the issue of weight in a non-dualistic way. Let's face it, who wants to 'lose' anything, unwanted or not? The body 'thinks' in a different way than the mind. If we can look at letting go of excess weight from the body's point of view, as if it were a separate entity that each of us shares consciousness with, and that the 'body-mind-spirit' philosophy is a practical, actionable perception, it becomes easier to achieve the goal of a healthy weight."

"Is there a particular dessert that is most effective? I personally hope that it is chocolate pie with whipped cream."

"All desserts can work. There will be a section on each category of the most beloved desserts beginning with French apple tart,

Chapter 7

my agent's favorite." I was elated. I sounded both confident and catchy. The shape of the book became a little clearer. I needed to find a way to reframe the weight-loss process.

How could I take the "loss" out of weight-loss? Straddle, control, management, administration. "Straddle" sounded the best, but it made me think of riding a horse, and suggested imbalance. Every word suggested its opposite, and that made the reframe tricky.

Selling "loss" as something desirable was similar to the spiritual con job the Catholic Church had gotten rich on by pretending that poverty was noble. Another cultural con job about how hard work assures success was when the Nazis placed a sign with the slogan "Work will set you free" above the gates of the Auschwitz concentration camp, a detail usually forgotten along with the 1.1 million people who died there. The price of peace is eternal vigilance, and that goes for weight ... straddling as well. One thing about Auschwitz, no one was fat. Maybe that was my next book, the concentration-camp diet...

My imaginary interviewer laughed uneasily, pushing her dark straight hair off of her pale, square-jawed face, adjusting the collar of her gray pantsuit and pushing her oversize horn rims back on her nose. She cleared her throat and said, "That could be brilliant, but let's get back to the book. What's the foundational psychology here?"

"Once physical hunger has been assuaged, that's where an intelligent person can see that their so-called hunger is for something more than food. By eating dessert first, we start out our eating experience with the reward. By not delaying physical gratification, we are free to look at our needs for emotional gratification. I believe this is where the confusion lies. We want to be acknowledged and rewarded, get our just desserts." I laughed at my own double entendre. But there was my hook, and the name of the book: *Just Dessert*, with the tagline "All things in moderation. Nothing in excess."

"Can you summarize your main points?"

"No. 1: Eat a small portion of dessert whenever you want one. Feeling deprived is a trigger for overeating. No. 2: It's not about food; it's about fear. No. 3: Reward or dessert? You're entitled to all the pie you want, and most of what we want isn't food; it's the reward of recognition by our peers that we are seeking. The book will help you figure it out, make better choices, and by having the taste of a physical dessert first, you'll eat less!"

"So is that it?" the interviewer asked.

"No, the reader must be willing to accept that the body, whose prime directive is to stay healthy, would seek the right food in the right quantity if free of mental influence. Any abuse of a 'trigger food' such as ice cream is almost always a compensatory emotional response from one of the aspects of the personality."

"How did you lose weight? I mean, become healthy?"

"I tried every diet, but nothing worked until I accepted that the issue wasn't food. I just needed to be appreciated."

"But what was the issue then? And how did you lose the weight?"

"I just told you! By making the distinction between physical and emotional hunger."

"I see. But what were the steps you took?"

"I studied psychology in college. We are motivated by two things: greed and fear. All seemingly self-destructive behavior comes from one of these two emotions. Greed is what makes us eat too much. But greed is another form of fear. To paraphrase the Book of Job, 'That which I greatly feared has come upon me.' Having to 'lose weight' triggers our primal fear of starvation. One day, I was eating a piece of cake and my father screamed, 'You'll never lose weight unless you give up sweets!'"

"That sounds about right."

"NO!" I leaped out of my chair, sticking my finger at my imaginary opponent. "NO! That was exactly why it would never happen. Why would I want to 'give up' or 'lose' anything? No one would. So as a result of how weight control is thought and spoken about, the body holds onto weight instead of balancing itself."

"You lost me there." God, this interviewer self was such a twit!

I sighed, sat down and said, as if speaking to a small child, "I attained slimness by reframing how I thought about eating, and took what actions were necessary to become healthy. As soon as I thought of 'losing weight,' it made me want to eat."

"I get that." The interviewer laughed. "That makes sense. Then what happened?"

I was scribbling as fast as I could. "I took stock of what I could change, and what I couldn't. I couldn't change my height, but I could change my weight. I looked ordinary as a mousy brunette, so I became a blonde. My voice was nasal and whiny, but I was inspired to change it by Marilyn Monroe and Katharine Hepburn, both of whom had created a stage voice for themselves as actors, separate from how they spoke as people.

"I ignored the fact that life hadn't worked out so well for either of them, and hoped that I would have a better fate. I read somewhere that Marilyn found her voice in a dressing room when she and her roommate, Shelley Winters, were shopping. Shelley was auditioning for some part, and was rehearsing her lines in a breathy, lilting voice. Marilyn asked Shelley if she could 'have' that voice. The rest is history.

"As a result, I'd lightened up my own voice, and mostly used a 'head' voice as if I were a little girl. This practical approach became my winning strategy.

"Next, I accepted how height-challenged I felt, and told myself that by not eating much I was becoming taller, because I looked taller. Food lost its allure, and I no longer had any interest in it. It was ironic that I ended up becoming a food writer. I thought of myself as a mandatory gourmet. But even slender, I was still my unlovable self, so I created a persona, an alternate personality that I called the 'Approval Rat.' She's who you see before you now, this soft-spoken blonde who takes tiny bites and wears high heels and fluffy feminine dresses."

I turned off the recording. I had my hook, and went shoe shopping — in my closet. I found a pair of pale-pink, suede stiletto-heeled pumps. They were a little big, which was probably why they hadn't been worn, and the metaphor didn't escape me: Could I be big enough to fill my own shoes? Sometimes the Creator was so corny! I put them on and went to work.

My fingers flew across the keyboard. Chocolate pie, apple pie, diet pie! Hooray, I'd successfully created a relatable if imaginary character, the way I did for my clients. The A.R. could no more write a book than any of my other clients could, and I had become her as I always did. A wave of relief washed over me, because, in this capacity, I never worried about the quality of the work.

As Dorothy, the professional writer, the sarcastic dumpy brunette with the nasal voice, I appreciated the irony that I would succeed by not being myself.

But there was another aspect that I would never share. This was Cassandra, a pimply teenage version of me who was honest, cantankerous, and refused to cooperate with anyone. Her favorite word was "NO." She was the scapegoat, the one who suffered for the other parts. Was this conscious schizophrenia, or was it common sense?

She was always ready for a fight, and slipped out if I drank too much. She always blurted out the truth, without a care for who might get hurt. She was the older sister I'd never had.

In my imagination, Cassandra rolled her eyes and said, "You'll never get away with this sophistry. It's crap."

"Watch me," I whispered, and mentally stuck my tongue out at her.

Chapter 7

"So, are you saying you're a schizophrenic?" The interviewer persona had returned unbidden and still British.

"Not at all. Things tend to be organized into threes: body, mind, spirit. Beginning, middle, and end. Spiritual, mental, physical. The Holy Trinity. The Three Stooges. I have at least that many aspects: myself, the A.R., and Cassandra."

The number three became a useful way of parsing my thoughts, if not reality. I'd concluded that for myself there were always several "selves" present and that my mind was often at a cocktail party with the aspects all arguing.

They didn't get full billing, but I tried to be exquisitely aware of their voices, so I distinguished between whether I was having a thought or whether it was someone else's. I read about the "collective unconscious" Jung spoke about, and it seemed that was like a radio station that played incessantly in everyone's mind. Once I understood that, I learned how to change the channel to a more pleasant one.

When I was a young teenager, my father constantly shamed me for my gluttony, and my mother let him. I became depressed, and fatter.

One night when Aunt Cindy came to visit, after she'd sat through the usual dinner where I was diced up like so much celery, she came to my room and we had a talk. She was very angry and told me that the layer of lard was insulation to protect myself from my father's relentless verbal abuse, since my mother offered no such protection. She explained that overeating was just a habit, and that a habit could be broken! She said, "There's nothing wrong with you. You just have a bad habit."

I was amazed at the possibility that I was not fundamentally deficient. "What do I have to do to change?"

"First, believe that it's possible. Then there are three parts of any addiction. The actual physical addiction, mouthy busyness, and friendship."

"I'm not addicted."

"Oh, no? Do you eat when you're not actually hungry?"

Ashamed, I nodded, "All the time."

"Do you eat when you're upset?"

I nodded again.

"Do you eat when you're bored or alone?"

"Yes. Okay, I'm a food addict." Tears spilled out of my eyes. Aunt Cindy handed me a box of tissues. I blew my nose as she hugged me. I got a little snot on her top. She wiped it off and winked at me.

"Don't get upset, Dotty dearest, it's over. You just did the big thing by admitting the truth. That's eighty percent! The next part is to accept that eating has been your friend and gives you something to do. We need another habit, maybe writing?"

"It will take forever."

"No, there's no secret to losing weight: Eat less of fattening stuff like sweets, drink more water, and focus on separating your 'friend' relationship with food. Think of food as fuel that keeps the car of your body running smoothly. When you're mad or sad, write it down, and if you're afraid that someone will read it, throw the pages out on the way to school." Her parting words were: "Just be true to your ideal of beauty. Ignore your dad, ignore everyone else. What do you want to see in the mirror?"

"And?" My imaginary interviewer leaned forward, waiting for the answer.

"That question still haunts me."

The A.R. stood up and pivoted in front of the mirror. She was perfect, if short: blonde, busty, bifocals, wearing an expensive pink sweater, designer jeans, and heavy socks with Yorkies embroidered on them to fill the shoes. I smiled at the image.

"What you see is what you get," I said. Cassandra roiled her chewing gum, blew a bubble and popped it. She knew I was lying.

Chapter 8

It was 10:30 p.m. and time to dance. There was a *milonga* near Times Square that offered two dance rooms, one that played traditional tango music and another that played alternative music. Alternative tango covers a wide range of musical styles, including jazz, rock, and blues.

I, Dots, danced to the alternative music, while the A.R. insisted on traditional music. Tonight, I was leaving the A.R. at home. The studio was on Eighth Avenue between Thirty-Eighth and Thirty-Ninth Streets, an area so dangerous that it wasn't safe to use the outside intercom and risk getting buzzed into a narrow hallway ripe for a mugging. I walked through the adjacent dive bar to the elevator. The long brass-railed bar was manned by Loretta, a blonde giantess serving tough-looking men with prison tats and their equally tattooed gal pals. Rap music blared. I waved and walked to the service end of the bar. Loretta smiled and handed me a to-go cup full of cheap white wine.

"Hey, Dots, looking good. No sign of that guy."

I handed her a twenty and sighed with relief. Peter wasn't there.

The studio was on the fourth floor. The elevator opened into a hallway that led into a mirrored studio on either side. The lights had been lowered and colored Christmas bulbs created a party atmosphere. I paid the entrance fee and walked into the alternative room, a big mirrored box with banquettes on one side. I changed my shoes as a new song began, "I Want a Little Sugar in My Bowl," sung by Nina Simone. I sipped some of the wine.

A short, attractive man with a goatee and a fedora looked at me and gestured with his head for me to join him. This was the *cabaceo*, the way a male *tanguero* communicated his desire to

45

dance with you. I smiled back and nodded. I stood up to meet him.

This was the critical moment of the dance where I was sure to fail. I was face-to-face with a stranger, and my only job was to get into the embrace in the right way. The truth was, I couldn't tune in enough to follow his lead. My lower half would go numb; I often had to guess what my leader was suggesting. Guessing is not the same as knowing, so there was always a private terror. I prayed that I could fake it. Horrible to know you're doing the thing you love wrong and have no idea how to fix it. He extended his hand, and I stepped forward so he could slide his arm around me. He began the dance. I was hammered by an onslaught of internal critical voices that pounded at me like gunfire. I countered by reciting numbers back from fifty to remain focused. I managed to follow at the end with a matching flourish. He smiled as a new song began, "Wicked Game," by Chris Isaak, a haunting rockabilly song about love and betrayal.

"Relax, just let me drive," he whispered.

"Okay, thanks." I took a deep breath and told myself, "Relax." We danced smoothly, a good connection. I was happy that I hadn't screwed up.

The song ended and he asked, "Another? And I'm Fred." I was about to nod when Natasha, looking sexy in black lace, and Bonnie, her best friend, a tall, rangy brunette in apple-green silk with short, spiky hair, came up to me, blocking my partner.

Fred smiled at me, shrugged, and went off looking for someone else.

Natasha grabbed his arm and said, "Sorry, you can have her back for the next one."

He looked uncertain, but I was amused. Natasha beamed at me because we could both read Bonnie's mind — she'd pegged Fred as the perfect man because his eyes came to the height of her breasts. "I'm going to enjoy watching him manage having to dance with my boobies," Bonnie whispered as she hugged me,

Chapter 8

and sat down next to me to change into her green satin dance shoes.

Stefan, a tall dapper baldy, wearing a black turtleneck and jeans, asked Natasha to dance. "Red House," a sexy Jimi Hendrix song with a fabulous electric guitar solo, began. Bonnie was a tango traditionalist. "I hear Jimi Hendrix. Ugh! I'm braving this horror music to see how you're doing with your grief?"

I leaned in and said, "You know, it amuses me that grief's treated as an ongoing illness in our society. If you took the metaphysical perspective, death is a release from the toils of school Earth, and when you die, you go 'home' to that better place. Is the earth separate from heaven? If the core teaching is that everything is really only the One Thing, then both are a part of God. I think of my dad as having gone home to a nicer place, one where Norman never has to deal with pets and has all of his toys."

Bonnie leaned in closer. "What? Sorry, I couldn't hear most of that over the music, but you seem good. I've organized a tango festival in Cancún. I got you a VIP pass and a great price on a room. It's next month."

I hugged her, and she fled to more familiar music.

Fred and I danced to the remainder of "Red House." It was as if he literally became someone else while dancing to this hard-rock song, which inspired him to "show off," leading me in kicks, lifts and wraps.

I stopped worrying about all of my issues. He couldn't have felt a connection if it hit him in the head, so I let the A.R. take over since she can't feel a connection with her partner, either. Perfect. I watched as she and Fred ripped up the floor.

"We" got a round of applause from the other dancers at the end of the song, but the truth was that what they'd witnessed was two phonies pretending to connect. An air-kiss of a dance. I left feeling empty.

"I want a little sugar in my bowl, I want a little sweetness in my soul..."

The post-tango blues were very blue. Of course, the A.R. was pleased at her performance, but I had not been fed.

I went home, took a nap and went to work before dawn. I had thirty days. The festival began just after my deadline ended. I decided to be enthusiastic about going to Cancún. Otherwise, the long winter stretched forward without a clear shape.

As soon as I put on my pumps, I had a brainstorm. I would use Fernando's mom as the inspiration for my discovery. She'd proved an idea that I had tossed off as a sarcastic throwaway to Suzanne, equating it with using henna for one's graying pudenda hair. Suzanne really did have a gift for finding commercially viable material, and wasn't just a parasite living off the talent of her clients. Taking my cue from her, I would embellish the concept by using the word "eat" instead of "taste," and could balance that by letting the reader know about calories and how to factor dessert into the whole eating regime. I had a shock of positive recognition because I actually did that to maintain my weight. I tasted, but ate little. I felt a wave of relief. This would be easy, and I didn't have to reveal any secrets other than this one. Now I needed to gather great recipes and test them.

I spent the next month writing, which I loved, and cooking, which I hated. I fed the birds. I wrote. I slept. I fed the birds. I wrote. I slept. I cooked. I went to the bar. I slept. I wrote. I fed the birds. Apple tart. Chocolate mousse. Chocolate-mint-chip cookies. Since my life had no other meaning, I invested the time in the holy grail of my own book, and the promise of sunshine in Cancún.

Here's what I came up with: "Weight balancing will set you free forever. I'm a former fatty who conquered my weight problem by embracing my love of sweets and learning to eat

Chapter 8

them in small portions. For years I went through a depressing cycle of abstinence followed by bingeing. Finally, I got tired of the routine and got off the hamster wheel by combining calorie counting with portion control. I learned that by having a bite or two of a dessert before lunch and dinner, I could control what I weighed as a lifestyle, not a cycle of gain and loss! Beyond the outward control of food, the secret is to accept that overeating is about feelings, not food. Overweightness is an outward manifestation of a state of internal unhappiness! The extra pounds work like insulation against feeling too much. If you're not eating out of hunger, or for the sheer pleasure of it, then why are you eating? The answers to this question will free you from weight worry forever and lead you to learn to weight-balance successfully through creative portion control.

"Once I became healthy, my friends wanted to know how I'd shed that extra ten pounds I'd been carrying. They kept asking me to share the how-to, and here it is: By eating a little dessert first, you can stay trim. And I mean a bite or two. Here's what a bite looks like."

How could I dramatize this? If it were an app, you could check the portion size on your phone. To make the point, I used my limited skills to create a page of realistic pop-out bites so the reader could visualize what she was up against.

Then I began to work on the table of contents based on six basic categories of dessert: cookies, cakes, pies, pastries, puddings, and general baked goods. I wrote a sample chapter about puddings that began "The owner of La Boca's mother, Maria, owned a restaurant and was always slim and beautiful. Her son, Fernando, the current owner, shared his mother's secret: Taste but don't eat. Her amazing flan is one of the many recipes that I will share." And I laid out the ingredients and recounted how Fernando made the flan.

I broke the book into four sections.

Part 1: Out and About. A compendium of commercial desserts and the calories in each bite.

Part 2: At Home. Food plans for days, weeks and a month of low-calorie, low-fat desserts. In their own castle, the reader was now in total control of their food intake.

Part 3: Strategies for Living. How to manage at work, at parties, with family, on holidays, and stress-eating.

Part 4: Recipes. Recreating the classics with new delicious low-calorie ingredients that were healthy-ish.

The outline wasn't perfect, but it was done. I sent it off to Suzanne, but with no sense of victory because it wasn't really my book any more than the others had been. It was Suzanne's idea. My contribution was the same as for my other books, although my name would be on this one. I'd massaged the unappetizing raw clay of myself into someone sane and relatable, a role model for women everywhere, as I had with Babette. I would succeed as I always had, but it would be a Pyrrhic victory. I would lose by winning.

Cassandra objected. "Cheer up, Dotty downer! Your name will be on the cover. Why can't you enjoy your success?" I had no answer. She was right. To paraphrase my late father, what I did was put lipstick on pigs, but this time I was the porker. Finally, I would get to be the bride, and not the bridesmaid. Could you curdle two metaphors? The best I could hope for was to be a piggy bride.

I realized I would have to hurry to make my flight.

Chapter 9

The Cancún Tango Festival would be three days in paradise. Natasha had a conference, so I went alone, and except for Bonnie, no one knew me. Cancún has a well-organized airport, and while strolling through it, I relaxed. I'd made it, and declared a holiday and a rest from constantly battling with myself. Bonnie texted that she couldn't meet me, but sent a car. I arrived at the hotel around noon. The resort was typical, tropical and sprawling. I walked through beautiful gardens and packed swimming-pool areas with outdoor bars, marveling at the warmth and beauty and the smiling kindness of the staff. As I neared my room, there was an outdoor buffet, and I stopped for a moment to look at the desserts, but they were nothing special.

I had a charming room with a big double bed and a large balcony with an ocean view. My pass and schedule for the festival were on my nightstand. I opened the colorful brochure and examined the lists of activities and practice sessions. A festival, which really should be called "camp," is made up of endless classes and workshops with star teachers, interspersed with practice sessions or *practicas*. At night there were group dinners, followed by the evening *milongas*, where the real game was played.

I studied the schedule. My biggest problem was how to get into the correct position with my leader before the dance began. The tango embrace required a body-to-body hug with a stranger. Without this connection, it was impossible to follow. Intimacy and hugs were both things I'd avoided until I took on this dance, but I believed that unless I could commit to being in that connection, I would end up unloved and alone. I would tremble before each tango because I knew I was wrong before the first step was ever taken, and hadn't been able to fix it yet!

There was a class called Mastering the Embrace. Here was my chance!

The classes were held in the main part of the resort on a concrete area covered with a portable wooden dance floor shaded by palm trees. Thirty people were gathered under a nearby portico, stretching, putting on their shoes or chatting. Bonnie showed up briefly, hugged me, checked names off against her list and hurried off. I changed my shoes and waited.

The three workshops I'd signed up for were named Mastering the Embrace — Beginning, Intermediate, and Advanced. The brochure guaranteed that by the end you would know how to do it perfectly.

Tara Bolivar was a well-known teacher who had won major championships with her now ex-partner, Carlos, who would also be attending the festival to perform as per contract.

I listened to the gossip around me about who Tara's new partner might be. There was a collective gasp as a striking couple wearing name tags that identified them as Tara and George walked towards us carrying a boom box. Tara was tall and lithe with frizzy chin-length blonde hair, gray eyes and a button nose. She wore a turquoise wrap dress and worn, high-heeled gold tango shoes.

But who was the mystery man whose name tag read "George"? He was tan, muscular with dark hair and eyes, and wore a white polo shirt and jeans. His Western-style belt buckle was inscribed HOUSTON FDNY, and his jeans held a tidy package. I was surprised to think about that! In my mind, the A.R. said, "How vulgar," and Cassandra sneered.

Most tango classes have this structure: The teacher or teachers explain what will be taught, demonstrate and then either have the class warm up by doing exercises or go right to the main event.

Tara gestured for us to come onto the dance floor and make a circle.

Chapter 9

"Hi, I'm Tara and this is George." George waved shyly.

"This class is about the embrace, the most fundamental part of tango. Without the embrace, you have nothing; it's just a dance. When you get into 'tango embrace,' the 'click' of connection is there, or not. There are levels of connection, and this class will improve wherever you are." She turned to George, who held out his hand. Tara took it and they stood in the embrace pose.

"Please notice where he is holding my right and left hands."

We noticed.

"Good. The most important part of tango is the initial meeting and how you get into the correct embrace, but before we can learn how to hold each other properly, we must be able to walk together. Grab a partner and walk. Try to keep time with the music."

Slow tango music with a clear beat played. We partnered up. A short guy with beady eyes, steely gray hair and wearing a festival T-shirt and plaid Bermudas smiled, and I nodded. He walked over. "Hi, I'm Brandon."

I nodded again. "Dots."

Once the class was in pairs, Tara said, "Good. Now walk together in teaching pose, our arms on our partner's forearms, back and forth across the floor."

She demonstrated with George. We followed and she watched us, then came over to several couples and made a few adjustments. When the song ended, Tara stopped the music.

"Again, but this time on the beat, people." The music began and we walked back and forth. Brandon was very confident, and I enjoyed the smoothness of his lead.

Tara watched us for another minute, then clapped her hands in delight. "Yes, you all have a good sense of rhythm."

I hadn't seen that with the men I'd practiced with, but encouragement is a good thing. "Now you're ready to work on your embrace. Let's make two lines, leaders and followers facing each other."

The students stood opposite each other, leaders in one line, followers in the other. Tara and George again demonstrated how to get into the correct tango embrace.

"The follower waits until the leader offers his right hand. She takes it and allows him to draw her to him. Her left arm wraps around his shoulder, and his right arm around her back at bra-strap level. That's what can be seen by the eye, but there is so much more: The placement of the head and neck, keeping the shoulders down, the sternum up. The tango embrace is a hug. While maintaining this hug, both dancers must each stay on their axis." She demonstrated with George.

"To the followers: while you can 'use' your partner's left arm to steady you, you must be so balanced that you could be dancing alone. Now try getting comfortable in the embrace."

Brandon slid his arm around my back. I laid my left arm on top of his. Tara looked over at me. "That's very good. Now be sure not to lift your left elbow on the turn. He needs the steady connection so he knows where you are at all times." She looked at the other followers. "That goes for all followers, and leaders, this is what you want from a partner. If she's not consistent, you can raise your right arm so that she will have to leave her arm on top of yours." Tara got back into the embrace, then deliberately lifted her elbow. George moved his right hand an inch higher, and the elbow came down.

"Now you try it."

Brandon turned me, and I noticed that my left elbow lifted on its own. He moved his right arm and hand up, and my elbow relaxed. I looked around the room and saw everyone looking happy and smiling. One of the many tango mysteries was solved!

Tara said, "There are two kinds of partner positions, 'open embrace,' when the bodies don't touch, and 'close embrace,' where from shoulder to waist the bodies are in constant contact."

Chapter 9

Tara and George demonstrated the two styles of embrace. Once in the open-embrace position, Tara looked at the leaders and said, "Don't do it the way George does it. Look, do it like this." She roughly moved George's hands slightly, corrected his posture and the angle of his head. I saw the flash of pain in his eyes, but then he covered with a smile. His eyes met mine, and he looked away.

"Okay, let's try it." As we got into the embrace, my partner's cell phone rang. "I'm a doctor," he said apologetically, and hurried out of the room.

Suddenly, I was the runt of the litter, a woman without a partner. Humiliated, I decided to go to the bathroom and not return. Tara caught my mood and smiled. She called out and pointed. "George, would you..." George walked over and extended his hand.

"Ready, everyone?" Tara started the music.

As we moved toward each other into the embrace, I stepped out of time into one of those moments you read about in a romance novel. He took my hand, and I felt a shock as if I'd been plugged into an electric socket. He wrapped his other arm around my back and pulled me close. Our embrace was like heated liquid mercury racing up a thermometer.

When a man like George is holding you in his arms, there's nowhere to hide. My ambivalence about intimacy rushed like a tsunami into my chest, choking me. I could never win against myself. Better to die on the spot, but the body fought for breath, my lungs thick with waves of watery grief. Somewhere along the line, I'd given in to my despair that I would ever dance well. My tango terror was a response to this deep, previously unconscious certainty that I would fail. Wow.

Tara walked over to us, looking pleased, and said, "Your name, please?"

Her voice snapped me back to reality. "Uh ... Dots." I was surprised at the approval in her voice, and the warmth of her smile.

"Dots has made a half-circle from left to right, using the left hand and arm to create a connection, which leads to the engagement of her upper back so the energy flows across her back and through her right arm and hand into his. This energy loop is what we want to attain. It will keep the connection throughout the dance. Now let's all try that. Change partners. Leaders move to the right."

George nodded a thank-you and moved to the next lucky woman.

Brandon returned and moved into George's spot. "Sorry! I'm a surgeon, newly divorced, and I live in Short Hills." I smiled and wondered why he was apologizing — it was a funny way to flirt with someone. I shared what Tara had taught, and Brandon was able to keep up with the rest of the class. At the end, George and Tara danced, demonstrating all of the elements we'd learned in class, and received a round of applause.

Tara said, "Thank you so much! There will be an hour-long *practica*. George and I will stay around to help."

Brandon asked if I would stay and practice with him. I danced a few songs with him and then he had another call and left.

George asked me if I wanted to dance. A romantic tango played. We got into the embrace. He corrected the angle of my right hand in his left. "Give me a little resistance. It will help your balance, and I will know where you are. Think of your hand and arm as al dente versus mushy pasta."

"Oh, are you a chef?"

He laughed and shook his head. I changed the angle of my hand in his, and we made the electric connection again. We shared a glance of joy, and then we danced.

Chapter 9

Suddenly, my mind went quiet. All of my aspects relaxed into silence; the A.R. didn't interject in her breathy Marilyn Monroe voice, Cassandra was quiet, and I was no longer a doormat. My wish had come true, and a blended version of me was dancing. All of me danced, able to attune to George's lead. No guessing what he wanted. I, or we, knew!

I blessed all the lessons I'd ever taken. I had enough technique to maintain our connection.

The song, "Volvamos a Empezar," or "Let's Start Again," was a romantic plea from a man asking a woman to start their relationship anew. The music was swooping and romantic, the smooth tenor singing with a catch in his throat. The song ended, and we stood locked in the embrace. A new song began. George let go of me reluctantly.

"I'd better circulate. You, too." I nodded, lost in a tango trance.

"Let's dance again later." George smiled and turned away.

Brandon reappeared, eagerly waving. He'd changed, and looked better in long pants than he did in the baggy shorts and knee-high striped socks he'd worn to class. He wore an expensive watch, just in case you missed how successful he was.

We danced well together, but I couldn't settle. I felt slightly unbalanced.

George came over for another dance. He held out his hand, and I stepped into his embrace. Kismet! After the first lilting song in the *tanda*, I noticed I was off-balance.

"George, I want to ask you something." He nodded. "How best to stay on my axis when I do a forward *ocho* with my right foot?" He led me in a forward *ocho*.

"Relax your left shoulder, stay back on your quads, use your ribs, not your shoulders. More floor pressure with your left leg." It worked, and my balance returned along with my confidence.

"You're a great teacher."

"I'm no teacher, just helping out my wife." Wife. Okay. Burst bubble. Also, a great bubble because there was no chance of any horizontal tango playtime. I glanced over and saw Tara dancing in very close embrace with her ex-partner Carlos, a darkly handsome Argentinean with curly brilliantined hair, dimples, and a thin gold earring.

The song ended and I saw a flash of anger in George's eyes. "Excuse me, I have to take care of something."

"I can see that." He looked at me surprised, gave me a lopsided grin, and hurried off. Brandon took his place. Life was good.

Chapter 10

It was time to get on the real dance floor. The *milonga* started soon. I wanted to both hide under my bed and have another dance with George. I looked to the A.R. for help. I got on the Internet and watched a clip of Marilyn Monroe singing "Happy Birthday" to JFK, and showered, thinking about George. I put on a filmy red dress with a layered, uneven hem that swirled when I moved. I curled my hair. Lipstick. Perfume. I posed and pushed my hair off my face in the gesture that cemented the A.R. persona. When I left the room, A.R. was in control. I was free not to be me.

I entered the ballroom. Tables and chairs lined the dance floor, and the DJ had set up his rig in one corner. The room was dim, lit only with tiny twinkling Christmas lights. The bar at the far end was packed. I counted more than 175 people. Couples sat together. The women sat on chairs on one side of the dance floor, and the men sat in chairs on the other.

The key to a successful *milonga* when going solo was getting to dance a *tanda* as soon as possible with a leader that the other men respected. If the leaders saw that you were a good follower, they were emboldened to approach. If a follower didn't dance early in the evening, she could sit for hours without being asked, a soul-crushing experience.

There must be familiarity, which is why it's key to connect in a group class. The math is simple. If one man sees you dance well, then the others will ask you.

Once I'd had a few sips of wine, I sat down in the women's section and put on my shoes. I looked around to see who I recognized. Brandon saw me across the floor and gave me a *cabaceo*. I smiled back. I was ecstatic! It would be a good night.

The A.R. piped up. "Ugh, are you serious?"

I fought back. "So, you'd rather sit out dances?"

"Yes. He's a loser. He wore shorts to class."

"Oh, c'mon. He's trying his best!"

Brandon reached me, smiled and said, "Thank you for dancing with me."

I smiled and stepped into the embrace. The A.R. was right. He was tentative and indecisive, the opposite to the way he'd been in class. The A.R. insulted Brandon and me, but I ignored her and enjoyed the dance. I drank more wine to shut up that voice, and had five good *tandas*, some with class members, and some with leaders who had seen me for the first time tonight. The wine kicked in, so I left and fell into bed.

Chapter 11

In the follow-up workshops, Tara taught us how to find and adapt the embrace with each partner, but it was George who knew how to create trust. Tara made cracks about George, but the leaders looked to him for approval, so she backed off. He understood that the leaders were fighting to make the women happy, and he supported the fight. It gave me a new insight and respect for all leaders.

After a long day of workshops and *practicas*, there was a group meal to get to know your fellow dancers, and then an hour break before the *milonga*. Bonnie came by briefly and pulled me off into a corner.

"So, how was the class? Did it seem like Tara and George were getting along?"

I nodded. "Aside from Tara's constant putdowns, yes."

Bonnie pondered this for a while then leaned in so I could hear her quiet words.

"As you know, Tara broke up with Carlos, her professional partner, who's also here. They were contracted to teach and star in the performance, the finale of the festival. He refused to teach with her, so she brought her husband. Tara wants George to go pro, but he's into being a firefighter. It's obvious to me that she's still in love with Carlos. I have a feeling we could be watching tango history in the making if Tara and Carlos get back together."

"Are you taking bets?" She looked confused, then laughed. "Is Carlos angry that she won't leave George?" Bonnie nodded.

"Does George know?"

Bonnie rolled her eyes. "I doubt it."

"I disagree. He probably came to keep an eye on her."

"Well, I hope he's better at putting out real fires." I followed her gaze to where Carlos was staring at Tara, who was deep in conversation with a student. George entered and went over to Tara, casually kissing her. Was I relieved that George was married? Yes, because then the connection was only about the dance.

At the end of the meal, George sat in the empty seat beside me and said, "You look pretty in green." I smiled, and he leaned in and said, "Save me a *tanda*." It was a dead-on flirt, and he was flirting with me, not the A.R.!

Dessert included a version of the classic tres leches cake, pound cake soaked with three kinds of condensed milk. Instead of being a single layer, this one was a three-layer confection. Instead of the filling being cream-colored, one layer was pink and the second, blue. The icing was a swirl of both colors garnished with raspberries and blueberries. Definitely a visual winner, and simple to make. It had to be tasted. I took a single bite, chewed for a moment then spit it out. The cake was nothing special, but the cream layers were amazing. They had been flavored with raspberry and blueberry jam. I took photos and added it to my list of reimagined classics. It would be easy to adjust the calories. Back at the room, I tried on everything green I'd brought. Nothing was good enough, so I turned on tango music to get myself in the mood. After changing my outfit a couple of times, I settled on a tight, pale-green-mint, low-cut top and a flowing iridescent skirt and my black three-inch stilettos with silver heels and ankle straps. It was my perverse version of a nun's habit, to mark my service to this most high God.

I affected calm, but underneath I knew that I was being run by my fear, or my greed. My greed for dancing was what was making me fearful of not having enough opportunities. Having a bustline generally guaranteed me attention, and for once I was pleased with my anatomy. Since this was the opening *milonga*, my expectations were low, but my anxiety about George was silly. He is married, I told myself over and over, willing my other aspects to remain silent.

Chapter 11

Once at the dance, which was already packed, I found a way to position myself so that, as the dancers circled the dance floor, the leaders would notice me.

My inner voice spoke up long enough to remind me that trying to please other people was a recipe for disaster, and the A.R. jumped in to argue that, no, it was the way to get everything. I didn't have the bandwidth to referee as I was hoping for some sign that George thought I was special.

When George asked me to dance, my heart pounded in my ears. "He's taken. He's married," I whispered to myself.

Cassandra sneered, "You still want to do him." It was true. And the A.R. said, "How married is he really?"

"Shut up, home-wreckers," I said mentally. The *tanda* began, and our connection was intense, and I counted backwards from one hundred to maintain calm. We danced to a romantic *tanda*:

"Tormenta," singer Mario Pomar (1954)

"Derrotado," singer Roberto Florio (1956)

"Soñemos," singer Roberto Florio (1957)

"Tenía que Suceder," singer Mario Pomar (1955)

At the end, we separated. Before I could say "Thank you," which in tango-ese means "I'm moving on to another partner," he took my hand and smiled.

"I really enjoy dancing with you. Let's do one more. It should be a *Vals*."

It was, and for once I was just able to dance, my mind blank except for the tango recipe, shoulders down, sternum lifted, chin slightly lowered, move from the bra strap, keep connection, wait for his lead, the legs begin from just below the rib cage.

This was our *tanda*:

"Mujeres (Solo Tango Orquesta)"

"Lágrimas y Sonrisas (Sexteto Cristal)"

"Vals de Invierno (Solo Tango Orquesta)"

At the end, we finished with a dramatic tango pose, chest-to-chest, my knee lifted to above his hip and pressed into his leg. I glanced over and saw Tara nearby, watching with hooded eyelids.

"Ahem," I said. "Your wife is not happy."

He winked at me and drawled in his best Texas twang, "Ha! She's never happy. But I thank you for a lovely dance," as he turned and headed to where she stood.

He offered Tara his hand, and she accepted with an angry look. The song began, and they danced. When Carlos danced by, she put on a smile and held George tighter. So obvious! I felt flattered that George thought I was a worthy choice to make his wife jealous with. I was glad that I'd worn green.

Chapter 12

Two long tables had been set up on the patio for our group dinner. White tablecloths, tropical flowers, candles and tango music coming through the outdoor speakers. I went to the buffet and made myself a plate, then took a seat at a corner table near the door. George saw me and smiled. At a nearby table, Tara was busy fawning over Carlos. George helped himself from the buffet and sat down next to me.

He whispered bitterly in his Texas-tinged baritone, "Yeah, she wants her career back."

Why tell me? Was I supposed to feel sympathy? Why do good-looking men assume that they can get that from women? I was annoyed. Wash your dirty linen in your own bathroom sink.

I glanced at him. "Would you mind pouring me a glass of wine?" He stood and grabbed a bottle from the center of the table, and poured me a glass of Malbec, and one for himself.

"What brought you to Cancún?"

"Vacation. Relax, have fun."

He laughed. "A worthy goal."

"Thank you. What were you saying about your wife?"

George studied Tara, who was chatting with Carlos and an attractive female student as he spoke.

"She and Carlos were partners before she married me. They'd won many competitions. They'd been in a show. He wasn't interested in her. Tara expects all men to fall at her feet."

"And did you?"

"Hook, line and fire hose."

"Do you always mix your metaphors?"

He grinned. "As much as possible. You don't get points for originality when you're trying to get someone to jump out the window of a burning building."

"Touché." Intelligent. Educated. I realized that the Approval Rat was a total snob. "How did you two meet?" Dorothy, the writer, told the Approval Rat to butt out. "You saved Tara from a burning building, and the rest is history? Sorry, clichés are catching." Or soon to be, I thought.

He looked surprised. "Are you psychic?"

"Actually, no, just sarcastic."

"Wow, a *tanguera* with a sense of humor. You know you're very rare."

"Thanks, so how did you two meet?"

"I wish it was dramatic. There was a fire in her laundromat. She was inside and got trapped in the restroom. I went through the fire to get her."

"Wow. Shame it was only a laundromat. I guess fires are less hot in that setting."

He laughed. "Yeah. But a fire's a fire. Okay, I know you're a writer so I'll make it a better story. It was a six-alarm. It wasn't a laundromat; it was a theater where she was performing. The fire was the hottest one ever." He winked at me as he poured more wine. When he poured, the lower curve of his bicep popped.

"When we got together, Carlos was a player, but Tara said that when it was clear that he would never change, they agreed just to dance."

"Only in tango would that be possible."

George nodded. "Yes, and after that conversation, he'd always been professional with her. That is, until I showed up. He got jealous and became very difficult. He didn't want to be exclusive, but he didn't want anyone else to have her."

"My aunt Cindy has an expression for that: If you go potty where you eat, it's going to be messy and hard to clean up."

George laughed. "I like your aunt Cindy. Once we were married, Tara wanted me to replace Carlos, become her partner. He's Argentinean-tango royalty, been dancing since he was in diapers."

Chapter 12

"Really? I can just see it. Little swarthy, hairy Carlos as a baby in a black diaper, a fedora, and tango shoes."

George drank his wine, then grinned. "Yep. Me, too. Anyway, I'm just a social dancer. I have no interest in competing."

"That's too bad for both of you. How long have you been married?"

"Three years. Sorry, and TMI. What do you do when you're not attending a tango festival?"

"I told you, I'm a writer. I'm writing a diet book."

He looked at me appreciatively. "Looks like you know your topic. What's it about?"

"Thank you. How to reframe how you think about weight control — you're not losing anything, you're gaining health and beauty. Trust your body. Trust your heart."

"What we never do in tango and need to."

I laughed. He'd just given me another good thread. "True. I'm attempting to employ the same techniques to improve my dance."

"You dance well."

"Thank you."

There was a silence while the waiter served food and refilled our water glasses. I watched Tara chatting away with Carlos.

"Why does Tara want to keep competing?"

He shrugged. "She enjoys it. She likes the challenge. She likes winning."

"Did you meet through the tango?"

"No. I only started dancing tango to please her." I could hear the sadness in his voice. Did Tara understand that she was losing him?

"You seem to love it."

"Thanks. I come from a family that likes to dance. More salsa or two-step, but in my world, real men dance, which made it easier to learn the tango. But I didn't realize I was joining a cult."

"More like a religious order."

"Ha! Tango can be a lot like that." We clinked glasses, enjoying a sweet moment of mutual understanding.

"Why did you start dancing?"

"I'd recently ended a bad relationship. A therapist friend suggested partner dancing."

"Yeah, I get that. Tara's a very good follower — on the dance floor. Maybe I'm not leading her well in life. We seem to want different things."

"So, you don't want her to get back with Carlos? I mean professionally."

"I just wish she'd give it a rest so we could start a family."

"And now? If she had a new partner, she'd..." He finished my sentence.

"She'd be practicing all the time. And not with me."

"Yes, and tango has a way..." I stopped. Not my business.

He gave me a wolfish smile. "There's risk in every choice you make. In tango, you take a wrong step and you bloody your partner's foot. In my line of work, you take a wrong step and you fall seven stories through a roof, or lose your balance and let go of the baby you're trying to save."

"Obviously, you can't equate them."

"I keep trying to explain that to her, but..." He gestured helplessly. "And she's always angry lately. I mostly can't get away when she goes to one of these things, but I had vacation time, and Carlos didn't want to teach with her, so I agreed to help her demonstrate..."

"And this is your reward. I'm sorry."

"Like they say, you make your bed..." His voice trailed off, and his dark eyebrows pulled together as he watched his wife fawn over Carlos. After a moment, he turned towards me so she was no longer in view. He moved my glass closer to his, and gestured to the waiter to take our plates.

Chapter 12

He spoke intensely. "I've lived my whole life in Houston. I come from a family of firefighters."

"Why would you all do such a high-risk job?"

He looked surprised. "To help people."

"And beyond that?"

"Because otherwise life is ordinary and I feel like I'm just marking time. The men in my family make a difference and live large. I don't want to live in some petty soap opera."

Cassandra leaped out of my mouth. "Like your wife using you as a club to get Carlos back."

He looked at me and looked away. I sipped my wine and explored the contents of my bag.

"I'd never quite thought of it that way, but you have a point."

"I could also be dead wrong, and remember that writers are liars."

"So, you don't think that tango has a drama factor."

In my mind's eye flashed an image of him as a little boy trying to get his mother's attention, but she flicked him away like a fly and said, "I'm watching my soaps." The little George looked so dejected that I reached out and put my hand on the grown-up George's arm and said quietly, "You deserve better."

"Maybe, but you don't choose who you love." So, he was here to fight for her.

Dinner was over. Tara came to collect George and they left together.

Later, same lights, same people, same music. Different dress. Black lace over a naked fabric dress with an open back and a bustle. I'd put my hair back, worn large hoop earrings, and dark burgundy lipstick to match my new shoes that I'd bought from one of the venders selling their wares at the festival. As I entered, a dramatic *tanda* began. The tenor sounded like his life was over. I found a good seat in a row of chairs on the far end of the dance floor, so all of the leaders saw me as I walked past.

I sat and changed my shoes. George caught my eye across the room. I smiled. He crossed the room and I stood up to meet him. We faced each other. He gently took my right hand in his left, and circled my back with his right arm.

I started to ask something, and he shushed me. "There's a rule against talking while you dance, especially when this feels so good." Wow. He was flirting. I reminded myself that he was married, so no danger.

At the end of the song, he said, "Are you sad?"

We stood in the embrace, waiting for the next song in the *tanda* to begin. I nodded.

"Why would you be sad?"

"I took care of dying family members. First my mother, then my father."

"I'm so sorry."

"Me too. I lost years of my life."

"You did the right thing."

"Maybe, but I'm done with putting others first now. I don't want to deny myself anything ever again — as long as it doesn't hurt anyone else."

"Nothing?" George asked as the next song began. His deep brown eyes bore into mine.

"Nothing." I smiled.

We danced in happy silence until the end of the song, "Vida Mia," the perfect accompaniment to the moment. Many tango songs are about loss, grief, and death, but this song expresses happiness in love and the connection that tango offers.

For the rest of the evening, George and I danced every other *tanda*.

Chapter 13

The finale of the festival was a performance by the various teachers and some of the students who had taken the advanced track of classes. I'd had a hunch that this tango show would be cringeworthy — a second-rate Catskills, maybe even worse — so I had declined to be in it. It was preceded by a lavish group dinner. The crowd of diners chattered about the show excitedly, and I wondered how I'd manage to sit through it. Wine would help. As if reading my thoughts, George sat next to me and poured us both a glass of wine. We clinked and drank.

I cut my food and took dainty bites. "Tell me about a recent rescue."

His face lit up. "Just before I left, a small hotel had a fire on the fourth floor. A mother was trapped. I ran through the fire in the hallway into her hotel room. She had a baby, which I carried over to my buddy, who had climbed up the outside. He started down the ladder with the infant as the flames came under the door."

"Oh my!"

"I tried to lead the woman to the ladder, but she screamed that her baby was still in there. I got her to climb down by promising to rescue what turned out not to be a baby but a French poodle, who wouldn't come out from under the bed. When I finally got hold of him, the floor collapsed and we fell to the floor below. We both survived."

He took out his phone and showed me a photo of himself proudly holding the dog. "The dog's named Poochie."

"That's wonderful. I love dogs."

"Me, too. At the firehouse, we have a Dalmatian." George showed me a photo of a beautiful dog posing in the cab of a shiny red fire truck.

It was too much for me, and I opened my phone and pulled up an old video of Toro doing tricks, looking adorable.

"This is your dog?"

"Was."

"I'm so sorry."

"Thank you."

"I know how you feel. Like losing your best friend."

I swallowed tears to keep them leaking out of my eyes. I remembered holding my little guy in my arms as the vet prepared to deliver the lethal injection. When I'd leaned down to kiss Toro for the last time, he'd given a happy bark, licked my face, and then lapsed into unconsciousness. George wiped my tears with his napkin.

"Remember the good times, and look forward."

The waiter cleared our plates. There was a sudden exodus of teachers and students. It was nearing time for the performance to begin. Tara swooped by with Carlos and shot me a dirty look. She kissed George possessively.

"Wish me luck, baby."

"Break a leg, hon," he said.

She hurried off towards Carlos with a wave.

The two of us sat in the deserted room. He picked up a wine bottle. I nodded and he refilled our glasses. There was a palpable silence, then he put his hand on my knee beneath the table. He leaned in and said, "I believe that everything happens for a reason, do you?"

"Yes."

"You have such satiny skin," he whispered. My sexual pilot light turned on for the first time since I'd broken up with Peter. George leaned towards me, and I felt his hand move up to my thigh and give a gentle squeeze. "So, does what happens in Cancún stay in Cancún?"

"Yes."

Chapter 13

"We have time. I'm not performing. She's dancing with you-know-who, and I didn't see you on the roster."

So, he'd been thinking about it, planning this. Beware of what you wish for. Which word did I keep to which self? I felt like an actress deciding which way she would play a scene. The A.R., who was based on Marilyn Monroe, someone who'd had an affair with a married man and was murdered for it, would walk away. If I were true to Dots, she would walk away because she'd been betrayed by Peter. Cassandra weighed in: "He belongs to someone else!" It was three against one. But some part of me rebelled. If I wasn't Dots, who was I?

There was now a new "me" that wasn't any of them. Was I now my Inner Voice?

The mental battle continued.

"What would make you happy?" That was its question, not "mine."

"Firefighters always get what they want," Cassandra said. "He expects you to say 'Yes.' Then he'll lose respect for you."

This new me felt a wave of rage. Inwardly I shouted, "Shut up! All of you!"

The voices stopped. In that moment of silence, I felt something shift in the four chambers of my heart. I was suddenly aware of a brighter, larger picture of a new life centered around a future version of me who looked like the A.R. with dark hair. She hovered outside a cave in some primordial forest.

"Come and save me, please," she whispered, beckoning with her hands. She seemed taller than I was. I understood. It was to her I'd made the promise. My true self. In my visualization, I walked over and saw she was still tied to a post just inside the cave wall. I untied her, took her hand and led her to a pool of sunlight.

"Don't abandon me again," she pleaded.

"I promise." We hugged and blended into one being.

I would call her Dorothy, the given name I rarely used. She didn't need to justify her behavior. (Where had she been all my life?) The old arguments that it was okay to commit adultery because he was unhappy were irrelevant. It wasn't about him. If I wanted a future worth living into, I had to make good on my promise not to deny myself to please others. I lifted my glass of wine, and smiled.

"What do you have in mind?"

He looked at me with a mischievous smile — were we not partners in crime?

"To meet you in your room. 113, right?"

"Yes. 113." He was a firefighter. He would know where the fire was.

I sauntered to my room. Once inside, I opened the terrace door, which overlooked the ocean. The moonlight shone on the sea, making it shimmer like liquid gallium. It was a cold beauty, just right for facilitating adultery.

George knocked on my door, and I went back inside to let him in. He stepped inside, and I closed the door behind him.

"Okay?"

I nodded.

He picked me up, and I wrapped my arms around his neck. He kissed me. "I've never felt this connection with anyone," he said.

Was that on the dance floor or off? It was a good line and worked on either level. I hid my amusement with a smile. Did he actually think I would believe him?

Quickly, we found our way to my bed. His sinewy frame cradled me carefully at first, but after a few kisses and caresses, we blended with force and sweat until we were spent. As the lyrics from "Vida Mia" said, "We were one heart." I fell asleep not knowing where I ended and where he began — a perfect horizontal tango.

Chapter 13

An hour later, Astor Piazzolla's plaintive ballad "Oblivion" blared from my phone alarm.

"We should get back."

He looked at his watch. "No, we still have time."

"Time for what?"

"I want to dance this tango with you." There were tears on his cheeks. I had a mental flash image of his mother pulling him on her lap. I could feel his pain as if I were him. He wrapped his arms around her and held on tightly. I was jerked back to the present as George threw his brown, fit legs over the side of the bed and stood up. He walked over to my side of the bed and extended his hand.

"May I have this dance?" I felt as if he were in a boat rowing on a river and couldn't stop until he reached the pier where I was standing. He took me in his arms, and I felt him tremble.

We each danced our own grief, him expressing the loss of his dream with Tara, and me grieving for that unresolved longing for my father's love.

As we danced, he led me in a series of slow leg wraps. I imagined that each twist of my leg around his became a flaming circle surrounding the earth. The sobbing violin strains seemed to bind our souls together into a single point of light. The lyrics were perfect for the moment:

"Brief, the times seem brief,

the countdown of a night

when our love passes to oblivion."

I felt the tips of my breasts brush against the soft hair on his chest. His calloused fingers cupped my shoulder blade. He kissed a spot behind my earlobe, and I got a whiff of sea salt and his semen. I shivered. The song ended.

"Again," he whispered, and we danced. This time he hummed the melody. Our bodies cast a single four-legged shadow on the floor as if the moon were sunlight. Mournful and slow, each movement a sob, every turn a sigh. At the end of the song, we stood locked in our embrace, lost in the dance.

"Again," he said. I started the song on my phone. If tango can be the fusion of two spirits in movement, we achieved this for another four minutes and forty-seven seconds. This was the culmination of my entire life, and maybe his too. But tango is its own beast — because at the best moment of my life, I lowered my left shoulder, still worried about my technique.

At the end of the song, there was applause from the recording, which jolted us back — the festival performance was only minutes from ending.

"Mi amor, we don't want to be caught." He held me like a beloved child, but I gently disconnected.

"You're right, George. Shower?" He followed me, and we talked as we soaped each other.

"I have never cheated on my wife before. Not in three years."

Three whole years! A saint! "And I've never slept with a married man before." Was that even true?

"I wish I were free. I would follow you to New York."

In the doorway, we hugged. George kissed my neck and muttered something with the word *corazón*, which means "heart" in Spanish, and left.

Alone, I felt hollow. Why was I bereft? Because he was married and would never be mine? Was I hoping against hope? In my mind's eye, Cassandra rolled her eyes and said bluntly, "That would be absurd, though a firefighter could get work anywhere."

I had a moment of clarity. Hope was a killer.

The purity of the tango connection was everything a child seeks from a parent: total acceptance. I now understood what I'd never had, and could never have with either of them.

Chapter 13

The Inner Voice spoke gently. "This is delayed grief. Let it release." Grief for my father? My mother? "No," the Inner Voice said, "grief for a life unlived." For once, I didn't shut it down. I let myself weep until I was done.

Chapter 14

I dressed with care in a metallic-silver and white dress that looked vaguely bridal. It seemed perversely perfect for the occasion.

As I hurried along the outdoor pathway to the dance stage at the far end of the hotel compound, the always listening "world radio" took over my mind, filling it with a choral symphony of breathless, horrible comments along the lines of, "George was just using you to get revenge on Tara. He didn't even fancy you. You were desperate, an easy mark. He had no respect for you; he thought you were an ugly whore. He cheated on his wife; he would cheat on every woman." I had a sick feeling about how cheap I'd feel on the plane ride home.

The Inner Voice interrupted the "radio" by shouting, "Stop listening to that rubbish! What if he was telling the truth? What if there's something special about you that he saw? What if you showed him what it was like to be with a woman who was emotionally honest? What if you give him the courage to find his own truth?"

Me, emotionally honest? That was rich. I wished that could be true about me. But the idea that maybe something good was possible cheered me up. Still, first I had to admit that I wouldn't have slept with him if he had been single.

I cringed and my left shoulder flew up to my ear, and my arm came up as if warding off a blow. I stumbled, and Brandon appeared at my elbow, steadying me.

He looked me over. "You okay?" I smiled.

"You look like an angel. I didn't see you inside. Where are you sitting?"

"Oh, all the way near the door. I needed some air."

"Me, too. Long show."

"Dance later?"

Chapter 14

"Sure."

Brandon escorted me inside, and we stood in the back. The show was reaching its finale. Bonnie came out onto the stage and announced the main attraction: Carlos and Tara. They walked out onstage, dressed in black and red outfits, and launched into a tango full of lifts, jumps and dips. Tango is a social dance that can become grotesque when pushed to Broadway-show performance levels. Tara and Carlos got a standing ovation.

Brandon whispered, "They were great, weren't they?"

"If you like trained seals."

"You don't think they were improvising?"

I shook my head. Brandon took this in sadly.

"I guess you're right. Too bad."

"I know."

"How about dinner and a *milonga* Stateside?"

Stateside? Brandon smiled at me nervously. Poor fellow, could he not see the disaster he would take on by dating me? I'd spare him the heartache.

"Actually, I'm not free," I whispered and saw his face fall for the second time in two minutes. He nodded tightly, and focused on applauding.

I felt eyes on me and turned. George was staring at me from another spot in the back, and we exchanged a delicious smile.

Later, at the cocktail after-party, Tara stood near the bar too close to Carlos, surrounded by a group of dancers, chatting away as she sipped a cocktail. George and I stood at the other end of the bar, and when she noticed us, she gave a friendly wave. We waved back.

"Melodía del Rio," a sparkling rhumba, began.

"We can tango to this," George said, leading me to the dance floor.

Carlos and Tara joined us on the floor, followed by several other couples. As George and I danced, he led me in a showy *boleo* and a *gancho*, then pulled me in close and whispered, "I'm kissing your pussy as we dance."

He then led me in a series of backward *ochos*, his hand burning a hole in my back. I pivoted and executed a forward *boleo*. He whipped me around and pulled me in close. Our chests touched, and I cradled the back of his neck. The song ended. Tara left Carlos and headed our way. She wasn't stupid, and sensed something between us. George and I shared a last moment, then I saw Brandon making his way towards me. I smiled, thanked George loudly, and moved away. I saw Tara whisper something to George, and he looked down at the floor. Too bad.

I arrived at the airport at 4:00 a.m. for a 7:00 a.m. flight. I checked in at the desk and then headed for security. I heard my name. I turned around. George hurried towards me. George in his white polo shirt, blue jeans, and cowboy boots. His eyes cried dry tears as he reached with his hand to tuck some stray hairs from my eye. He took the copper bangle from his wrist and slid it on mine.

"You started a fire I don't want to put out." I almost laughed outright, then remembered that he *was* a fireman. He took my hand and pulled me close.

"Someone might see us," I said.

"I don't care." He kissed me, but I kept my lips together. George looked heartbroken.

"We shared a moment," I said, comforting him. "It was wonderful."

"Not just a moment."

"Okay, we shared *the* moment."

"... of my lifetime."

Oh dear, this was getting messy. I gently pushed him away.

"There's a convention in New York. Can I call you?"

I sighed. "Oh, George, we agreed. What happens in Cancún..."

Chapter 14

"Stays in Cancún."

Mercifully, my flight was called and I hurried to get on the plane. He stood and watched. I turned and waved at him.

Once the doors closed on the plane, I put the bangle in my handbag. I downed the glass of bubbly the flight attendant offered and toasted to whatever. Thank God! I didn't feel anything. I was so relieved. Love involves loss, and I had a wound in my heart as deep as the spear in Jesus Christ's side. Thank you not, Peter!

While my parents had spent the preceding two years circling the drain, I'd had a love affair with one of the best *tangueros* in the city. Peter had taken everything from me. I had no cushion. We'd had a magic connection when we danced, but off the floor, our interaction had been tumultuous, verbally violent, fabulous and terrible. Peter was jealous and couldn't handle my dancing with other men, although that was the structure of the casual vertical promiscuity of any *milonga*. Peter danced with as many women as I did men, and I didn't see why there was a difference. On top of our fights over whom I danced with, his ex-girlfriend, Nona, stalked him, made scenes at parties, and the cherry on the whipped cream on the icing of this cake was a New Year's Eve where he kissed her instead of me at midnight. True, Nona literally pushed me out of the way to get in the line of the kiss, but by then the point was moot.

Peter and I met dancing at the Luna *milonga*, held on Saturday nights at a dance studio in Chelsea. Today would have been our anniversary, and it was also the anniversary of Annette's successful suicide attempt.

She'd overdosed on her pain meds and passed in her sleep. It was so typical of her to make it a passive-aggressive event where the poor nurse would be blamed. Annette hadn't left a note, but I knew in my bones that it was no accident because she'd made two prior attempts. I'd thwarted my evil stepbrother Brad's plan to ruin Bridget, Annette's nurse-companion, by collecting the many unsolicited emails that Annette had sent to me complaining about how she couldn't stand dealing with Norman and the unbearable pain she felt at her wasted life. It pleased me that her annoying, unsolicited Internet garbage helped to keep a decent caring person like Bridget safe. Bridget was a pretty, heavyset woman with a lilting brogue, three teenage kids and a drunk husband who'd been out of work as long as I'd known her. She had a working relationship with Mother Mary Magdalene, and had taught me Mary's prayer after my first breakup with Peter.

"Hail Mary, full of grace, the Lord is with you. Blessed art thou among women, and blessed is the fruit of thy womb, Jesus. Holy Mary mother of God, pray for us sinners now and at the moment of our deaths. Amen."

I felt a warm presence close to me when I recited it, but Bridget had an ongoing conversation with Mary, and I did not.

Peter and I parted a year ago today. A year of heaven, a year of hell, followed by this past year of misery. How had I stayed with him so long? Peter had a side that was irresistible, an adorable, funny, blond, wide-eyed, square-jawed man-child that peeked out and melted my heart at the oddest times.

Before Annette died, she'd made clear she wanted to be cremated. Typical of her to be so mean-spirited and cheat the earth that had supported her. Burial in the ground was paying it forward, but cremation was an insult to the cycle of creation. Whatever. It was time to dance. I put on a black lace top, tight jeans and high heels. As I was leaving for the dance, Thad called to tell me that my father's cancer had reached stage four.

"Hi, Dots, sorry to call with bad news. I'm on speaker."

"That's terrible, Thad. I'll get an Uber. Tell Dad I can be there in an hour."

Norman yelled into the phone, "Fuck off, Blots. What good can your sour face do?"

Chapter 14

Thad said, "I'm sorry, he's pretty upset."

"Okay, Thad, call me if anything changes."

I confess, a few tears slipped out of my eyes in the Uber on the way to the *milonga*. I expected that I might have to wait for a dance for a while because of my emotional state, but as soon as I changed my shoes, I looked up and Peter, a stocky, tanned blond with a bull neck and cerulean eyes, stood before me, extending his beautifully shaped square hand, not using the *cabaceo*.

"Dance?" he asked in a velvety baritone.

Peter was an insider and one of the most sought-after dancers, and I was thrilled. One *tanda* turned into two, then three. He drove me home in his white SUV. When we pulled up in front of my building, he tried to kiss me. I moved out of the way and reminded him of the tango rule about not mixing dancing and love. He smiled and said, "What if we go on a regular date, no dancing?" He had me at "date."

The evening went well, dinner in a French bistro near my house, and we started to meet regularly.

After the third date, he suggested that we add dancing. We went to a *milonga*. He was greeted like the mayor of Tangoville, and everyone wanted to know my name. Heady stuff. Then when we danced, the other dancers applauded. Good chemistry? I, dumpy Dots, was dating the quarterback. I was finally being accepted, and the other "good" dancers were now asking me!

At some point, he asked me not to dance with other men, and that was the beginning of the end.

In the tango world, unless an agreement was made determining which *milongas* each ex-partner would attend, they were often at the same dance. Since neither of us would give up our precious dance schedules, we both frequented the same places as before our breakup. I refused to dance with him for a month or two, but gave in, because magic is magic, and sexual chemistry is all that. At home, in the bed we'd often shared, I would mourn for him and cry myself to sleep.

The first time I broke off with him was after discovering that he had been sleeping with his ex-girlfriend throughout our relationship. He pointed out that since he'd invited me to live with him and I'd refused, what did I expect? Twisted logic, but he had a point, so I couldn't completely damn him. At the time, Peter lived in New Jersey, near to where my father would be buried. I didn't want to pass that graveyard every day for the rest of my life. I'd suggested that he move in with me, or that we find a new place, but he wasn't interested.

The first time I ended it, we had a bitter, angry parting. There'd been no actual trigger for the breakup, just one more text from his ex while we were about to make up after some fruitless argument. I'd danced with someone else, and he'd had a tantrum and accused me of flirting. He said, "I didn't like the way you danced with him. He held you too close. I saw him kiss you."

"On the cheek, after the *tanda*. I saw you kiss your last partner, too."

"He wanted you."

"For twelve minutes. That's how long a *tanda* is, in case you forgot."

"Yeah, well, I saw the way you pressed yourself against him."

"That's an illusion."

"Oh, bullshit."

"Peter, you know the tango is about intimacy, not sex."

"Fuck you. Drive yourself home."

His text-message alert went off. He pulled his phone out and read the text, typed something. I could tell from his face it was his not-so-ex ex. I felt like a guitar as a string snapped.

"I can't do this anymore, Peter."

Chapter 14

"Do what?"

"Seriously?"

"I can't control her texting me."

"You can if you block her number."

Silence.

"If you love me, do it now."

"I don't want to hurt her feelings."

Wow. No need for physical violence. I realized that she'd metaphorically been in bed with us the whole time. He apologized and offered to drive me home. I got a lift from other friends.

Peter fought hard to win me back by proving he'd left the ex and offering to move to the city. He bought me a pair of diamond earrings as a "pre-engagement" offering and succeeded in convincing me that his intentions were serious. I was thrilled until I learned that he was now living with his cleaning lady. Grace had cleaned for him for as long as I'd known him. Now, according to him, he was bartering living space for services. He claimed she only cleaned for him, but I knew she was cleaning his clock as well. Grace, such an ironic name. I'd met her and it was clear she saw him as a meal ticket. His explanation was a variation on a familiar theme — it was my fault. I'd broken up with him, so what did I expect? Again, the twisted logic that somehow made it all my fault. Was my father whispering in Peter's ear from that nearby grave?

This second betrayal broke something in me. I was like the little stuffed duck I'd loved as a child that quacked when I pressed its belly. At some point, it stopped working and was silent. I felt just like that doleful little toy.

The tango world is like a remote mountain village full of judgmental people gossiping and criticizing their fellow dancers. They were nosy, and whenever Peter and I danced together, the other dancers would ask me if we were back together. My negative answer would constantly elicit, "But you dance so well together," in an accusing tone. Somehow, I was the villain of the piece because I'd broken the golden rule of tango, "Don't date where you dance," and I paid dearly. I wondered if I would still want to dance with him after my "moment" with George.

The plane began its descent.

Chapter 15

When I entered my apartment, I thought, Who lives here? The place was simple with white furniture, a faux black-and-white calfskin rug and throw pillows, high-tech chrome fixtures. The A.R. lived in this fancy place, not me, lowly Dots. I had a moment of cognitive dissonance, and I felt my brain bend as if I'd stepped into an alternate reality where I was an extra in a series on the streaming platform that the A.R. programmed.

When I looked around, everything reminded me of the past — but whose past? When something is over and you try to recall exactly what happened, you can't, and really, did it even ever happen? And what does "happen" even mean?

I put my handbag down and turned on the computer, where my writer self lived, intending to work, but I felt suffocated, and unable to be in my own skin. What to do? I was trapped by my own persona. I needed a way to reorganize my reality.

I thought of the Japanese woman whose book created a cult based on keeping around you only the things you loved. Her theory was that by touching each thing you owned, you could quantify the emotional charge, positive or negative. That was the answer: I had to clean house.

The book suggested that you work through your stuff category by category and you place everything in one section on the floor. I went into the large bedroom closet to see what was there. On one side, color-coded clothes and shoes, accessories in bags by color. I looked through the stuff. Easy to know what to throw out: anything I'd ever worn with my father or Peter. All my stuff was in the beige and gray family in stark contrast to my colorful tango clothes. I'd probably worn half of what was in there, and took out a few things I'd never really used. A ruffled cashmere shawl my stepmother had given me, a gray pantsuit I'd worn once or twice to an interview, a strapless cocktail dress in gray velvet that I'd worn to a wedding Peter took me to. I easily found the accompanying accessories and put the lot into a garbage bag. I felt great, much lighter.

On the beige nightstand was a big white scented candle Peter had given me. Honeysuckle. I'd never lit it. In the nightstand drawer, I found matches from a French place he'd once taken me. I had a flash of us dancing at a tango bar on a Saturday night. I remember people cleared the little dance floor for us, and we gave them a pretty good show. We got applause and free drinks, and would have made new friends except that Peter loudly remarked on some petty mistake I'd made. I hustled us out of there, but then he had a full-blown tantrum on the drive home because I'd accepted a dance from the owner of the bar and hadn't asked Peter's permission.

"How could you do that?"

"You danced with the owner's wife."

"I told you not to dance around."

"We're not married. You have no claim on me."

"You made me look like a loser."

"No comment."

"Are you saying I'm a loser?"

"You said it, I didn't. Just drop me off at my place."

"Just get out." He stopped the car. We were at 14th and Eighth Avenue.

"It's not a good neighborhood."

"I don't care."

"Fine." I got out, slammed the door of his expensive car and hailed a cab. When I got home, he was parked in front of the house and had bought flowers. I paid the driver, ignored Peter and walked to the door of my building. Peter rushed up, got on his knees and held the flowers up.

Chapter 15

"I know they don't make up for anything, but I'm sorry. I followed your cab to make sure you were safe. Can I come up, please?"

And I let him. Dots the doormat!

Later, after consummation, he whispered, "Live with me."

"Not going back to the burbs. Come to the city."

"No." And then he was asleep, snoring gently.

If I'd said yes just then, would we still be together?

Why, oh why did he have to be damaged beyond repair? Why hadn't being in love mattered enough for him to be transformed? I inhaled the sweet smell of the candle, and a dizzying longing for him came over me. I imagined the smell of his citrusy cologne, the veins in his buff arms, his squinty eyes when he laughed. I wanted him in spite of all the facts.

Peter seemed to offer unconditional acceptance, but it was a ruse. The truth was he ruled through criticism, and had frequently shamed me when I forgot to "collect" my feet when we danced. I could hear his growl. "Collect your feet, dammit. It's so simple for the follower. What's your problem?" I felt a wave of fury that choked me. Damn him. It could have been so good. I found the shoes. They were old, the suede faded, the heels chipped. I found the flowing black lace dress with a red lining. They went into the garbage bag.

I lit the candle and sat on the floor to think. I couldn't face getting into a bed I had slept in with him.

I fell asleep curled up next to my bed, and when I awoke, the candle had burned down and dripped wax all over the nightstand onto the floor. Yep. That was Peter. His underlying hostility was present even in his candle.

Okay then, time to detox. I wanted this to be short and sweet, to use joy versus bad memories as my touchstone. I threw all my regular clothes on the floor, then emptied my dresser, separating my tango underwear and tops. I was so upset about the candle that I just wanted to throw all of my tango stuff away. It was best to tackle that another day. I put all the tango stuff in the closet with my dresses and shoes. I closed that door.

What had occupied my "regular" life? Work and my father. I felt okay about my work. I found myself hanging stuff back up until I came across the clothes I was wearing when I tried to rescue Hector. Black tailored slacks, a white collared silk shirt, and a long black sweater. As I held the garments, I remembered the shriveled version of my father, chest heaving in spite of the oxygen feed, his gray bulging eyes filled with terror, staring at me like a drowning man. "I love you," he'd whispered as I stood at the end of his bed.

Next was the outfit I wore to the funeral, a lipstick-red halter-top dress with a deep V-neck, empire waist, and flowing pleated skirt. My head began to hurt. This was some rabbit hole I'd fallen down.

I bid the clothes farewell, but something was triggered, and I found myself stuffing all of the other clothes that were associated with Norman's illness into the same garbage bag. I checked the pockets and found notes in his spidery handwriting. *Blots, pick me up this. Blots, order me that.* And I'd never been able to find the right thing, of course. I felt resentment pile up in my guts like acid reflux.

The most important discard wasn't clothes or shoes; it was my nickname. Dots/Blots was the bad daughter, the fatty, the mousy brunette with the whiny voice, the manless wonder, the loser. Ugh.

I put on tango music and went into a zone. Suddenly it was noon, and I had ten bags of stuff. Clothes, shoes, sentimental objects, photos, everything. I'd bagged everything neatly. I knew if I hesitated, I would backslide.

I threw out most of my sheets and towels because Peter had used them. Then I realized a new bed and furniture would have to be purchased to replace anything with memories. Would I

Chapter 15

have to move? Yes. Eventually. This was a torture chamber, not a home.

I made a few calls, and miraculously the Salvation Army people came. I got rid of all of the furniture in my bedroom as well as the clothes and shoes.

I ordered a new mattress and frame online for same-day delivery. I'd wanted to throw out the bedroom rug, but I knew that it would take weeks to replace, so I shampooed it to remove any trace of Peter's footprints.

Afterwards, I went to feed the pigeons. It was overcast and cloudy, but as I opened my bag and cast seeds to the birds, a ray of sunlight shone through the clouds and lifted my spirits. I was proud of my decisiveness. It was the candle that had been the trigger, and had allowed me to understand that the villain wasn't Peter. It was my father, who'd confused me into thinking that abuse was love.

Henry, my feisty little sparrow, came to the edge of the circle of feeding pigeons and gave me a cheeky look as he cocked his head at me. I threw him a breadcrumb. He swooped and caught it as it bounced.

The A.R. was charmed. "We may survive this after all — if you stop making such self-destructive demonstrations; you just threw away thousands of dollars of perfectly good stuff."

"I can afford it!" I crowed and threw a handful of bread out for the sparrow. Seven other sparrows joined him, and I watched them feast. This is what it's like to be in the "now," I thought, then laughed at the impossible conundrum: knowing it undid it. I was giddy and forced myself to breathe. Charles arrived and sat down gingerly on a bench, his head between his hands. His plight snapped me back.

"What's wrong, Charles?"

"I'm so ashamed. Someone gave me spoiled food, and I soiled myself. I need money to do laundry." That's why he'd sat on a faraway bench.

The look of misery he wore reminded me of me. I found some money and placed it on the edge of his bench. Forty dollars. He folded it carefully and put it in the inside pocket of the army jacket with his name on it. I wanted to ask what war he had served in, but I'd never seen him in this state before.

"Don't be ashamed, Charles. It could happen to anyone."

"Thank you, now I can do laundry and also buy a new set of sweats. I owe you a poem."

"No, get yourself together first. Bring a poem next time. Do you need help?" I moved toward the bench, but he held up his hand, palm facing me, and said, "No. Stay back, and here's your poem:

Our work then is to ward off the two thieves of life's sweetness

our regrets about the past

and our hopes for the future.

All we own is our time.

Be present in this and every fleeting moment

Does the act of smiling make you happy

or do you smile because you're already feeling good?

Does happy mean you're not sad,

or is it only a thin covering for the grief that is life?"

I applauded, and smiling, he slowly walked off, holding his guts.

As I returned to my loathsome flat, it began to rain, and my good mood fled as I contemplated the current facts that remained unchanged by my purge: My father was still dead. Peter was still contemptuous. My bedroom was unrecognizable and nearly empty. The good news was that if the bed didn't arrive, I could sleep on the couch, which I'd kept because it was the first "real" piece of furniture I'd ever bought, before the A.R. was born. I went into the kitchen and had fun breaking every glass and dish that Peter might have touched. I hoped Charles was feeling better. I certainly was!

Chapter 16

Aunt Cindy was why I'd become a writer. She'd been a journalist for a local New Jersey newspaper, and a ballroom dancer. Aunt Cindy never married or had children but confided with a twinkle that "she'd had a lot of fun and didn't have some doddering old man to look after, or bratty grandchildren to babysit for." She was a free spirit.

We sat on the fern-green corduroy sofa in the lounge area of the home that had floor-to-ceiling French windows. I looked out on a stark winter landscape.

"To what do I owe the pleasure of this visit?"

"Can't I just visit?"

"The Sherlock side of the family always has an agenda." It was true.

"Aunt Cindy, I thought you'd want to know about how Norman died."

"Are you sure he's gone? Can you kill demons?"

"Yes. I touched his dead hand and made sure there was no pulse. Twice."

"Ha! Good riddance to bad rubbish. Your mother was fine until she married him, you know."

"That was blunt."

"When you're my age, you have no time to mince words. Here's my eulogy: He was a man who if he shook hands with you, you'd better count your fingers. Ashes to ashes, dust to dust, and garbage to garbage. Amen."

She took my hand and held it. I looked into her eyes that looked like ships on a stormy ocean. She pursed her lips and said, "You look all in. Grief will sap the life out of you."

I felt a wave of love for her. I would never have to count my fingers after I held hands with her.

"How about relief? Doesn't that make you tired as well?"

She belly-laughed until tears filled her eyes. I joined her. Concepción, her aide, brought us a cart with tea and cookies.

"What about the will?"

"I don't know."

"Call Frank. Maybe there's enough so you could write your own book."

"What would I write about? Nothing ever happened to me."

"Anyone who had a childhood with your parents has at least one book in them."

"I write nonfiction."

"Write a memoir then. They're very fashionable. You know, *Mommie Dearest*, et al."

"What would my message be?"

"That which doesn't kill you makes you strong."

"Nietzsche already wrote that."

"He didn't write it in a novel."

"I write memoir-cookbooks."

"Perfect. Your father was a recipe for disaster."

"Is that the headline?"

"No, it's the title, as in *A Recipe for Disaster*, or maybe *Daddy Dearest* would be more enticing. You know how it is: If it bleeds, it leads."

"On your tombstone."

"I'm too close to that to appreciate the reference."

"Sorry."

"I'm just teasing you. Relax! Get some spine! And thank you for not dragging me to the funeral."

"I wasn't even invited."

"Some people have all the luck." My hurt feelings about that caught up with me, and inwardly I was crumbling like a stale muffin. I fought long overdue tears.

Aunt Cindy handed me a plate of cookies and mimicked the Oracle character in the original *Matrix* movie.

Chapter 16

"Have a cookie. By the time you've finished it, you'll feel as right as rain."

I'd seen the film with her, and enjoyed her assessment that the film was a documentary. I took a bite.

"I'd like to see you catch a break; you have been through a lot. First your mother, then him. Can you get away for a week? Somewhere warm?"

I was somewhere warm. I felt seen. I felt as if I were actually in my life. It hadn't occurred to me to take another vacation.

"I'm fine. I went to Cancún to dance after he was in the ground."

"And...?"

"I had an adventure."

Aunt Cindy's face lit up like a toddler eyeing a lollipop. "Do tell."

"I danced a tango in the nude with a married firefighter with a Western twang."

"That's wonderful!"

"Yes, it was." I was suddenly back in that room, and felt George kiss my neck. I shivered.

"He won't leave his wife, you know."

I blurted out, "I'm counting on it."

"Wow. That was fast."

I shrugged. "I'm doing a little redecorating." Ha! That was the understatement of the century.

"Good, but don't try to change the subject. Your soul is weary. One project after another with no rest."

"I know."

There was a pause. This wasn't the first conversation we'd had on the topic.

"You need a boyfriend or at least a paramour. What about that Peter tango dancer you liked so much?"

I shook my head and sighed. Aunt Cindy nodded as if I'd said something eloquent.

"You know what I hear all day long? Regret, for all the things these oldsters I'm surrounded by didn't do. They're all scared to death of death. Because they feel they wasted their time here. I regret nothing, and I'll let you in on a little secret. I don't mind dying because I know I'm going home."

"Home?"

"Back to spirit, back to the Creator, back to heaven where we all start from. We should celebrate at funerals and cry when a baby is born. This life is like taking a trip somewhere, and at the end you return to your home."

That was a new idea. Concepción returned.

"It's time for your physical therapy, Mrs. Cindy."

In the car on the way back to the city, I left Suzanne a message that I was back, and declared, "I swear by Hector's feathers that I will deliver *Just Dessert* on time."

I needed a nap, but the bed had not arrived. There was an email with a song and dance about the delay, but I was too tired to care. I'd taken a pillowcase from the hotel that smelled of George. I put it on a throw pillow on the couch and fell asleep. I dreamt of being on the river in a rowboat, with George rowing me as I lazed back under a white parasol, like a French Impressionist painting. My job was to move back and forth and balance the boat as he rowed. I woke up with the answer to what to call my system of weight control! It was "weight balancing," not "straddling," and the crux of the matter was anxiety versus fear because a specific hunger can be handled, but generalized free-floating fear of starvation cannot. Thank goodness for dreams. I never could have found that by thinking. And the phrase came with such a great metaphor about finding balance, not just with food but in all things.

The word "anxiety" was a marketing term that described a condition of the fear of fear, whereas fear was a biological response to a specific stimulus.

Chapter 16

I'd conquered my fear of food by analyzing what I was afraid of. I couldn't control how much I ate, so I measured everything I liked to eat to see how much of it I could eat and maintain my weight. Portion size was the building block of all weight balancing. How many calories did a bite of a doughnut or cake have?

I revised the outline a touch so that part one became a brief tutorial of how the body processed food, and how every stomach was of a definite size, roughly the size of a person's clenched fist, and could hold no more than two fistfuls without getting stretched. It was easy to gain control if one understood the body. I created a quiz, as I know people enjoy taking them, which was a hidden diagnosis sheet. The carrot (pun intended) was that by answering the questions you could jump-start the getting-slender part. It flowed, and I put everything, including tango, on hold.

Suzanne chose that moment to call me. "Don't go off topic" was her opening gambit.

"Are you psychic?"

"No, but after all our books together, you think I don't know how you're going to try to sabotage yourself?"

"That was subtle." She had some nerve: "our" books?

"Maybe not, but let me have the conversation with you. Sock puppets. Left hand: How's it going, Dots? Right hand: Great, I just had a fantastic insight, and am redoing the table of contents so that it makes more sense. It'll be better, and maybe coming up with a new title?"

She had me. "But..."

"Let's do the cost-benefit analysis — will it be so much better that it was worth missing the deadline and creating drama with the client?"

"No, but this is my book. I'm the client."

"No, a publisher is the client. You're the product."

"But..."

"No buts, if you want to change anything, send it to me first. Read. My. Lips. Eating dessert can help you become thin and beautiful."

"Not exactly. More like eating a bite of dessert before each meal."

"Whatever." I could imagine the dismissive wave of her hand and the frown that would accompany it. "I can sell this based on your delivering exactly what was in the proposal, and no one will write a check till they see the book. This time I can't cover for you. Your name is going on the cover. If you want to miss your chance, keep improvising. Remember, I've got you on my voicemail promising to meet the deadline."

"All right, Suzanne. I'll get back on track." So much for the upgrade.

"Thank God. When can I see it? A month?"

I looked at the tangled mess of half-finished chapters. "Maybe three."

"Good. And stay away from you-know-who."

I put aside the pages I had written in a fever and reread what I'd already written. My previous insights seemed pedestrian compared to what I knew now, but this was my chance to become a brand. By reminding myself that I was the ghostwriter of my own book, I was able to maintain the imaginary distinction that I was one of my subjects. Because I kept my emotional distance from myself, the work flew.

Working off my proposal, I created a rough outline of each chapter with the key points laid out in the text.

I ignored the outside world, which meant no dancing. This was a speed pregnancy. Giving birth is an accurate cliché used to describe the act of creating a book. I didn't get out of my bathrobe except to buy various desserts to see how much of each was a "bite" and to estimate the calorie count. The common wisdom is that a sedentary woman needs to eat 1200 calories to reduce body size. That is not a lot of food and then

Chapter 16

to whittle away calories for dessert at dinner would challenge the most determined dieter, so I got out all my baking stuff and experimented with low-calorie versions. I'd worked with several food testers in the course of my career and knew how hard it was to be accurate. With all of the new non-sugars like stevia and monk fruit, much more was possible. But what if my audience were not bakers? How could I come up with simple stuff like "Bad Girl Pie," yet deliver on the book's promise of classic favorite desserts, which were rarely easy to make?

I'd worked on a diet cookbook as a newbie and had spent six excruciating months delving into the legalities of recipe creation, so I knew the ropes, which is how I'd been able to predict an end date. I'd kept my notes, which luckily included many recipes. While I couldn't use them as they were, I had a framework. Recipes were generic, like the ones for chocolate pudding or apple pie. There were a million variations, and this is what made them unique.

I knew that once a food book is sold, every recipe is fact-checked, so I wasn't worried. I just needed sexy names like "French Dancer Tarte," not "Just Dessert Apple Tart," but Suzanne was the master of the hook and would find the best frame.

I was unmoved by the smells of caramel and chocolate. I was slim because I'd been able to disconnect emotion from eating. It was the same reason that tango was hard for me, because I had to risk being emotionally present for an entire *tanda*. But when I reread the pages, my writing was flat, and I knew it was because I was so emotionally distanced. What to do?

I called Aunt Cindy.

"I'm stuck."

"Okay, tell me."

"I'm writing my own book, *Just Dessert*."

"Wonderful! I love it and it's about time. It's your memoir, right?"

"No, it's a diet book with recipes."

"Go ahead, tell me the story of how it happened." This was a childhood bond, telling each other about our real lives as if they were stories.

"Once upon a time, the Ugly Duckling was driving back from her dad's funeral. She called her agent, the Fox, because Ugly didn't want to die without something with her name on it. The Fox told Ugly to create a diet book where eating dessert before a meal helps people lose weight. Ugly wrote the book and lived happily ever after."

"Cinderella would have been a better choice."

"Yeah, yeah. Whatever."

"It's deliciously ironic that the pie hater should write a book about dessert."

"It's not really mine. It was Suzanne's idea."

"I thought it was your joke that gave Suzanne the idea."

"It was."

"So, she just did her job — she took your original idea and dumbed it down to something commercial. It's still your idea."

I sighed and shook my head. "No, she told me to write it."

"You provided the spark. She just built the firepit."

"I wish that I could believe that."

"Please, Dotty doughnut, let yourself win once in a while. Please. Just this once. Stop your negative self-talk — it will kill you. At least Cinderella overcame her self-imposed victimhood. The Ugly Duckling became a swan on the outside, but it didn't change how she felt about herself. Be like Cinderella. She shared her struggles and received divine intervention. If you share your own struggles, your readers will relate to you better, and then maybe you can forgive yourself."

I nodded, and knew she was right.

"It's a good story you can tell when you're interviewed on TV: your dad passes, and you get the opportunity for the book. I remember reading somewhere that Danny Glover got the part in that movie with Mel Gibson on the day his mother passed."

"I'm just writing a diet book."

"What does 'just' mean? All books have value. We write because we can't help sharing something we've learned. Share what your past taught you."

"I have no past."

"Don't be absurd."

"Aunt Cindy, you're the one who taught me that. You taught me that to look back on or talk about the past made it happen again."

"Yes." I could feel the warmth of her smile. "And that's precisely why every great writer must look at their past in order to project a future, and then change it. That's why writers get crazy."

"So, you're saying that writers do need to revisit their past."

"Yes, but not as part of a continuum. You have to call on your own experiences briefly to write your own story."

"That's opposite advice!" I stamped my foot like an angry child.

"Yes, it's a paradox. Grow up! You shouldn't have to look backwards, but sometimes you do have to. Your success depends on it."

I had no answer. "I don't remember much after my sister died."

"Which is a blessing. But you must share how you used your techniques successfully. And some of Liz's desserts. The one thing she did well." A grim chuckle escaped her.

"Her desserts made me fat."

"No, you made you fat. No one held a gun to your head. You chose to eat all that stuff, and then you made the choice to get slim. I remember you telling me how you succeeded in stopping eating that chocolate-pudding pie you loved so much. You made the mental equation that it looked like shit, and would become shit, so why would you eat something that would also make you feel like shit and get you fat."

"That's not going in the book, because it's the reverse of the advice I plan to give."

"No. You're wrong! It's bad advice, so you share it, then give them the right advice. They will trust you more if you admit that you are human."

"No, I'm making the whole book up." My spirits plummeted. "But I get your point. If I don't use myself, I'm writing a one-woman show with no star. But I didn't do anything special."

Aunt Cindy laughed.

"Jesus, Dot, the hell you didn't. How about how you cut all of your food in eighths and quarters for months?"

"Pretty desperate, huh?"

"No, I thought it was very ingenious. And your fat freak of a father made fun of you for even trying."

"I can hear his sneer, 'Once a fatty, always a fatty, why even bother?'"

"Yet, you persisted."

"I still feel the shame."

"But it worked!"

"That's why I'm happily married with kids and my own writing career."

"Be patient. If you want to know what you want, look at what you already have. Your problem, if you choose to have one, is with what you want. Change what you want by letting the few good food memories in briefly, and the book and your life will be much better. Don't forget to include some of those desserts that got Norman fat. They were as sweet as your mother was sour."

"How do I control what I remember?"

"Do what you always do: get a pair of their shoes. Maybe buy the shoes of the future cookbook diva, Dorothy Sherlock. What would she wear?"

Chapter 16

She had me at "shoes."

"Okay, love you."

"Love you, too. And get to work!"

I steeled myself and made a list of what I remembered. *The Betty Crocker Cookbook*. Cakes from mixes. Lemon-chiffon pie. Chocolate layer cake. Bread pudding with whipped cream. Chocolate-chip cookies. Opening tins, cutting apples, chopping nuts. I remembered our yellow-and-white kitchen with its linoleum floor and harsh lighting. I remembered Toro at my feet, throwing sticks for him, and walking him in the autumnal woods behind the house. I remembered my dad before he became obese. A moment when my parents were happy after eating chocolate-pudding pie. (I was forbidden to eat it. Of course, I raided the fridge late that night and got slapped.) Making cookies with my mom, which of course I did wrong. But I remembered the recipe. Her secret? A chocolate liqueur in the batter. I pulled the dictionary on my lap and imagined holding Toro that fateful night, waiting for Dad to come home to take my mother to the hospital when my sister was ready to be born … I shut the mental book. I hoped I remembered enough.

I put on tango music and danced around until I felt better, and made a list of desserts. I began to hunt down recipes. As I often had to do with my other clients, I airbrushed the trauma out of those memories and turned them into Norman Rockwell–esque stories of a wholesome only-child suburban story. But something nagged at me. I heard Cassandra's voice snarl, "For God's sake, tell the truth, just this once. Honor me, dammit!"

I pondered how much of my father to leave in, because trauma was fashionable, and what used to be called "constructive criticism" was now called "fat shaming." But then, there were actually happy moments when my mother was hopeful and cooked dinners for Norman. How long did I have to pursue those memories? It wasn't too bad until the event of the fatal birth of my sister, stillborn when I was eight, which ruined everything. No more baking parties, no more happy moments. I don't think I would have survived without Toro. The mechanics of suburban life went on, but the heart was gone. My father was always late, and half the time Mom had gone to bed drunk. How many evenings did I sit at the kitchen table with Toro at my feet waiting to eat dinner with my dad? While waiting, I had snacks with my imaginary older sister. My sister was to be named Cassie, which I thought lacked class, so I upgraded it to Cassandra. In my imagination, she looked out for me in a way my mother never did. Liz, my mother, was tall and willowy, like her older sister, Aunt Cindy, and regarded me as a mistake on the Creator's part, an ugly mockery of female beauty. Liz had been a nasty drunk, and never missed an opportunity to remind me that I was to blame for all of this. Enough. I mentally closed the book of the past. I wrote down what I remembered from the cooking part of each experience and researched the missing ingredients.

I had two and a half months of productive solitude, and then Peter texted me. "I miss you; I made a mistake. Isn't it our anniversary soon?"

I laughed aloud.

"So many mistakes," I texted back, but then erased it.

I visualized us dancing in close embrace to some slow bluesy tune. I could almost hear his gravelly voice reverberating in his chest as he sang along, and felt my heart turn over at the memory of how his chest hair revealed by an open-necked shirt had tickled my nose.

I texted back, "Sure we can dance sometime after I hand in the manuscript."

"How about Valentine's Day?"

"Okay, I got to go." I turned off the phone.

Chapter 17

The book was to be roughly 30,000 words plus recipes. My outline called for twelve chapters and forty recipes. I wrote between a thousand and fifteen hundred words a day. I would begin by editing down what I'd written the day before. The chapters needed to be fifteen pages or so. The preferred length of the entire manuscript was a hundred and twenty pages, to allow room for roughly forty recipes and photos.

I wrote the chapter on "Pies, Tarts and Flans," which I described as "a type of dessert with a yummy center encased in some kind of pastry." Flan was the ultimate dessert as it was all filling, no pastry. It amused me that Fernando and Suzanne's desserts ended up in the same category. It seemed perfect that Suzanne's favorite was contained in pretentious pastry whereas Fernando's was all sweet filling.

But where did I fit? What would I have been if I were a dessert? I plunged into a dark place. I had no category. And I was certainly not sweet. I'd done such a good job conditioning myself not to react to food triggers that I'd wiped out a part of myself. How could I recapture the passion for food that made diet books successful? It was an unsolvable paradox. How could I risk revealing myself without revealing myself? I was skating on thin ice, trying not to land in quicksand. Jumble much? Mixing metaphors was like stress eating for other people.

I wrote in a constant state of queasiness. I lost five pounds because I just couldn't bear to eat after a day's writing. I was being clobbered by my self-doubt, and evil voices inside my head screamed, "Stupid! Stupid! You have nothing original to say. That's why you're a ghostwriter. You're nothing, you know nothing, you have nothing to say." Curiously, my whiny writer self was unmoved. The sock-puppet dialogue went like this:

Writer self: "Hey, Inner Critic, shut up! Evil voices! Get lost! I don't care! I do have something to say. I'm the poster child for the techniques I advocate in this book."

Inner Critic: "Once a fatty, always a fatty. Like an alcoholic writing a book about drinking in moderation. And you could fall off the wagon in a heartbeat."

It was right, and I'd have to stop and talk myself down. I'd get some writing done, but then there would be another attack, which one of my supportive parts would rebut, but which would then rinse and repeat with an increasingly critical Inner Critic. This caused a fatigue I'd never experienced before when writing. I imagined that it was like carrying a difficult fetus, and dragged myself forward by focusing on the successful book with my name on it appearing in bookstores.

On top of this, I couldn't write away my disappointment over Peter. There was no reckoning the depth of the connection between us. I woke up with a physical ache for him.

The daily calls from Suzanne were a good push. At 8:00 a.m., she'd call and I would tell her how well my writing went for the day that hadn't yet occurred. Then we'd talk at the end of the day and I'd report what I'd done. Telling the story backwards was something I'd used in my real life to gain control over eating. Suzanne was a good friend.

Three days before my deadline, I was able to write, "The End."

I went to sleep for twenty-four hours, got up, and treated myself to steamed broccoli and egg drop soup. My fortune cookie read, "He who knows he has enough is rich."

I went back to sleep for another day. I awakened at dawn and remembered that I could see the river from my window, and pulled up the shade. I saw Charles writing on the bench, and the birds looking for food. My apartment looked like it had been ransacked, so I cleaned up. The manuscript was in the printer. When Suzanne called, I had good news.

"It's done. On time."

I sent her the draft. I went to feed the birds. It was summer. My heart lifted when I saw the sunlight glittering off the water of the Hudson River. I walked down to my bench. Charles was there and happy to see me.

"I thought maybe you moved to Argentina."

"Not yet. Just gave birth to my new book." The pigeons remembered me, and I gave them a good feed. Henry, my lovely sparrow, swooped in amongst them, fearless and free.

"Do you think he knows his size compared to them?"

"Is that rhetorical?"

"Yes, because I wrote a new poem."

"Okay, let's hear it." I was suddenly impatient, squirming at this social obligation. I threw some crumpled soup noodles outside the feeding pigeons, and my sparrow dove for them like a cat playing with a toy.

I felt in my pocket and handed Charles a five-dollar bill. His eyes filled with tears, and he started to walk away.

"Wait, Charles, what's wrong?"

"You don't care. You didn't even let me read my poem, and it's for you."

"Thank you. I'm so sorry. Please."

"Okay." He dug in his pocket and brought out his notebook and struck a pose, then tore the piece of paper from the notebook and crumpled it.

"Never mind, it wasn't that good. But here's the point: You're a sparrow, Dotty, and so am I." He looked me over carefully. "Don't be too hard on yourself. You'll have to get in line."

Chapter 18

The first draft was done. It was Valentine's Day, and I was alone. I felt very bad.

I got a text from Peter. "Let's dance at Nocturne tonight, and be my valentine."

I wanted to see him, but not to set off the gossip machine or Peter's constant jealousy when he saw me dancing with other men, so the best way to resolve that was to limit our date to the private sphere. I invited him over. I texted back, "How about my place, remember our deal?"

I got an effusive emoji cluster back.

Peter arrived at my apartment bearing a dozen long-stemmed red roses, a huge red heart-shaped box of chocolates, wine, a joint, a marijuana cookie, and some gummies, just in case. He wore a big smile that showed off his smile lines and perfect teeth.

"Wow, nice outfit!"

I was wearing what I referred to as my "virgin outfit," a pleated white silk dress that looked like a Greek tunic with a gold wrap belt and matching shoes.

He raked his eyes over my physique in palpable, nonverbal appreciation. I felt as if I'd stepped into a pool of sunshine on a beach.

He was so handsome. Tanned, craggy face, big shoulders and Bam-Bam arms. Navy blazer, jeans, and a crisp white shirt.

"Thank you."

"I like to be prepared." Peter handed me the goodies. He kissed me hello. I turned so the kiss landed on my cheek. He gave me a forlorn look and said sadly, "Happy Valentine's Day, honey."

When he spoke, the rumble in his chest affected me like a drug; I became deaf to my Inner Voice or any of my aspects.

Chapter 18

"Thank you." I opened the wine, he lit the joint, and we smoked. On this evening celebrated by lovers around the world, we moved all of the remaining furniture in my living room and danced the tango. We drank a bottle of champagne. We ate cookies and smoked. I opened more wine, he lit another joint, and we made love standing up, leaning over a table. We made love on the sofa, and on the floor. In between, we danced. We danced to "Sentimientos" by Linetzky & Romeo, a pulsing, instrumental, and sensual alternative tango with a mournful violin lead. Perfect to express the finality of tarnished love. Peter ended our final dance with a flourish, turning me and leading me into a back *gancho* with my back to him, leg lifted and pressed against his inner thigh.

"I could sleep here tonight," Peter hinted. "And every night." He gave me a sweet smile.

"All night?"

"Yes. I can stay till six."

"That's fine," I said and poured more wine.

We clinked our glasses and he took a gulp. I felt a wave of grief wash over me. It wasn't all night, though more than anything I wanted it to be. I glanced at the clock and it was 1:00 a.m.

He kissed me and said, "You're so beautiful."

I was happy. This was the dream, fulfilled.

"Time for bed?" It was a flirt.

I posed in what I hoped was a sexy way in the bedroom doorway. Again, he offered a wave of silent appreciation, then frowned. Another wave, this time of fear, washed over me, and I tried frantically to remember what I could have done wrong. I was drowning. I felt fat, out of shape, ugly.

Peter smacked himself in the forehead with his hand. "Ugh!"

"What's wrong? Are you okay?"

"It's not that — it's just, how did I get myself into this mess with Grace?"

"You couldn't resist a bargain?" I was only half-joking. Peter could be insanely cheap. I hoped the evening wouldn't devolve into a therapy session with the victim comforting the perpetrator.

"She's been driving me crazy."

"Is she still cleaning for you?" He nodded.

"I have no sympathy for you. None at all." I smiled as I said this, but I wasn't kidding. And he smiled, too.

"I have to call her. I don't want her to be worried. You could talk to her," Peter teased.

"And say what? That you're a jerk, but you're a good lay?"

"Ha. Ha. No, Grace is a tease. It's always tomorrow."

So, were they *not* sleeping together?

The A.R. was upset. Tears, a victim. She asked, "How could he do this to me?"

Cassandra rolled her eyes. "What did you think, stupid?"

I said, "Okay, Peter, that's enough. One more word and I will start telling you about what and who I have been up to." Peter's eyes flared with fear. So, he did still love me.

"No, please. Sorry, I guess I should call her. What should I tell her?"

"How about you won't be home and you'll see her for breakfast?"

"Okay." Peter picked up his phone from my living-room coffee table and began texting. When he was done, he smiled and held out his hand.

"Now play our song."

Our song, the first one we ever danced to, was called "Historia de un Amor," by Héctor Varela. It told the story of a failed love affair. I hadn't taken the hint from beyond.

The translated chorus was:

"You're by my side no more, my love
and in my soul all I've left is loneliness

and if I can't see you anymore
why did God make me love you?
just to make me suffer more?"

"I love you so much," Peter murmured as we danced. He kissed my ear, my neck, my shoulders. I was stoned and drunk. I felt myself wobble, and he caught me. The next thing I knew it was four a.m., and Peter was scrambling into his clothes.

"What's wrong?" I asked. "I thought you were staying until six." My head was throbbing.

"Grace called my sister, said she was calling the hospitals! She said I didn't call her."

"Really? I thought you texted Grace and told her that you were going to be out."

"I did." He'd always lied easily and without strain. I'd forgotten how gifted he was at it.

"Really? Show me the text." I looked him in the eye. He looked down, hiding his phone. "Don't bother explaining. Nice to see you. Now please go. You know where the door is."

He sadly picked up his dance shoes and put them in his leather shoe bag.

"I'm sorry. You know I love you. I had a great time." He took another joint from his pocket and handed it to me. I took it, nodded my thanks. He smiled at me, hopeful as a naughty puppy hoping he wouldn't be slapped for pooping on the floor.

"Bye," I said, my voice a verbal slap. I opened the door.

"I'll call you." He went in for a kiss, but I stepped back.

"Don't bother."

He shot me a wounded look. "Don't be like that."

"How should I be?"

Peter looked at me with pleading in his sky blue eyes. "I told you, just look away sometimes. Just look away."

"I can, but not when my nose is rubbed in it. Next time, lie better."

He smirked at me, as I realized my slip — "Next time." Was I insane? I closed the door and stood listening until the sounds of his steps stopped.

I looked around the trashed room, furniture in one corner, empty wineglasses, a crimson spill on the rolled-up rug and two roaches in an ashtray. I wished that I felt cheap and like I'd been "played," but instead I felt an unreasonable elation, and lay down in my mussed new bed, still damp from our endeavors, hugging the undershirt he'd left behind in his haste.

As I fell asleep, I asked myself, "What would he have to do to me for me to be able to cut the cord once and for all?"

Cassandra had a good answer: "When you stop sharing his contempt for you." Ouch.

I awakened at 7:30 with a hangover. I went for a walk. It was misty, and I couldn't see the river from my window. Outside, it was cold and rainy, a sound blanket to smooth the after-flush of a night of pleasure. I put on a trench coat, leggings and flats, big sunglasses. It was my best Audrey Hepburn imitation, but there was no Tiffany's for me to go to, so I walked gingerly and aimlessly on my swollen feet, punishment for wearing my highest, four-inch, gold-sequined tango shoes the night before. I felt immersed in the scenery, the slippery sounds of the cars and trucks driving along the West Side Highway creating a soundtrack for some moody, foreign-language film. My phone buzzed. It was a text from Peter.

"I had a great time. I'm going to ask Grace to move out. Wait for me."

Woo-hoo! I needed to talk to someone, but I couldn't talk to Natasha, who would berate me for seeing Peter. I needed sympathy, not therapy. It began to rain hard, so I went home and straightened up. Or, rather, I napped on the sofa, the detritus untouched.

Ernest Hemingway is reputed to have told an interviewer about his writing habits, "I write to the first drink." I decided to

Chapter 18

reverse his plan. At 11:00, I pulled myself together and went to La Boca to see Fernando.

"How's your day going so far?" he asked.

I made a face. "That good?"

I shrugged.

"Are you hungry?"

"No."

"Then talk to me."

I told him about Peter. He listened, and when I was done, he said, "Don't blame yourself, Dots. There's no crime in wanting love. Here's the line: Do you feel better for having seen him or not? Loneliness can be a crippling emotion."

"Yes, better." I did feel better — about Dorothy, the true self part of me.

"Good. Now draw that line in the sand — behind you. Stay on the side that feels better."

"You're right. Thank you. What did you do for Valentine's Day?"

Fernando sighed. "I was here, then I was home alone, but I spoke to my kids. My ex hates me. She's made them hate me, too." The sadness in his eyes pulled at my heart.

"I'm sorry, Fernando. You know I love you."

He came around the bar and hugged me. "I love you, too."

Chapter 19

"Grace is gone. Come to San Jose to the festival."

There was hope!

I texted back, "Yes, but I want my own room." I didn't want to be stuck in a room with a jealous oaf.

"Let me pay, then."

Peter bought tickets to the festival and booked himself in a hotel room next to mine.

The morning of our trip, he was an hour late, unapologetic in his white Benz SUV. When we arrived at the airport, we had to rush to get onto the elevator to the baggage check-in kiosk. As the doors opened, I hurried to the desk to present our tickets to the attendant. There was still a prayer we could make it.

The elevator doors closed on him as he was wheeling our bags out. He began to harangue me when he caught up to me at the desk.

"You didn't hold the door for me," he accused. "I can't believe you did that. What the hell is wrong with you?"

"Just shut up a moment. If you'd been on time, we wouldn't have been rushing." My father hadn't ever taken me anywhere, but this was what it would have been like if he had. This thought was like acid rain on a rather dejected parade. On top of that, we missed the plane.

Instead of apologizing and offering to cover the additional travel fee I'd have to pay to catch another flight, Peter got angry with me for asking him for the compensation. I was speechless. He had been crass about money before — the more time I spent with him, the more I saw that he was constantly pinching pennies — but not to this extreme. I paid my own fees. Thank goodness our newly assigned seats would be far apart.

As we were waiting for our new flight to board, I called the hotel to change my room, to be further away from him, but no

Chapter 19

one answered. With that, I turned around and suggested to Peter that he simply go home. He tried to undo the mess he had made, by offering to reimburse me for the extra fee, but it was a no-win. If I let Peter pay, he would feel that I was beholden to him, and if I said no, he would be thrilled that he hadn't had to spend money. Merely contemplating this made me feel ill.

"Peter, this was a mistake, and maybe if you stay in New York, it would give us time to heal."

"I already paid for this ticket — and extra at this point — and no way am I going to miss out. And I'm not going to let you go meet some other man there."

"Is that an accusation or a prophecy?" I asked. "Considering the way you're acting, I can only pray that I do."

"So, there is someone!" he shouted, oblivious to my innuendo.

"Quiet down."

"You're going to meet someone. Who is it? Do I know them?" he shouted in my face.

"I'm not meeting anyone," I sighed.

Two security guards walked toward us. I hissed, "Unless getting strip-searched by men in uniform is your fantasy, you'd better cool it."

We smiled at the guards, two burly men with serious expressions. "It's all right, officers, he was just telling me a story. It was *sooo* funny."

They stood for a moment, and then slowly turned away.

Peter waited until they were out of earshot.

"So, who are you meeting?" he asked.

I shook my head helplessly.

"You're the one who invited me! You're just making a scene to avoid having to deal with the fact that it's your fault we missed the plane. You were an hour late picking me up, so just accept it. You should have offered to pay the overage. You should be on your knees begging forgiveness. You are a cheap and nasty person, and I wish I'd never met you."

"You don't mean that." The announcement came that the plane was being boarded from the back. I'd been upgraded to business class.

"See you there, honey. I'll meet you at the baggage claim. It'll be okay." He gave me a peck on the cheek and walked away. Boarding for my row was announced. I began to cry. I struggled in my handbag for tissues, wiped away my tears, and picked up my bag. I couldn't stop. I was pathetic. Gina, a flight attendant, gave me a concerned look as I stepped onto the plane. She was my body double, with dark hair and a mole on the corner of her face beneath green eyes.

"Are you okay?"

I took a chance.

"No. Man trouble," I managed to get out without the sobs resuming. I went into the restroom to calm down.

When I got back to my row, there were two vodka miniatures tucked into the seat pocket. I chugged them both. Gina walked by, checking for proper takeoff protocol. I smiled my thanks. She leaned in.

"The best way to get over a man is to get under a couple of other ones."

"I'll keep that in mind."

I fell into a deep sleep almost right away. I awoke as we began our descent, and was chilled to the bone. My throat was sore, and I felt a cold coming on.

The captain announced that instead of it being seventy degrees as promised, it was forty outside. After we landed, things got worse. Peter was contrite, had found flowers somewhere, and was waiting with them in the baggage-claim area. When we arrived at the hotel, I didn't have the strength to put up a big fuss. On top of this, there were no other rooms, so we were left with our original room arrangement. I was feeling poorly, and I let Peter hail us a cab so that I could pick up a fifth of rum to use in a hot toddy to clear my sinuses and warm up. We argued about which liquor store to go to. Peter didn't seem to care in the least about my health.

The next day, the festival began. It was freezing, and I was bundled up in everything I'd brought.

The organizer of the festival and a well-known teacher, Jon Temple, a beanpole of a man who affected a 1950s beatnik look with a goatee and beret, taught the first class. I knew no one and was very nervous, but I was away from Peter. I couldn't stop smiling.

Jon employed me as his demonstrator several times, and other students warmed to me as I fumbled and struggled. We rotated partners throughout the workshop, so I made a lot of new acquaintances. I wasn't the only one who was afraid to change weight just before I turned and froze, effectively stopping the dance.

The secret was to trust the leader. If tango were a metaphor for life, I saw the larger problem. The two words "Peter" and "trust" could not be put in the same sentence. It was his job to help me to complete my weight change, and I wasn't always getting a clear invite. In the moment of transferring weight from one leg to the other there is a moment of suspension, which filled me with terror because it was like being in a speedboat where no one was driving. In spite of my annoyance with Peter, I was excited to share with him what I had learned, but he was nowhere around. I texted him.

He responded via text: "Tired. Taking a nap."

There was a *practica* after the workshop before dinner, and I happily danced with new leaders. After I got back to my room and changed clothes, I went to Peter's room to collect him for dinner. I hoped that we could find a way to have a good time together. I discovered that he was drunk, having used the medicinal bottle of rum to make us a traveling cocktail that he'd stored in a Diet Coke bottle. He'd already drunk half.

"Before you go off on me, Dots, just remember I have no pot with me. I'm just using the liquor to try to get my balance. So back off."

He was a pothead, not a drinker, and I had never seen him drink more than a glass or two of wine. The rum, which mellowed me out, made him contentious and rowdy.

Dinner was held in a large room with a blue-and-white nautical motif filled with the inviting smells of a buffet. As we helped ourselves to the food, I said hello to some of my new friends, but Peter just nodded curtly and refused to take off his sunglasses. He was also very possessive and kept making overt gestures of affection, a no-no in tango world.

That night I ignored him and danced with others. Each time Peter asked me for a *tanda*, I declined. He kept apologizing and said he was sober. I left the dance before he did, and slept.

Over the next few days, I took different workshops than Peter and avoided him except when we were in our rooms. He would rap on my door, and stupidly I would open it. We argued about everything. Don't ask me why I agreed to share the final night's dinner with him. At the table, he started lecturing me about how I had danced too closely with someone the previous night.

I stood up and said, "Enough!" I began to leave, and Peter grabbed my arm. I stared at his hand, and then said, "Take. Your. Hand. Off. Me. Now." He dropped his arm, and I stormed out and into the hotel lobby to take an express elevator to my floor.

Back in my room, with the door between the rooms locked, I paced back and forth. "How the hell do I get out of here?" I wondered. I checked but couldn't find a single available flight

Chapter 19

on the airline I had flown on back to New York City that night. I gave up on my escape plan and went to dance.

Once at the *milonga*, which was held in a ballroom at the hotel, I had a great time. I avoided looking around too much and hoped that Peter would be so drunk that he'd gone back to his room to sleep it off. But, no, he showed up at 11:30 and either didn't see me or ignored me. He went straight for the bar and started chatting to a tall blonde who sat on the barstool next to him. I got the message. This was tit-for-tat city, and back to our old ugly dance. Peter flirted because he was jealous of any man I danced with. Okay, two could play.

When I finished the *tanda*, I was dancing with a cute guy named Sergio, a lawyer from San Jose. I said, "Thank you," and kissed him on the cheek.

Sergio lit up and gave me a sexy look. "I really enjoyed our dance. Would you like to go have a late supper?"

I considered Gina's words about how to recover from one man by bedding another, and was about to accept. Peter must have sensed this, because he appeared at my side and said, "You promised me the next *tanda*."

The music began, Sergio slipped away, we danced a few steps, and I could smell liquor on his breath.

"Did this guy dance better than me?"

"No."

"I saw the way you looked at him. You wanted to fuck him, didn't you?"

"Maybe, but you made sure there was no chance."

"You're a fuckin' whore."

"That's a new low, even for you."

I pulled myself away from him. His eyes got dark, and I could see no whites. He raised his hand as if to strike me, and suddenly my hands were clenched in fists waiting on his next move.

A blonde *tanguera* in pink carrying a basket of noisemakers and party hats interrupted us. "Please, help us celebrate."

I accepted a paper tiara and a horn, and Peter, a pirate hat with a plume and rattle.

The music stopped, and Jon, now wearing a crown and carrying a whistle, proudly announced the end of the festival.

"Thank you, one and all. This is our most successful year so far, with over 250 dancers! There will be free champagne at the bar!"

I blew my horn, joining the other revelers. Peter stormed off. The music started, and I lost myself in the crowd. As the party wore on, I danced with every man who asked me, much to the A.R.'s dismay. Sergio avoided me, understandably, but I was disappointed at his lack of courage.

Around 1:00, Peter approached and asked me to dance.

"I'm sorry about before. I was out of line."

Curtly, I nodded and kept my emotional distance — no mean feat when your chest is pressed against someone you long to throttle.

"How can I make it up to you?" he whispered.

I shook my head and sighed. We executed a complicated figure of a forward step, pivot, and a backward *boleo* followed by a *gancho*.

"I don't know."

"C'mon, let's go back to your room to talk," he said.

"No," I countered as he pivoted and I executed a series of kicks. "I don't see the point."

The tango ended, and I pulled away.

"You know how much I love you," he said.

"You have a funny way of showing it."

"Please," he said, "I want to make it right."

By the end of the festival, my sinusitis had worsened, and I was definitely sick by the time we had to travel back to New York.

Chapter 19

Peter and I were sitting together on the plane — one more indignity. I liked to sit with strangers so I could relax and think. As the stewardess demonstrated the safety measures, I was grimly amused. If the plane goes down, it will be redundant, I thought. My heart had already crashed.

Chapter 20

I hailed a cab. Suzanne worked in a tall glass building on Sixth Avenue in the Fifties, across the street from Radio City Music Hall. In the elevator, I was surrounded by businesspeople in business clothes, talking in low voices. I got off on twenty-three and walked through the heavy glass doors into the reception area of the Dorn Agency, where Suzanne was a partner.

Lucien, the chiseled receptionist, smiled. "I'll see if she's free." He picked up the phone.

The inner glass doors leading into the suite of offices swung open, and Desiree Jones, a bone-thin, arrogant woman poured into an expensive red suit and flanked by two assistants carrying garment bags, hurried towards the elevator. She was the former host of a cooking show. Desiree gave me a cold, appraising glance that said, "I'm thinner than you and you are trash," and continued on. I felt like a toad. Again, the former First Lady Eleanor Roosevelt came into my mind's eye and said regally, "No one can make you feel inferior without your consent." Evidently, I was giving my consent. How was I to stop doing it? A needle stabbed the back of my skull. Didn't Peter do the same thing? Ouch.

Suzanne came out to greet me. She was tall with short red hair, big "artsy" earrings, a winter white suit with a short skirt, high-heeled boots and a black sweater with a plunging neckline. She was a self-described "piece of ass," but I found her overall gestalt to be strident and reeking of trying too hard. I wanted to flee, but the Inner Voice comforted my queasy gut. "Focus! She is only your agent."

Only my agent. My sadness calmed me down. She hadn't come to Norman's funeral or apologized for the late arrival of the funeral wreath.

Chapter 20

"Great timing, Dots," she said. "La Vierge. My treat."

We walked to the little five-star French bistro around the corner. The maître d' greeted her by name and took us to a secluded table in the back.

Suzanne ordered glasses of red Bordeaux for both of us and, as soon as the waiter brought them, took a big gulp.

"Ah, what a morning! I needed that." She looked at the menu, and I followed. Suzanne gestured for the waiter. She ordered an omelet, and I followed suit. Suzanne leaned back in her chair. "So?"

"I broke it off with Peter. I saw what you meant. I saw the contempt. I saw how I played into it." A couple of tears dripped down my face.

"I assume those are tears of relief."

I laughed and blew my nose. "Was that Desiree Jones? The woman in the red suit who came out just before you?"

"Yes. She's why I'm about to have another glass of wine."

"A new client?"

Suzanne rolled her eyes. "Yes. You've seen her on the Food Channel?"

"Didn't she have a dessert show?"

"Yes. Until she got fat and they dumped her. She had a bypass and lost 35 pounds. She wants to reinvent herself as a diet diva and stop making dessert, but I convinced her that she had to be the comeback kid, and use her desserts as part of the package, that she lost the weight that way."

"I know the feeling, except that I need to invent myself in the first place." I felt a pang of envy. Always the bridesmaid, never the bride.

Suzanne chugged her wine. The waiter brought the omelets.

"I sold your book." I leaped out of my chair to hug her, but she held up her hand.

"What?"

"Sit down. Eat," she said.

We ate in silence for a few minutes, then she put down her fork. She looked at me.

"You're not going to like this. I sold the book — to her."

I didn't get it. When did Desiree become a publisher? Then I got it. She'd sold the book as if I were still a ghostwriter. I felt like I'd been slapped across the face for the second time in one day.

"Desiree is going to pretend to use your diet to lose the weight, and the book is her journey."

"You can't. It's my journey."

"No, it's the agency's. It was my idea, remember?"

"So what?"

"I know. I'm sorry, but you'll be getting beaucoup bucks."

"For selling my birthright. Like in the Bible. Jacob and Esau. How did that work out for Esau?"

"Esau lost out. Jacob won, through cunning."

"He must have had you as his agent."

"Ouch, that's not fair."

"Maybe, but do you really think you're in a position to say what's fair?"

"Look, I know you'll see this as a betrayal, though no ghostwriter will get the kind of dough you're getting."

"For selling my unborn child."

"C'mon, Dots, you're fertile as hell. I'll make the next one a bestseller, I promise, even if it's awful."

"Cold comfort. I could get hit by a car, and then poof! On my tombstone, 'Dots did nothing, died here.'"

"You've done a lot."

"For other people."

"You got paid."

"Not enough. I won't do it, Suzanne. It's my book…"

"No, I told you. It's not yours."

Chapter 20

I was genuinely shocked. "That's illegal."

"Go and reread your contract. It's the same one as your others, and states that this is a work for hire, meaning you don't own the material. We do."

"Give it back."

"I can't. I don't own it. The agency does."

"I thought I could trust you."

"I got you $25,000 more. And let's be honest, I know it didn't take long to write."

"No, just the last ten years and three months."

"$25K on top of the usual fee isn't nothing."

"So that's what I'm worth to you."

I gave Suzanne a look. She had not done well enough by me to take that tone. "You got me a competitive rate. It's nothing compared to what creating a brand could be."

"It's still a lot of money."

"You're missing the point."

"I've always looked out for you."

My stomach lurched. I was so angry, I was dizzy. I took a deep breath.

"You never push for me."

Suzanne got angry and hissed, "Goddammit!" and slammed her fist on the table, rattling the dishes and cutlery. She leaned forward until our noses almost touched.

"Don't take this too far, Dots. I love you, but I'm a businesswoman. You've written more than a few of these, so write another one with your name on it, and I'll make it up to you, unless you can't come up with a new idea. If that's all you got..."

"I should sue the agency."

Suzanne looked at me coldly. "If you do, I guarantee you'll never work..."

"... in this town again." I finished the old chestnut.

"For one thing, you will lose. The contract's airtight. So next time, pony up for a lawyer. I told you to do that, but you always said, 'No, I trust you, Suzanne.' You get what you pay for."

She was right. I'd accepted the judgment that I believed that I wasn't worth spending the money for a lawyer. I should've called Frank. I reached for my bag.

"I'm sorry, Dots. I. Had. To."

"Really?"

"Yeah, Desiree's the niece of the senior partner. She's going through a lot, and has MS."

As if this was supposed to soften my heart. The old Dots would have sympathized. The new me was going to work this horror to her own advantage. No lentil stew for me. That's what Esau sold his birthright to Jacob for. Suzanne wiped her eyes.

"I'm really sorry about this." Not sorry enough not to do it, but okay. Two can play.

"Okay, Suzanne, here's the deal: I won't make a fuss over this, and in return, and in writing, you get me a pre-sale on my newest book."

She smiled eagerly. "What's it about?"

"I'm not going to tell you."

She laughed uneasily. "Please."

"No."

"Good one. C'mon, we go back a long way. Now tell me what it is, the mocktail diet? The oral-sex diet?"

She was baiting me, but I wasn't biting.

"No. I get the message. Business is business. But here's a hint: it's even more superficial than *Just Dessert*."

"You're not shopping it to someone else?"

"Maybe. Probably. Yes. I intend to keep my next book." My tone was cold, bitter.

"Please. I promise to make this one a success, no matter how bad it is." Could she open her mouth without insulting me?

Chapter 20

"Sorry, I can't tell you. Does your legal department have a confidentiality agreement? If you and I can sign one, then we could talk."

"Of course, we can sign."

I nodded. "And I want to be treated well. For my silence. For not outing our little princess Desiree at the perfect time. Look what happened with Milli Vanilli."

"You can't. It's in your contract."

I sat back and raised my eyebrows at her. "It's always better to ask for forgiveness than permission."

"You wouldn't."

"Don't test me, Suzanne. I'm pretty sore about this."

She was quiet and ate her omelet. "I hate cold food."

"So do I, but Shakespeare tells us that revenge is best eaten that way."

"Ha."

I felt sick. I excused myself and barely made it into a stall before I threw up. I was trembling and weak. I wasn't breathing, and I just wanted to disappear.

"Breathe," the Inner Voice commanded. I took a breath and tuned into the soundtrack. It was the "Flower Duet" from *Lakmé*, a great writing tune, an angelic duet for soprano and contralto, the opposite of the one Suzanne and I were singing. I splashed water on my face and repaired my makeup. I wanted to curl into a ball and cry, and I also wanted to pick up one of the upholstered chairs and break it over Suzanne's head. I walked back to the table.

"I didn't realize what time it was. Sorry, I'm late for another meeting."

"I understand, and *Just Dessert* will need some revisions. You'll get extra moola, I promise." She smiled at me, as if that was the fix.

Did she know I had nothing? I felt humiliated, as if it were somehow my fault not to have another idea in the pipeline.

Mark Twain wrote that you should put your eggs in one basket and watch that basket, and I had done just that, but now I had no eggs and no basket.

"Focus on survival," the Inner Voice whispered to me. "Pay the bills."

"Thank you for lunch."

She started to stand for our usual hug, but I left without looking at her. As I walked out the door, I glanced back and saw the waiter placing another glass of wine in front of her. I hoped she would choke. Suzanne must have been working on this deal since Babette told her my joke.

Chapter 21

I had left my body and was in some dark limbo above and could look down and see myself standing outside the restaurant wearing the blank look that survivors of disasters have when being interviewed on the TV news.

I wanted to kill Suzanne. I imagined myself going home, getting the rifle, bursting into her office and blasting her the way my late father had taken out Annette's curio cabinet. I imagined her blood and brain matter splashed across the cool white leather sectional and shag carpet. Then fast-forward to her head on a plaque above my nonworking fireplace, like one of my father's deer. That was one way to get a brand!

I couldn't breathe. I panicked. I couldn't feel my body. Where was this horrible black vacuum I was stuck in? I had to ground myself, fast.

I remembered the moment when I'd blindly signed the contract and sent it back to Suzanne. My despair over my father had made me foolish. Even in death, his malice had leaked from the other world to destroy me. He was gone but he wasn't done. Maybe he'd never stop, even from beyond the grave, until he brought me down. How I despised him at this moment, and how I loathed myself. How could I have been so idiotic as to love my tormentor? Did I get a hall pass because he'd been my father? Didn't all little girls love their fathers? Would it ever stop? In therapy this process is described as "working something through." Talk therapy. Two words that created a non sequitur and wasted years of my pointless life, trapping me in the fantasy that something that had already happened could be changed. I was still trying to move back in time and rewrite everything. Trying to fix the past shut me out of the present and contaminated my future. Suzanne had stolen my book. What was I going to do about it? There, a breath of calm as a solution presented itself. I'd send the contract to Frank, but I knew it was an empty gesture, and that he'd charge me.

I stepped out onto the crosswalk. A huge red, green and silver oil truck made a sharp turn, nearly crushing me, ripped my handbag out of my hands and knocked me down. If Suzanne was the truck, then the symbolism could not be missed.

I got up carefully, relieved that I hadn't twisted my ankle. It began to rain, a bone-chilling downpour. The icy water brought me back, and I walked home, one careful step after the other.

As I walked, I felt a stab of fear. My message was so trivial. Who was I to get on some high horse? I'd put all of myself in the book, but all I had to say was that portion control and thus self-trust was the secret to weight balancing. It wasn't like I'd been shot in the head like Malala, or died of anorexia like Karen Carpenter. My tragedies were both petty and non-life-threatening. I knew how shallow I was. I was focused on my own food intake without ever relating it to something larger. An image came into my mind of me as a small child in the kitchen, arms crossed and refusing to eat. The dark shadow of an adult loomed above me, and I "heard" my mother say, "No, Norman. No point in hitting her." The shadow would recede, but I could smell her wine-tinged breath as she leaned close and berated me. "There are starving children in Africa. You should be grateful for the food you're being given. Count your blessings." Maybe this endless conversation is what made me hate clichés. I would retaliate by suggesting, "Okay, let's pack this up and send it to them."

"Don't be fresh" was accompanied by a slap from Norman.

I would be sent to my room, and the same food presented until I ate it.

I didn't deserve anything more than being a ghostwriter since I could only parrot what others knew. I was nothing, and it was my own fault. I hadn't read the contract, and I had

Chapter 21

previous evidence that Suzanne could not be trusted not to steal other people's material.

Suzanne had been approached to represent a book by a well-known business consultant that posited that rather than trying to sell something, you should share the benefits that the purchase would have with your customers to create a win-win situation. There was a self-help book from the 1930s called *Be a Go-Giver* — the original book had fallen out of copyright, and the so-called author stole the entire text and put his name on it, without bothering to even change the title! Suzanne bragged that she'd sold it without any concern for the original author's family. I should have listened more closely. It was a living parable with the same moral as the story of the scorpion and the turtle crossing a pond. The scorpion convinces the turtle to carry him on his back, promising not to sting the turtle. When they get to the other side, the scorpion jumps off and savages the turtle. As it dies, the turtle asks, "Why did you sting me when you promised you wouldn't?" The scorpion replies, "It's my nature."

Chapter 22

I stood in the doorway of the apartment. The room stank of rancid pot. There was a half-empty bottle of champagne on the floor near the front door. I swigged some, but most of the wine landed on my coat as my teeth were chattering too hard to swallow. My hands shook from the cold as I emailed Frank the contract. By the time I'd taken off my wet things, he'd sent back a terse reply: "The contract is ironclad. You're stuck. Next time, call me first."

I emailed back. "Can I sue?"

He returned with, "You'll lose."

I sat on the sofa that the A.R. had bought and looked around the trashed room. Was I even in my life? The A.R. danced, the whiny writer wrote, Cassandra criticized, and the Inner Voice dispensed wisdom. But what did I do? Did I even exist as an identity, or was I just an observer of the hen party in my brain? My future stretched out like a desolate highway across a desert. Mourning for my unlived life wrapped me in a dank and turgid mist, what Kierkegaard had termed "the sickness unto death." I was already a phantom, so why not just give the body early retirement? No one would miss me.

I went on YouTube and found a station with fifteen different versions of "Oblivion," the theme of the nude tango I'd danced to on my balcony with George. I googled the lyrics.

"Heavy, suddenly they seem heavy
the linen and velvets of your bed
when our love passes to oblivion
Heavy, suddenly they seem heavy
your arms embracing me
formerly in the night
My boat departs, it's going somewhere
people get separated,

Chapter 22

I'm forgetting, I'm forgetting
Later, at some other place in a mahogany bar
the violins playing again for us
our song, but I'm forgetting
Brief, the times seem brief
the countdown of a night
when our love passes to oblivion
Brief, the times seem brief
your fingers running all over
my lifeline.
I'm forgetting, I'm forgetting."

I summoned the comforting memory of George, but shared the forgetfulness of the song. I couldn't conjure his face. I couldn't have picked him out of a lineup. I left the music on anyway.

I'd swiped two bottles of Oxycontin from my father's medicine cabinet. I poured out the bottles and counted the pills. I had twenty chalky-white, round, ten-milligram tablets. I had a plan, but I didn't want to make a mistake in dosage and wake up in some hospital with a tube down my throat. The dosage on the bottles was one every twelve hours. The potential of permanent release made me calm, and I got on the computer to get information about the best way to overdose on Oxycontin. I couldn't get the exact dosage that would create death, but I learned that by crushing the pills you were able to enhance the effectiveness of the dose. I emptied the bottles into my mortar and pestle that I used to pulverize herbs. There was the faint smell of basil as I crushed them. The end could be quick and painless, but I'd heard that taking a lot of pills at once could make you throw up. I wouldn't want to be found suffocated in my own vomit. Instead, I imagined myself dead, stretched out on my couch, wearing my best tango outfit.

How delicious to not have to deal with loneliness, old age, and failure. I stirred the crushed pills into a glass of Coke Zero.

I took a sip. Bitter, but I felt the relaxing effect of the drug right away. I went into the bedroom. The new bed was soiled by Peter, as the old one had been. One positive feature of my plan was that I wouldn't have to replace it.

I clumsily put on the tango outfit I'd worn with George. I definitely had a buzz, and had trouble buckling the straps of my shoes. I walked unsteadily to my computer and sat down, my feet on my rug. I took a second small swallow of my potion. Note or no note? I was a writer, after all. I hoped for something profound, but all I could come up with was "Goodbye, Toro." I paused, waiting for inspiration. Nada. Crickets. The final indignity: writer's block on my deathbed. Should the W in writer's block be capitalized?

I took another sip, and then a swallow. I almost gagged. I was fading. One more sip to go.

Chapter 23

I woke up on the floor, groggy, with a brutal headache, and threw up all over Toro's mat. There were no second chances. The spilled contents of the glass had been soaked up by the doggy rug, which was now covered in puke. Not only had I failed to kill myself, now I had to shampoo the carpet. I was too weak to move much and passed out. When I came to, there was daylight. I hurled again. I was too dizzy to stand just yet and curled up into a fetal position. Later, it was dark. I was able to move, and crawled painfully to the bathroom, trying not to gag on the smell of aging puke.

Suzanne texted me. "Desiree is on *The Daily Scene*. Check it out."

The Daily Scene was a morning show hosted by a cabal of vicious media witches, and whenever I watched it, I was embarrassed to be a member of the same gender. They were loud and contentious, made stupid illogical remarks, and competed with each other on-screen. Of course, Desiree would be their darling. The sound from the TV reminded me of a chicken coop I'd once visited on a school class trip.

I watched a commercial for feminine diapers and another for a depression medication whose side effects included psychotic breaks, then the segment I dreaded began. Desiree sat on the couch looking fabulous. I felt like death.

The doorbell rang. I opened the door, and an old, stooped Black man stood in my doorway holding a package. He saw my sadness, and as I tipped him, he said, "Look, honey. You woke up this morning, didn't you?" I nodded glumly. "Did anything hurt?"

I shook my head. He laughed. "Then praise the Lord."

Point taken, but I just felt worse. I knew my reaction was self-destructive, but when I opened the package and saw the spiffy book and glossy press kit with Desiree's name on it, I wished that my suicide attempt had been successful. I flipped through the book, my book, and felt bitter pride that the work had been printed exactly as I wrote it. I was thanked in the acknowledgments as a "source of inspiration." This was my worst nightmare. I was a spook. I heard my father's voice say, "You see, I was right. You're nothing."

"Ef you, Dad," I shouted, but didn't feel any better. I had done this to myself. Did that make it better or worse? Either way, I was still the victim — of my low self-esteem. All my failures were tied to this one flaw. I had accepted my father's judgment of me. I couldn't blame Suzanne, and I couldn't blame Desiree. There was only one player in this game of my life. Me.

I watched as Desiree mouthed my words on-screen so precisely that I wondered if Suzanne hadn't secretly taped and transcribed some of our conversations. I wished that I could have gloried in her success as I had that of my other celebrities, but this book was supposed to have been mine.

Desiree was joined by Missy Smythe, a lithe Black tennis star wearing her tennis whites. Desiree flipped her hair as she parroted my words about the body's wisdom and how, if you began with a sweet each meal, it would steer you away from overeating. *Just Dessert* was about to become the new holy grail.

With maybe eight percent body fat, Missy listened with reverence and then proceeded to testify how Desiree's coaching had changed her life. So much so that Missy just had to read a key passage from my introduction aloud: "I wrote this book to help others balance their bodies so that a life free from the stigma and health risks of being overweight can disappear from people's lives. The way to accomplish a new state of happiness and peace in your physical form is to engage in a new relationship with yourself and your body. The path to transformation is listening. In this book, you will learn how

Chapter 23

to 'hear' and use your body's signals to adjust portion size to allow yourself to move into balance. Portion control holds the key to receiving our just desserts."

Wild applause. A standing ovation. Finally, when the applause died down, the chief hen applauded and said reverently, "Desiree, you are so honest. It's so inspiring for everyone in our audience to realize that it's okay to get real with yourself about food."

This mutual self-congratulation lasted for a half-hour, culminating in a pitch for Desiree's new show on the Food Channel. I had to marvel at Suzanne's savvy. The phone rang. Suzanne. Did I answer? Could you kill people over the phone?

"What could you possibly want?" I asked. "Unless you want to offer me more money."

"Yes."

"For my silence but not for my talent."

"Dots, this is merely a gesture to encourage your discretion."

"Send me a proposal." It was my turn to hang up on her.

I alternated between feeling weepy and furious at myself. What a loser I was. I couldn't read a contract, I couldn't hold a man, I couldn't even kill myself. I knew that each negative thought was scorching my nervous system. I, and I alone, controlled my mind, didn't I? Obviously not. I wanted to destroy Suzanne and Desiree. I wanted to go on the show, barge onstage, punch Desiree in the jaw, grab the mic and rip off her dress, revealing the gastric-bypass scar. I had a moment of elation, and then felt sick. What if the positions were reversed? I'd once seen a large, poisoned rat climb onto a subway platform at Times Square writhing in agony. That was the moment that I saw that all living things were connected. What had been the rat's crime? It had just wanted food and warmth. Wasn't Desiree desperate for those same things? Was she a rodent? Yes, or maybe I was insulting the rat! Or maybe I was like the rat, toxic from self-hate.

What does anyone really need to do? Die and pay taxes. I couldn't help but giggle at my melodramatic gesture, and that the best I could come up with as a legacy was "Goodbye, Toro." The giggle expanded into unstoppable laughter. Tears rolled down my face and my side ached.

I texted Suzanne.

"Get me more money, and I'll sign an NDA."

What did I care? I'd been given something more precious: the perspective that comes with a good laugh. My near-death experience had given me the possibility of a different experience of being alive, and a specific task: find my next book.

Natasha texted me that Hector had moved into the same cage as Anna. Hooray!

Chapter 24

I went to La Boca. The warm food smells and Fernando's smile made me feel three-dimensional.

"Any requests?"

I shook my head.

Fernando hummed the opening of the song "Fragile," by Sting. "For all those born beneath an angry star lest we forget how fragile we are." He sounded like Julio Iglesias if he were a baritone singing Sting. Funny, and touching. Without meaning to, he'd sent an arrow straight into my heart. Oh God, I thought, can I ever write, say or be something original? An arrow, really?

"Dots, are you okay?"

"Hard day." I smoothed my hair, the cue I realized was the code when I transitioned into the A.R. persona.

"Yes, me too. I haven't heard anything about your bird lately."

I told him about Hector getting together with Anna.

"I love the idea of dating cages!" He was intrigued by the tango analogy.

"What made you think of Hector?"

"I know this guy who has a studio and needs to write a book."

"Sorry. I'm only working on my own stuff now." Yeah, right, I had nothing.

Fernando looked sad. "This guy is my friend, and he has a new studio. He needs help."

But the A.R. is a pleaser. She asked, "Is he a dancer?"

"Sí, for many years. He's based in Queens. Tomas Gardel."

"Wow. But I've never heard of this guy, never seen him on a tango website."

"No one has. That's the point, Dots. You help put people on the map, you give them a voice."

Bad Girl Pie

"Thank you. I can talk to him, see what's involved. This could give me the opportunity to deepen my understanding of tango."

Fernando smiled. "Yes! If you would learn, study; if you master, teach."

A good point, but also, there was no place to dance in the city without the risk of running into Peter. But he would never lower himself to go to Queens, so there was hope. There was no website, so I called the number.

"Hello, Gardel Studio, Tomas speaking." His voice was smooth like Fernando's flan, and pleasantly accented.

"I'd like to try a lesson. What is the cost?"

"There is no charge for a half-hour introductory lesson."

"Thank you. How is 2:00 p.m. tomorrow?"

"Perfect. It's on the second floor 22-24 21st Avenue. Take the N to Astoria-Ditmars. See you soon. Ciao." The line went dead.

The next day I took the subway to the studio in Astoria. It was on the main drag on the second floor above an Argentinean tapas restaurant. I rang the buzzer and entered a narrow hallway. I stopped for a moment and enjoyed the sound of tango music wafting from the top of the stairs.

I entered the studio. The entranceway was filled with a large white reception desk. Beyond the desk, there was a square room with floor-to-ceiling windows facing out with views of the river. The fourth wall was filled with a larger-than-life-sized mural of a *milonga* in progress: dramatically lit, ten couples danced, each couple dressed formally in red and black. A man suddenly stood up from behind the desk, holding scattered papers.

"Sorry, I dropped a file."

Tomas, five foot seven, slim, muscular, with shoulder-length black hair threaded with silver and a broken nose that made him look like a boxer, peered at me with soft brown eyes from behind the desk. He cut a sharp figure in a white V-necked

Chapter 24

T-shirt, black pants, and white dance shoes. He gathered the papers and put them in a red folder.

"Hola, you are the one who called about the lesson." He smiled. "May I know your name?"

"Dorothy Sherlock. This mural is really something."

"Thank you."

"You painted it?"

He nodded.

"Wow, are they real people?"

"*Sí*. They are people that I have danced with."

"All of them?"

"Mostly. Some are gone, so I need to update the mural every so often."

"Is that you?"

I pointed to an illustration of a man wearing a red open-necked shirt and short black hair slicked back with brilliantine. He was dancing with a tall woman with waist-length raven-black hair and sparkling eyes. She wore a plunging red dress and glittery stiletto-heeled tango shoes.

"Is that your partner?" I asked.

"Was."

There was a constellation of sadness in that one word.

"As I said, the mural needs to be updated. What is your goal in taking lessons?"

"I want to learn to dance well enough so that the better dancers ask me."

"How do you define 'better dancers'?"

"You." He smiled at the compliment.

"Thank you. Now, before we begin, do you understand the concept of having a dance identity?"

"Not really."

"How do you see yourself in terms of dance?"

"I'm a follower."

"Not a partner?"

I thought about it. "I should be, right?"

He nodded. "Not should, want to. We each have multiple roles in the dance. Leader, follower, and also partner."

Tomas walked out from behind the counter, and I followed him onto the dance floor.

There was a freestanding ballet bar against one wall next to a piano and four folding chairs. Tomas gestured toward the chairs.

"Please. You can change into your shoes there."

While I put on my practice shoes, tired black lizard low-heeled spikes with an ankle strap, he pulled the canvas drapes closed and made a few clicks on his phone, and music flowed from a series of speakers. The song was "Cascabelito," by Di Sarli, a lushly orchestrated lilting tune in which the singer is asking his partner to run away from the "crazy carnival" of life.

He walked toward me and held out his left hand in the classic invitation.

There was something odd about the shape of his hand. It felt like a paw. It made me think of Hemingway's cat who'd had extra toes. There was an animal vitality about him. He looked at me, his eyes so dark I couldn't see a pupil. Sorrow leaked out of his smile. We danced the song.

"You dance well."

"Thank you."

He smelled faintly of cologne and Irish Spring. His grief flowed through his hands, and I thought of summer rain in a forest. He was easy to follow.

"Beautiful," Tomas said when the next song ended.

I dismissed the accolade. He was just trying to get me to sign up. He adjusted my right hand so that our palms were perfectly aligned. He gently pressed my right palm with his left.

"Now meet me."

Chapter 24

I pressed his palm, trying to match the pressure. I felt more balanced. We danced another song.

"See, you don't have to rely on me for support. A follower leans, a partner creates the illusion, but a partner relies on their own axis. That's why you can use me as ballast when you turn, but you're turning on your own balance. Now add to that and imagine that, when we turn, your left arm is supporting me."

"I'm supporting you?!" I'd never thought about tango as a truly collaborative dance.

"Wouldn't you support someone you love?"

"Of course."

"If you mean that, and act on it, your dance will transform. Each partner is someone you love for the length of the *tanda*."

"So, it does matter who you dance with."

"Ultimately, you're dancing with yourself, but that's not what I meant. I mean that whatever the reason you are dancing with someone, they deserve your support during the dance, the way a partner deserves that support in life."

Had I ever thought to protect or support Peter? "So, your partner is like your spouse during the dance."

"Yes. Americans dance tango like they are getting divorced; we should always dance as if we were newly married."

I relaxed my left arm and hand. He moved my hand so it curved around his shoulder blade.

"Hug me. Use your hands to make a soft frame for the shape, and use some pressure from our palms so you can feel my lead. Relax your shoulders, then drop your chin slightly. Stay focused on this while we dance."

He lightly ran his finger down the back of my neck from the hairline to my shoulder. I shivered and felt my neck go long and my head and torso rise out of my shoulders.

Tomas led me into a basic figure called the *molinette*. The woman circles closely around the man, who leads her to take a back step, a side step, and a forward step. Back. Side. Forward.

Together. On the turn, the follower steps back, then to the side. We did these five times. His face wore a dreamy smile.

"Your *molinette* is spectacular."

"Thank you so much! How do people get chosen to be in the mural?"

"They were all people who were part of the scene and who were colorful in some way. Maybe one day you will be in the mural yourself." He winked at me. "There's nothing wrong with your dancing. It speaks well of you that someone who dances so well would take lessons. That's how you get into a mural."

"Thank you. Tango is about refining the fundamentals."

"True." He looked at me, thoughtfully considering his next words.

Tomas said, "You'd make a good teacher."

"No, I'd never be good enough to teach." I felt my brain actually twist behind my eyes.

I imagined myself as Tara leading a tango class, with Tomas as my helper. "Teacher." The word caught in my throat, until I got a mental flash of me as a disappointed old spinster with a cat, but at least there was a living creature for me to love.

Tomas's phone rang, and he excused himself and went into the small office at the far end of the studio. He returned with a big smile.

"That was Fernando."

"How do you know him?"

"I worked for him as a waiter. That's how we met. How do you know him?"

"I frequent his restaurant."

"Now I understand. You are the infamous ghostwriter, the master of the emotional recipe. You came undercover pretending to be a student to see what I had to offer. Will you write the book for me?"

There it was. All of my beingness fled, and tango was ruined for me forever. I shook my head no.

"Why not?"

"I have to write something with my name on it."

He looked confused. "*Bien sur*! Of course. But you will write the book about me, not for me."

"'Tomas Gardel teaches the Tango,' by Dorothy Sherlock."

He nodded. "Perfect!"

I sat back, dazed. I had a vision of the finished book. The cover had the title superimposed over a photo of the studio mural with me and Tomas dancing in front. My new brand. Then I thought about how Suzanne would see the project, and I crashed into a wall of despair. No one cared about tango outside of its tiny community. I got angry at God. This was no replacement. This was like killing off a lover and sending me a dog. Fuck God and everything else.

"I'll think about it. I'm sorry, I have to go. Late for a meeting."

I ran out of the studio, saw a cab and jumped in. The song that played was Tina Turner's "What's Love Got to Do with It," matching my sour mood exactly. I wallowed in self-pity and started to spiral down into a dark cave, but as we entered Manhattan from the 59th Street Bridge, I remembered the story about the drowning man.

"God will save me," he said and turned down the assistance of a sailboat, followed by a motorboat, and then a yacht. As the yacht pulled away, a voice boomed from the heavens: "Who did you think sent the boats?"

The man realized he'd completely missed the point. Didn't some great wise person counsel that you should do what you love? I loved writing and I loved the tango. This could be a double win. Sometimes you need to bottom out before you can come back. I was coming back like a cork pushed down in the water.

I stopped into La Boca, and Fernando waved. I sat at the bar.

"Yes? Or no? Malbec or prosecco?"

"I need a contract."

"So, get one. I will pay the lawyer. You have one that you have used?"

I nodded. The joke was that Suzanne was the right person to get the actual contract for an author. I'd avoided her for weeks, and maybe this was a way to reopen communication. And I'd call Frank.

Fernando poured Malbec.

"I don't want to jinx anything by celebrating too soon. The paper should say that I am hiring you and Tomas to work together to make this book. The proceeds can be split three ways, and you will also get a fee. You are my friend. I don't know how to make that decision."

Being treated with respect felt good.

Chapter 25

We drank coffee in Tomas's office, a tiny room with a window. There were no personal items save for a framed black-and-white photo of a little boy dancing tango with a beautiful woman in a tango costume. The frame was very heavy. Tomas said, "That's me with my grandmother, Carolina, when I was eight. My grandmother and grandfather danced tango and knew all of the great musicians and taught me to dance when I was a kid."

"So that's your pedigree."

He laughed and said, "I'd never thought of it that way, but yes."

"Why is the frame so heavy?"

"It's gold underneath the paint. When Perón came in, people hid their wealth." He winked at me, as if to say, "Not true, but fun."

"Wow." Pedigree, indeed. "Well, let's get the idea organized. The key is that the book explores the nature of partnership. When you asked me about what my dance identity was, it was something new that I'd never heard before. If people see tango as a way to be a better partner, the book could have broader appeal."

Tomas was pleased. "Yes, I agree."

"The book should have four parts: The basics for leader and follower. How to learn as a leader, how to learn as a follower. Finally, dancing together as a partnership. I'd like to know a little more about you. You were born in Argentina…?"

"Born in Argentina, raised in Sarajevo."

"That's exotic."

"Not to me. I'm a citizen of the world, but which world? I fit in nowhere. That's why I'm here. How long have you been dancing?"

"Two years. I'm a beginner."

"Aren't we all?" He smiled. "I think it would make sense to organize the story into lessons."

"How many lessons are needed?"

"I'm not sure. I focus on mastering the basics."

"What is your most fundamental belief about tango?"

"If you can walk, you can dance."

"Simple. I like that. Is there more?"

"The embrace must be mastered. The dance is won or lost on the first step."

I squirmed. That was where I had so much trouble. Too anxious to be able to receive the lead. Maybe he could help.

"How is a partnership won or lost? It sounds more like a battle."

"Exactly. A battle to give and receive. A battle to share a unique moment in time. The incredible intimacy of creating something together."

"Like having a child for twelve minutes?"

He nodded. "Let's dance."

I followed him into the studio. He held his hand out. I took it, prepared to be disappointed.

"I need you to help me turn this into words." I stepped into his embrace.

He tapped my right shoulder. "Relax this shoulder." I lowered it. He tilted my hand and pressed his palm against mine.

"Match the pressure I'm exerting."

I pushed my right palm against his left and felt a surge of energy. I felt the space between my shoulder blades light up as if my shoulders were wings.

He clicked on music from his phone, and we began to dance. By using the right hand to hug his palm, I was suddenly dancing at another level. I was no longer just a follower — I was a partner.

Chapter 25

My first writing assignment had been to create a how-to book of simple Chi Kung techniques for a Tai Chi master who barely spoke English. In his energy system, instead of chakras or meridians, there were three brains: one in the head, one in the heart and one in the gut, and the power source for these brains was the tinderbox of our perineum. "Love Your Perineum" had been a chapter heading, and was about how contracting the perineum area between the front and the back was a path to enlightenment.

While I was relieved not to have my name on the book, I'd learned how the two nervous systems in our body work. One that we were aware of, and the other, unconscious, located in the back of the body, which controlled all of the automatic functions of the lungs, heart, ribs, and other organs.

When I contracted my perineum, energy shot up my spine, and then down through my arms into my hands, and by Tomas's smile, I could tell the energy surge extended into him.

He led me in a series of effortless turns because I remembered to keep my chin slightly lowered and my head over my standing leg. Who knew that squeezing your butt was the secret?

The dance ended. We stepped apart and smiled at each other.

"How about we go downstairs and have some empanadas and talk?"

"Sure."

We walked downstairs to Tapas. It was a simple diner with plastic checked tablecloths, linoleum floor, and faded framed travel posters for Argentina on the wall.

I pulled out my computer and set up a file. I reminded myself that this wasn't the old situation where I had to become invisible.

"Beyond your pedigree, what experience have you had that gives you a special insight into your craft?"

"During the siege in Sarajevo, I was injured and blinded by a bomb. I had to learn to get around, unsure whether I'd ever be able to regain my sight. Learning to 'see' without my eyes has allowed me to work with students at a deeper level. The tango saved me. I dance to remember, and to forget. To remember that there is always hope, and to forget all of the tragedy and hardship I've experienced."

"How did it happen?"

"The siege went on for four years, and there was constant bombing, but after a while we ignored it. Life resumed. One day, I was coming home and a bomb exploded near my house. I was knocked out, and when I came to, I was in the hospital. There was bombing every night, so the hospital staff would flee to the bomb shelter in the basement four flights down, leaving the patients to die.

"I trained myself to navigate the route. One night, the hospital was hit badly. There was complete hysteria around me, and I was so scared that when I ran, I made a wrong turn and smashed against a wall so hard I knocked myself out. That's how I got this." He pointed to his flat nose.

"Oh, I thought you were a professional boxer in the old country." He laughed.

"Miss Sherlock, why do you dance?"

"Dots. To try to understand men."

"What does that mean?"

"I feel that my relationships don't last because I can't follow their lead."

He laughed again. "In dance, there are rules. The leader leads, the follower follows. If there's a problem, it's the leader's fault."

"Okay, but does that work in life?"

"If every relationship can be likened to a dance, then yes. Whether the leader is the man or the woman, whoever is leading must do that well."

I really had to think about that. What if all of the misery I'd endured with Peter wasn't my fault?

Chapter 25

"Now tell me more about your life. Your grandparents taught you tango?"

"Until I was twelve, then we moved to Sarajevo to open a restaurant. Then my only teacher was my mother."

"Such an advantage to be taught to lead by a follower."

He nodded. "It gave me a tremendous edge."

"So how old were you when you were blinded?"

"Sixteen. They sent me to Germany after to recover. I went to junior high school there and lived with my father's parents. They were also very devout."

"Why didn't you get your nose fixed?"

He laughed. "You must have money to do such things."

"The siege ended in '96?"

"Yes. My parents moved to Munich as well and opened another restaurant. I worked as a waiter, busboy, cleaner, whatever they needed."

"Are you an only?"

"I have a brother who died."

"In the siege?"

"No. He had SIDS. He suffocated in his crib." Tears slipped down Tomas's nose. "He was eight years younger than me. Enrique. Henry."

"I understand. I lost a sister. She was born dead."

"Is it worse to never be born, or to die as an infant?"

"I don't know." We shared a moment of silence for our dead sibs. "That's rough. What about your parents?"

"My mother got very ill. She's in a hospital in Munich."

"And your dad?"

Tomas whispered. "Dead."

"My God. How long ago?"

"He killed himself on what would have been my brother's twenty-first birthday."

"I'm sorry. You've been through a lot. How have you supported yourself?"

"You don't stop, do you?"

"No, I never stop." I'd googled him when Fernando offered to connect us. There were no YouTube videos of him, no listings under his name. He didn't exist on social media.

"I've done all the positions in a restaurant. Manager, waiter, bartender, bookkeeper. I practice martial arts."

This man was like a pillow book. He just kept opening to a new page. "How did you get into martial arts?"

"I was a manager at a restaurant. I closed. One night someone held up the place, and I did nothing. The robber shot the cashier. I was so ashamed of my cowardice that I decided to become like my favorite action hero, Bruce Lee."

"Did you ever get the guy?"

"What guy?"

"The one who held up the restaurant."

"Yeah, I picked him out of a lineup, and he went up for manslaughter. He swore he'd come for the owner's family. And I'm ready, anytime." Tomas struck a comical martial-arts pose.

I felt a cold finger on my spine. "You're a marked man. Karate to a gunfight? I'm not sure you'd win."

"We're all marked. We're all born with a time stamp."

"True."

He looked down at the floor. There was a long moment of heavy silence, then he jumped up and smiled.

"What is the purpose of dancing the tango?"

"To experience joy?"

He laughed. "It's interesting that you would turn that statement into a question."

"What do you expect? I'm a writer."

"Okay. What else do you want to know about me?"

"When did you first teach tango?"

"I wanted to date this girl. She liked to dance, so I took lessons. Six months in, my teacher asked me to assist. At a *practica*, one of the male students asked if I would help him. I said I would try, and soon I had many students. Ever since then, I've been teaching."

"The senior teacher didn't mind?"

Tomas laughed. "Oh, he minded. He told everyone I stole his students. That's why I came to NYC. You can hide here, and no one will find you. He would still like revenge on me."

"Is that why you haven't connected with the Argentinean crowd here? And why you're not on social media?"

"Exactly. The tango community, like many others, can be vicious. If one wins, the other must fail. So, by being better, I made him less, by their logic, and he was a legend. It's like when you catch crabs, you throw them into a pail. If one starts to climb out to escape, the others pull him down."

"Would you like to hold a regular *milonga* or *practica*?"

"Yes, of course. But they know about Buenos Aires."

"So how do you get students?"

"Word of mouth. Fernando always talks me up, and I have other friends that refer me."

"What's this teacher's name?"

"His nickname is Cho-Cho. He owns a hotel in San Telmo and is a major player." I'd heard of him.

"Is there more?"

"Like what?"

He reached over and shut the lid of my laptop. "Yes, but enough for now."

We arranged to meet the next day. I was early. The teaching area behind the reception area was blocked off with a curtain. Tomas buzzed me in and gave me a big smile.

"I'm early. Sorry."

"No, this is great. You must have gotten my text."

"No…"

"Joking. I was just wishing that I had sent one. I'm about to begin working with this couple, and it might be helpful to watch how I teach." He disappeared inside the curtain and then returned. He nodded, and I smiled at the middle-aged couple who were changing their shoes near the door.

"This is Dots. She is going to write a book about my teaching."

I smiled, offered my hand. We all shook hands awkwardly. They were both fiftyish, slender, and dressed in muted colors. Maureen had a heart-shaped face surrounded by a bell of wavy red hair. Zevi had close-cropped hair, sideburns, and a long face with a square jaw. Both wore gold bands on their left hands.

Tomas pulled back the curtain and put on tango music. The couple looked at him expectantly. "Maureen and Zevi, why don't you dance a couple of songs so I can see where you are?" They hesitated, and Tomas grabbed my hand.

"We'll all dance."

I wasn't wearing the right shoes, so I kicked off my boots and danced in my socks. Maureen and Zevi timidly began to dance. I followed Tomas and noticed that he was watching them closely.

Zevi was quite skillful, and led easily. Maureen was more self-conscious, and stiff in her high heels. I watched her struggle to follow the lead, which seemed very clear to me. The song ended. I had a disturbing realization: I often guessed at what a leader would want, rather than having received a clear signal!

Tomas led me back to the chair I'd put my laptop on. "Thank you," he smiled and walked over to Zevi and Maureen, who stood nervously awaiting judgment.

"You both dance well. You have the most important thing, which is a good connection. Please get into the embrace." He glanced at me as if to say, "Write this down." I opened the computer and began to type.

He gestured for them to get into position and then walked around them, studying every angle. He took Maureen's right hand and Zevi's left, then pressed both hands together.

"The two hands are also embracing. Listen to his hand. The partnership begins here."

Chapter 25

"Is it alright for me to touch your neck?" Tomas lightly stroked his finger from the base of Maureen's hairline to her shoulders as he had with me. I watched as her shoulders dropped and she sighed. He slid her left arm around Zevi's shoulder.

"You're hugging him, but keep your shoulders down." He started the music. They moved much more smoothly than before the instruction. The song ended.

"I thought you were going to teach us some new steps," Zevi said. He was a man who liked being in control and resented Tomas for transforming their dance without there being a "product."

Tomas shrugged. "Of course." For the rest of the class, Tomas taught a showy sequence with a sweeping turn and a leg wrap. Maureen followed but looked bored, and I was, too. Tomas caught that and winked at me.

After the class was over and we were alone, Tomas sighed. "They never want to learn the tango. They just want to learn steps, performance tango."

I typed. He continued.

"Tango is about moving together as if you have one body and two heads and four legs. Tango is having enough technique so that you can focus on creating this improvised experience that lasts only as long as the song, then vanishes, forever. A series of moments ordered by the leader, but manifested by the follower."

I typed. He looked pleased. "It is an equal partnership."

A fleeting thought passed through my mind — that he was the burglar, not the hero of the story he'd told me. Same with Cho-Cho. Was he really the innocent victim or a sleazy student stealer? After the debacle with Suzanne, my trust in anyone was shattered. Even my lawyer had been an aspiring pedophile.

I looked at his hands, which still made me uneasy. He caught me. I looked away.

"This is not tango stuff but, when I was born, I had six fingers and six toes."

"What do you make of that?"

I shrugged. "The surgeon did a good job and yet you sensed something different. Bring that sensitivity to the work, and write from the body that is dancing. The words are the map, not the territory."

"But without a map the treasure cannot be found."

"Do you always speak in parables?"

"Analogies. Try not to." He grinned.

I pondered how I could be objective without paranoia. Aunt Cindy's maxim bubbled up, and I imagined her twinkling eyes beaming at me from beneath the straight line of her silver bangs and her throaty cackle.

"When you catch someone in a lie, it's never the first or the worst."

"You don't trust me."

"I have no reason not to."

"Good." He handed me back the signed contract.

"Thank you." I handed him the outline.

Tomas studied the pages. "This is impressive. I teach in a different order, but this is a good place to start."

I pressed the point. "Doesn't everything start with the embrace?"

He opened the drawer of the reception desk and pulled out a stained, much-folded piece of lined notebook paper covered in neatly printed blue ink.

"That's it?" I was taken aback.

He nodded and smiled. "No."

I was relieved. "What else do you teach?"

Tomas read over the list using his finger as a pointer and moving his lips. He held up three fingers.

"Three more things. Circularity, the three-part body (disassociation), the pause, and partner identity."

Chapter 25

"That's four."

"Just wanted to see if you were awake." A big smile.

"Can we make a copy?"

He handed it to me.

"Make me one." I tucked it into my folder and stood up. Tomas shook his head.

"Now, let's begin. Sit. Put on your shoes."

I laughed. "But I don't write with my shoes."

"With any luck, you will."

"No, I will need a pair of yours. It's like having a four-leaf clover, they will bring me luck." He nodded, and went behind the counter, and handed me a forlorn pair of tattered white leather dance shoes. "They're my only spares. Don't lose them."

"I will treat them like gold." I put them in my bag, sat down, and took out my shoes, which today were silver with double ankle straps. He held out his hand, and I gave him my shoes. He knelt down and slid my feet in one by one, and then tenderly closed the buckles. It was the most erotic moment of my life.

"These are lovely shoes, and you take care of your feet, which is very important. I'd like you to put something in the book about it."

Who was writing this anyway?

"Please, don't take what I say as I say it. I would never mean to tell you what to write. English is not my first or even second language, but my ability to rub people the wrong way is something my mother told me was a gift."

"A self-deprecating *tanguero*? As rare as a Yeti."

"Thank you. When I work with someone, the goal is to encourage what they do well, not look for things to criticize, fix, and make more money giving lessons. The book should reflect the power of positivity when learning with me."

He stood up and held out his hand. I stood up, still giddy from the intimacy of having someone wrap the leather straps around my ankles and buckle my shoes. Only in the land of tango.

"Don't worry," I smiled, disarmed. He smiled back, and I saw relief crinkle his dark eyes.

"Great. We'll dance now, and you act as if you were a beginning student, then afterward, you'll make your notes."

He put on a classic tango song with a weeping male vocal and held out his hand. I took it, and we moved into the embrace. He pivoted me around himself to the right, and I stepped forward on my left foot and turned. It felt awkward, and when I completed the half-turn and faced him, I felt clumsy and unaligned. Had I always felt this way?

"You're afraid," Tomas said. "What are you frightened of?"

"Of making a mistake. Of you finding out I'm a fraud."

"Wrong. Humans are afraid of two things. Falling and noise." He let out a yell, and I jumped. "See?"

I nodded.

"Tango is an improvisational dance. How can you make a mistake?"

"By not understanding his lead, and what he wants me to do."

"Like Maureen?"

"She was so nervous."

"No, self-doubting. She's afraid she can't do what's expected of her."

"I worry about that, too."

"Why? A lead is an invitation, a suggestion, not a command. It's one side of a two-way conversation."

"I never thought about tango that way."

"Most don't. But it's necessary to understand the relationship of the partners to the dance itself."

"How do I overcome my fear?" He held out his hand, and we got back into the embrace. He led me in a series of slow turns as he talked. "Your fear's not the problem, except it makes you give up before you try."

He was painfully right. I wanted to disappear.

"You're so sure you'll fail that you don't actually listen to how he leads. You don't believe you can succeed. Here's what could change things: form an intention that you're going to align yourself so that your body can understand his lead. Tango is like two snakes curving around a caduceus. It is not you parallel parking your partner like he's a car. That's why the embrace is so critical."

"Okay, great, but how do you cope with the anxiety? I mean, fear."

"They are two different things. Fear is more a concern that you might fall, and the solution is to make sure you fully transfer your weight each step. That will keep you balanced, and the fear will leave when your body's sure there is no danger. Anxiety is complex because it uses the past to create a bad future. The solution is to be in the moment and to focus on completing the step or the turn. When you are making a turn, what happens in your mind?"

I thought about it. "When I feel the lead turn, all my technique flies out of my head. I panic, then I guess."

He was quiet and said, "Dots, you're a brave person to admit that. We can change guessing into knowing. Guessing comes from a lack of faith that you can know something."

"I understand. That's a chapter for the followers!"

"And the leaders."

"Amen. How to address it?"

"See each other as an equal partner. Not enemies. Not people to impress, not to judge, partners — two people dancing around each other in order to create a living work of art. The leader's not a bully who's trying to throw you off your balance. And here's where I can bring the lesson back to your outline. We must resolve our anxiety in order to achieve the embrace. How can you hug somebody who might make you fall?"

"Isn't that fear?"

He shook his head. "A leader's goal is to make sure his follower is comfortable and enjoys herself."

I had a flash of insight. "I see, it's the follower's ability to stay balanced that will determine how the dance will happen."

He looked pleased. "Precisely. One more dance? No talking, I promise."

As we danced to "Que Falta Que Me Haces" (The Way I Miss You), by Miguel Caló, a ballad with aggressive violins and a dramatic serpentine melody, my mind sorted the many men I'd danced with into two piles: partner-leaders who danced with their follower, and narcissistic leaders, like Peter, who used their followers as a prop for their own fantasy. Peter was a bully, a user, not a leader. Thanks, Dad.

The dance ended, and we separated with a smile.

"Where did you go?"

"What do you mean?"

"You were not with me."

"Yes, sorry. I'll get my laptop." I sat down and opened my computer.

"The embrace reduces fear because you make a connection with your partner. Connection creates a relationship, and relationships require trust. There's a relationship between you and yourself, between you and the leader, you and men in general, in the past, in the present. How do you perceive the fundamental relationship between you and men? How does a man feel about women off the dance floor? These personal beliefs color the dancer's tango. Then there's the relationship to the music. For me, the music is the third partner of the dance, and as a Catholic, I believe the music creates the Holy Trinity."

"Is leading harder than following?"

Chapter 25

"They're both hard. Leaders have more technical stuff to learn. There's the added responsibility of initiating the dance and being the designated driver on the dance floor. But the leader gets to decide what the dance will be. For the leader, tango music offers more than the 4-4 of ballroom. I can lead you to the melody or the rhythm. The follower has an equally hard job because she needs great technique and she needs to be able to interpret any suggestions he makes. Most importantly, she must support him as he supports her."

The follower was supposed to help the leader dance? Tomas had just redefined the parameters of partnership for me. Again.

"That's a new idea. And I'm sorry I wasn't in the dance."

"Don't make yourself wrong here. Maybe you solved some big problem."

I went to La Boca for a glass of wine. Fernando was behind the bar. It was sunset and the burgundy and orange streaks were reflected in the big mirror behind the bar. There was something heartbreaking and final about the mellow, jewel tones of the sun going down, and of life descending into winter and death. What if death were dawn, birth was fall, and childhood winter? That was a prettier picture. Then being born was the nadir, and our allotted span was a joyous movement, and old age was a summer? Maybe the concept of a happy childhood was a canard — because for all of the goo-goo stuff, we were all trapped in these useless little bodies, unable to be independent. That was certainly my definition of hell, and I was still trapped in a little body. What would it be like to reach the top shelf without a step stool? To sit on a barstool without having to climb up?

Fernando burst into song, singing along with some rock anthem that was blasting from the speakers. He placed a glass of something bubbly in front of me.

"Hola, mi amor, we're celebrating."

"Okay, what's the occasion?"

Fernando clinked. "I've decided to take singing lessons." He was so happy, I wanted to have a piece of that sunny pie. I watched Fernando humming along with the background soundtrack of the restaurant as he happily served drinks and made up orders for the table. He was someone for whom nothing was ever wrong. Tomas had pointed out that I made myself wrong. I accepted that being in the wrong was inevitable. Because my thoughts controlled the prism that shaped how reality occurred for me, I was a time bomb ticking down to the next wrongness. If I felt that something was always wrong with me, then something always was. There was no mystery as to how I came to that conclusion in the first place. What was hard to imagine was how my life could be if I was good enough, if I wasn't always about to fail.

I looked up, and Peter stood in front of me. He smiled charmingly. I remembered that smile, an early dating smile. I counted mentally back from "O" to "T."

"Can I buy you a drink?" He gestured at Fernando, who gave me a concerned look.

"It's okay, I'll have another bubbly."

"Same," Peter said. That damned baritone rumble of his voice. It invoked the worst memory I had, of Peter kissing his ex in front of me on New Year's Eve, but I still got moist.

The wine came. "What's the occasion of this visit?"

He laughed. "I always loved your sense of humor." Huh?

"Can't I just want to hang out and chat about the meaning of life instead of the weather?" He winked at me, letting me know he remembered one of my core complaints.

What if there were no duality in my assessment of Peter, and I reframed the relationship without blame and without assuming that something must be wrong? Was it the wine? He suddenly looked so much more attractive. What if the history between us were negated and we saw each other freshly? What if there had never been a Grace? What if I'd never endured his cruelty? What if I didn't know that he'd been raped by his babysitter when he was nine? That his father had written him off as stupid and bought him property to manage with the money that would have gone for college? What if I were not a desperate middle-aged woman made foolish by misunderstanding that tango could lead me to find the love I was seeking?

Peter reached for my hand and said in a low voice, "I'm sorry about last time. I know that this is a once-in-a-lifetime thing. I know your worth." His sad eyes pleaded.

"Was," I said, and patted his hand, but didn't take it.

"Is." He insisted.

"When is Grace moving out?"

"Soon. She's looking for a new place."

"Okay, so what did you have in mind?" Absurdly, my heart leaped in my chest. This time, would I be willing to move to New Jersey? Was he going to propose?

He took my hand and leaned forward, and paused. I waited, hope against hope. Would he get down on one knee?

"Want to get together tonight and hang out? I have some new great weed. Smoke and do the wild thing and dance?"

I felt as if I'd been kidney punched. "Does Grace have a deadline?"

He looked away, admitting the truth. This was going nowhere. I came to my senses. Who had characterized me as a "desperate middle-aged woman"? I had! No one else was calling me names. And this was his idea of continuing our "once-in-a-lifetime connection."

I had to laugh, and that laugh saved me. He was treating me like I was a pity fuck, a ghost with tits, and had all along. I felt dumpy and humiliated. Suzanne was right. Every breath Peter took was toxic.

"C'mon, honey, you know we'll have fun."

Honey. Fun. I couldn't help it. I flung the wine in my glass at him like some actress in a TV movie.

"You bastard, I fucking hate you." My words were as sharp as a wire cutter.

He looked genuinely confused as he mopped his face. "What did I do?"

"Just get away from me," I hissed.

Peter looked at me with Yorkshire-puppy eyes. "Oh, c'mon, Dots. This is bigger than both of us."

"Really? Is that your best shot?"

He scowled, offended. "What? I know it's corny, but it's true."

"Please go."

His eyes searched my face. I glared at him. "I mean it. Get the hell away from me."

"If I leave now, I'm never coming back."

"Promise?"

Fernando hovered protectively.

Peter threw money at him and said, "You know what, Dots? You're a sarcastic fuckin' bitch, so fuck you." He stalked out.

Through the window, I watched as he walked across the street. He stopped and looked to see if I would run after him. I held my hand up in the classic third-finger salute. And stuck my tongue out at him for good measure. He returned the salute. He got into his white SUV and drove away. "You got to throw out the garbage," as Aunt Cindy would have said.

I was delighted with myself, but the A.R. started screaming that I would never find another man so loudly that I couldn't think. I crossed my arms across my chest against her. "Shut up," I whispered. Fernando came over to clear our glasses.

"Whew. I'm glad you like me," Fernando said.

"I like anyone who doesn't have contempt for me."

"I approve." He poured wine for both of us.

Chapter 25

"To freedom." We clinked and drank.

When I got home, I checked my phone. There were a bunch of texts from Peter, apologizing for cursing me out, talking about a future. I deleted all of them and blocked his number.

The next morning when I arrived, Tomas was eagerly waiting for me. "Put on your shoes, put on your shoes."

I took out my shoe bag, and he grabbed it.

"Sit," he commanded, and helped me put on my shoes.

"What's going on?"

"I need you. Remember Zevi and Maureen?"

I nodded.

"They are back, and I need you to help demonstrate where the problem lies with them without being direct."

"What's the problem?"

"She doesn't trust him." I laughed aloud. This was just too coincidental. Aunt Cindy believed that a coincidence is the Creator's way of making a miracle happen without having to take responsibility for it. I was ready for some divine intervention.

Zevi and Maureen arrived a moment later. We exchanged greetings, and they sat to put on their shoes. Tomas pulled the curtain that separated the reception area from the dance floor.

"Dorothy, I need you in here." And to them, "Come through when you're ready."

I followed him inside. Tomas started the music. Classic tango with a vaguely military beat.

"What is it, Tomas?"

He came close and whispered, "Whatever I say is for them. Don't take it personally, okay?" I frowned, and he reached out and ran his finger over the frown lines.

"Don't worry, just promise me, you'll appear to be calm." That I could do. Zevi and Maureen entered. Tomas smiled.

"Let's dance to this song to warm up." They moved toward each other and into the embrace. Tomas put his hand gently on Maureen's left arm.

"Relax. Lengthen your neck and rest your arm lightly on his. Hold onto the skin of his shoulder with your palm." She moved her arm. He moved her hand a little lower. "Enjoy his back. His shoulder will lead you. And do you feel how you are now supporting yourself?" To Zevi, he said, "Now lead her in a slow turn." He did, and she followed him smoothly.

"Good. Now let's dance." A new song came on, and he offered his hand to me. We danced, and he watched Zevi and Maureen closely.

He whispered, "Watch how she glances down on every turn, how she hangs on him when he turns her. She betrays her own balance out of fear." Ouch. Yep. "It defies common sense, unless you understand that she doesn't feel she can maintain her own balance, for if she did, there's no way she would forfeit it."

"Why does she dance with him then?" I said, painfully aware that I should draw my navel and my thighs back, drop my shoulders, and lift and stretch my own neck to maintain my own balance.

"Let me tell you a story. When I was a boy, my father taught me to ride a bike. When I would make a mistake and fall, he would torment me. After a while, I stopped caring, so when the bike got away from me, I would just let go of the handlebars. Why fight if you were going to fail?" He sighed deeply.

"So, you don't ride?"

"I do. My mother saved me. She told me to fight. 'Your father is cruel. Keep your handlebars straight, no matter what he says.'"

"The next time he told me I'd never learn, of course, the bike started to get away from me, but I grabbed the handlebars and straightened my arms. I didn't fall! The bike righted itself, and voilá, I could ride."

"So, Maureen feels powerless to succeed?"

Tomas nodded.

The song ended, and Tomas applauded.

Chapter 25

"Very good, Zevi, I can see you've been practicing."

Zevi glowed. "How did that feel, sweetheart?"

Maureen smiled at her husband. "I felt more balanced." She looked at Tomas. "I didn't know I was allowed to hold onto him."

"But you're not. Before you were holding on because you were trying to keep your balance. Now you are using him as ballast. By changing how you use your arms and hands, you are now on your axis. Very good work. Now let's change partners and do the song again." He started the song, and Zevi held out his hand to me in a courtly way.

"May I have this dance?"

I nodded and moved into the embrace. As I wrapped my left arm around Zevi, I saw that I had the same reluctance as Maureen to actually rest my left arm along Zevi's and connect with the elbow.

Tomas came over to me and made the same adjustment he'd done with Maureen. He said kindly, "You don't have to trust your leader much, just for the *tanda*. Just focus on dancing a step at a time. Wait, I will change the music."

He put on a tango with a measured beat. Zevi began the dance and I followed. Though Zevi was awkward at moments, I felt as if I were inside a jeweled cloud and my arm was soldered to his. The song ended. And Maureen and Tomas applauded. I was dazed. It wasn't Zevi.

After the lesson, which I'd recorded, I went to pack up my things. Tomas put on music and pulled the curtain back. He'd turned on the tiny, twinkling Christmas lights hung around the windows in the main room.

"Would you like to dance?" I looked at him, and he smiled. I nodded. The dramatic strains of Pugliese played. Tomas held out his hand, and I stepped into the embrace.

We danced as the light faded into darkness. Slowly I relaxed into a state of trust. The tragic melody was shared by the violins and the bandoneon, unraveling like a furled flag at a funeral. Loss, death, tragedy, grief, our dance expressed all of these emotions. He had no need to lead in the traditional sense. It was as if we were a two-headed fish with four gills undulating underwater. Each step Tomas led had its own momentum that flowed into the next step, and the next.

When the music ended, we stood in the embrace for a long moment, and then he hugged me. "Now that was a tango!"

I smiled. "Did you forget the past?"

"No, but I'm remembering a new future. I felt the ice in my heart melt, and open to love."

This was a moment of thrilling connection, but after Peter, the tango couldn't seduce me. I felt the wave of Tomas's emotion, and it was a beautiful moment, but I planned to end up in that elephant graveyard by myself.

The look in Tomas's eyes showed me he was smitten, and he leaned in for a kiss. I deflected it onto my cheek. I separated myself and walked over to where I'd left my shoes, changed, stood up, and walked to the door. He walked towards me. I held up my hands in a "stay" gesture. It took every ounce of willpower to remind myself that I did not date where I danced!

"No, Tomas, blame it on the tango. It's not me." Every molecule wanted him.

"Don't be so sure, my dear Dorothy. We have an amazing connection."

"Yeah, yeah, yeah," I heard Cassandra sneer. "There's a man who's trying to get you to steal defeat from the jaws of victory." The A.R. protested, "But if he likes you, you should go with it..."

"Oh, shut up," I said crossly.

Tomas heard. "What did you say?" I realized that I'd spoken aloud.

"I said, I'll see you tomorrow." I ran out of there and felt his longing follow me like a hungry dog. I hesitated on the stairs,

Chapter 25

the A.R. flooding my heart with images of us sharing romantic moments, but I snapped off the mental screen like an angry mother turning off the computer when she wants her kid to do their homework.

The Inner Voice made a dramatic entrance and spoke like the Oracle of Delphi: "The definition of insanity is to repeat the same behavior and expect different results."

Crazy maybe, but not insane.

Chapter 26

As I waited for the train on the dark platform, I felt despair. Had I missed the great chance of my life? Was that worth my principles? I hadn't thought twice about committing adultery with George.

Once on the train, I looked around for something cheerful. Two motherly Spanish ladies giggled together and whispered in each other's ears. I imagined them as little girls in pinafores, dark hair tied up in pigtails, which made me smile, but the tragic strains of "Oblivion" played in my mind, an ironic musical counterpoint to joy.

I wanted to have intimacy with a woman friend. Although Suzanne and I weren't chummy in that way, she was the closest girlfriend I had. I missed her.

What madness had made me trust my literary agent? Realizing I was blaming a bug for being a bug, I decided to forgive Suzanne. You can't fault someone for being who they are, or to not expect to be betrayed by someone whose nature is to destroy.

I once asked my Aunt Cindy how she put up with my mother, her sister.

She laughed and said, "You just ignore what's happening and hold the ideal of them in your heart. If I could see her as a good sister, you can remember her as a good mother even in the midst of a memory attack. Every so often, Liz would get the message and do something nice that allowed me to forgive her until the next time. And on the other side, your mom will be grateful for your forgiveness." I loved her kindness, and owed her a visit.

I called Suzanne from the 14th Street station.

"You cashed the check" were her first words. "I take that as a gesture of truce."

Chapter 26

"Okay. I didn't know we were at war."

"Oh, please, don't start with the hairsplitting. I'm really happy you called, so let me buy you dinner."

"Yes, how about you meet me at La Boca? They make a mean steak frites."

"Well, it's kind of a trek for me. Why not meet at La Vierge?"

"I understand, but let's face it, not much fun eating at the crime scene." I could feel her biting down a barbed retort.

"Okay."

She was a half-hour late. I'd anticipated the power move and brought a book. When she finally swanned in, Fernando treated her like a queen, leading us to the best table and holding our chairs out for us. Fernando asked what we were having.

Suzanne glanced at me and said, "We'll both have the steak frites and a bottle of that Malbec I keep hearing about."

"How would you like that cooked?"

Suzanne answered for both of us. "Medium rare."

Fernando looked at me, surprised. "I'll have the salmon instead."

Fernando smiled, reassured.

"Sorry, I forgot you were vegan."

"I'm not. Just no red meat." A fleeting memory flashed through my mind. Norman kneeled behind me, grabbed my arms to aim my rifle, squeezing my finger on the trigger — the sound of the shot, and the doe stumbling and falling as it was hit.

The wine came, and she took a sip.

"So, how are you?"

"As well as can be expected mourning the death of my child."

"Always so dramatic."

I couldn't speak, so I didn't. I felt my stomach lurch. I pretended to take a sip.

"You'll be pleased to hear my report."

I couldn't help laughing. "I doubt it unless you're going to give it back to me."

"Second prize. I'm trying to get you royalties. The book went to auction, and Desiree's getting $500,000. The diet plan is being franchised into a boutique website, and people are lining up to be trained to teach your system. There's been no press as yet, because the publisher wants to roll it out on all formats." She stood up and twirled around. "The diet's brilliant. I've lost five pounds so far."

"You'd have made a great *Judenrat*."

"What's that? Some kind of sex worker?" She smiled.

"If you're into BDSM. No, they were the Jewish traitors in the concentration camps. The Nazis would reward those Jews who turned on their own and carried out their nefarious orders."

"Keep your voice down. You're yelling."

Yelling? I felt invisible, voiceless. I looked over at the bar, and Fernando shook his head. I took a breath.

"This is supposed to be a truce."

"Then why are you rubbing my nose in her success? Trying to buy me off with $25,000 is a total insult." I stood up. "That should be me in the spotlight."

"I know. I can get you another, better writing job in a heartbeat."

"For someone else?"

"SIT DOWN."

Fernando grabbed a bottle of wine and followed the waiter, who set our food in front of us. He kicked me hard in the ankle. I sat down. He refilled Suzanne's glass.

"On the house, ladies." As he leaned over to refill my glass, he hissed in my ear, "Remember, draw a line in the sand behind you."

Suzanne held up her glass. "To our next success." I didn't raise mine.

"Oh, c'mon, stop being a spoilsport. Truth be told, the book was my idea. You made the joke, but I turned it into gold."

Chapter 26

"Then why didn't you just hire me?"

"I was trying to be nice because your dad had passed."

"Throwing me a bone, was it?"

"No." Her tone gave her away. It was a no that meant yes.

"I just want to know if you'd already sold the idea to Desiree before you suggested that as my topic?"

"No, of course not. That's paranoid. It would have been cheaper to just hire you."

"Just because I'm paranoid doesn't mean you weren't out to get me."

We ate in silence. As I chewed, I mentally recited t-a-n-g-o as a mantra. Fernando came to the rescue with flan, espresso and the check.

When he left, Suzanne took a bite and put her tearful oh-poor-me face on. She'd completely destroyed my future, and somehow, she was the victim. UGH! I wanted to scream with rage, but instead rearranged my face into what I hoped looked like sympathy.

"I couldn't help it. Desiree had a deadline, or she'd have lost the opportunity until next season."

She saw the look on my face.

"I was staring bankruptcy in the face." Suzanne teared and sniffled into her napkin. "Gus lost everything, and more. It's not an excuse, but I really need my job."

"So, this is his fault?"

"Yes."

"What about your moral bankruptcy? Like stealing someone's book? What Gus did to you justifies what you have done to me?" I bet myself a dollar she wouldn't address that.

"Bankrupt. Nada. Nothing."

I won my bet. "I understood that. To be in your late forties and living paycheck to paycheck must be terrifying, so maybe you can understand what you're condemning me to."

173

My comment registered. In the soft light of the candles, Suzanne looked drained. Maybe the karmic bill had been prepaid because Suzanne had spent her adult life loveless, with a creep who hadn't cared about her enough to control his addiction. And now she'd cut off my love as well. Until this debacle, we'd spoken almost every day, sisters from different mothers.

No more sympathy. This was a performance, her "turning on the waterworks" as Norman used to say whenever my mother got upset. No matter how good Suzanne's portrayal as a grieving, destitute widow was, she would be fine. She'd gotten her way. It was bad enough that she'd stolen the book, but I vowed not to give her the double victory of ruining any more of my life. How could I reframe what had occurred? Einstein suggested that you could never solve a problem from the level you were having it on. How could I change my perspective? I could take her behavior as either a total personal betrayal or ... what?

Were most people evil? No, they were weak. What if I saw Suzanne that way? What if *Just Dessert* didn't represent everything I wanted to share with the world?

The Inner Voice said, "What Fernando said."

"Oh, shut up," I thought crossly. I groaned. Suzanne blew her nose loudly.

"Is there a new book?"

The dreaded question had not been asked. I had no answer, so I made a joke.

"As it happens, yes. It's a ... dance, no, a tango book. How the dance is a recipe for life, and by learning to tango, you can improve personal relationships, make great food and lose weight." I managed to keep my deadpan.

There was a silence, then Suzanne laughed. "Good one. You almost had me."

"No, I'm serious. Tango as a way to navigate and improve your romantic relationships."

"Are you telling me that Peter made you into an expert?" What a cow she was. No offense to cows. Suzanne continued, "If you weren't breaking my balls, I'd say that there are two ways to go. Do you want to teach tango? Or become a relationship expert using tango as your metaphor? You can't do both."

She was right. I would have to become clear about my role, but I had no interest in being either. Still, maybe I could appeal to Suzanne's guilt. My joke had teeth.

"I'm not sure yet, but the promise of my continued silence about Desiree should inspire you to help me figure it out."

"Remember, the contract is ironclad, and this would ruin your career as well. Besides, I just said I'd help. What's the point of bringing this up? You can trust me."

I laughed. "Seriously?"

She looked offended. "I told you I had to."

"Everyone has a choice. I don't accept your rationale."

"How can you say that? You know what I've been through."

"Yes, I do. What doesn't kill you is supposed to make you stronger, not turn you into a traitor. The point is I don't trust you anymore. I have to protect myself. So please know that I can tip off the right person anonymously if I have to. Send them that recording."

"What recording?" Suzanne choked on her wine, spilled some on her designer top and frantically dabbed at the stain. I enjoyed her discomfort.

"I recorded the lunch where you admitted you were giving the project to her."

Suzanne was silent. She looked at me as if I had grown devil horns and a goatee.

I sat wearing what I hoped was a Mona Lisa smile.

"You're lying."

She was right, but I remained calm and said, "Do you really want to hear yourself sell out?" I picked up the bill folder to distract her from wanting to hear the "recording."

"No, give me that." She held up her hand for the check. "Okay. You've got yourself a deal. But I need you to sign an NDA."

I smiled. "My word is my bond. Let's make sure yours is, too. When you send me the new contract outlining our book deal, I will send it to Frank, and if he deems it wise, I can sign it. Once I receive the check for the advance, I will be considering signing an NDA for *Just Dessert* retroactively."

"You want me to get you an advance for a book on an unknown topic? I told you twice that I'd make something happen, but I have a right to know the topic."

"A right? Oh, really. I just wouldn't want to force you to pre-sell it to another diva."

"What're you saying?"

"Oh, c'mon, Suzanne, you know you pre-sold *Just Dessert* before I even wrote it. No one can write faster than me."

Guilt flashed across her face.

"Then you blamed the victim."

"I did not."

I nodded. "Yes, you did. You rightly pointed out that by trusting our friendship and not hiring legal counsel that I'd allowed this to happen, so it was my fault. Well, lesson learned. Thank you for dinner. By the way, what would it take for a tango book to be successful?"

"A miracle. Some connection to a star."

I stood up and left. I was shaking so badly, I could barely turn the handle of the door. Outside the cold air calmed me down.

"She was weak, she was weak, she was weak. Not evil." I repeated this over and over as I walked home. I really would miss those daily calls.

Chapter 27

My cell phone rang. It was Natasha, crying, her accent so thick I could barely make out the words.

"Hector very sick. Doctor says he must be put down. Please come."

When I arrived, Hector was propped up against the wall of the cage. Anna sat next to him, grooming him. He looked at her with dull eyes, unresponsive. His feathers seemed to be shredded, his colors faded. I'd seen a deathbed before.

"When did the vet want you to bring him in?"

"They wanted to do right then." Natasha's eyes filled with tears. She put a little food in front of Anna, who ignored it. "She won't eat."

"So?"

"I wanted to give them last night together, before I take him in." Natasha wiped tears. "Let's have vodka." She cracked open a large bottle with a label written in Russian and brought out two oversize shot glasses with the word "Samovar" painted on them. "This is new good place for tango. Maybe you come one night?"

"Sure."

"Great. To love," she said in Russian. When I looked blank, she translated. I clinked and said the one Russian phrase I knew: *Na Zdorovie.*

She knocked her shot back like a champ. My throat burned and my eyes watered. She laughed, and then wiped tears. We drank again.

"I'm fond of him. It is a pleasure to watch a male behave well, in any species. I want to take video and send to ex-husband for training."

She'd never mentioned having been married. She noted my surprise.

"For twenty years and two children. My patients make problems bigger by talking so much. Divorce was like spa vacation. Every day I wake up and thank him for getting me away from him." I was suddenly worried about her kids. She smiled and tapped on her phone, proudly showing me two strapping young adults in ski clothes, a boy and a girl flashing the same smile Natasha wore. "Twins, Nikita and Nicolai. They live with their father in Moscow."

"Do you see them?"

"We FaceTime or Zoom. They are both at university. She will be an engineer like her father, and Nikita is studying to become a psychologist like me. I help them when I can."

I flashed back to my father's supercilious expression and hatred of the bird.

"I'm glad he's had a good life here with you."

Hector slid down the wall of the cage and lay on his side.

"What time does the vet open?"

"You think it will matter?" She poured us another drink. She looked over at the two birds. Anna was sheltering Hector with her wing.

We sat sharing our grief with the birds. Anna "talked" nonstop but Hector didn't respond. Natasha opened the cage, and Anna came out and sat on Natasha's finger.

"She's so cute. Would you like to hold Hector? Might be last chance."

Natasha gently lifted Hector out of his cage. She placed my hands together with the pinkie fingers touching then opened them. My palms were side by side as if they were a bed, and Natasha gently laid him there. His wings were soft, and I felt a wave of love towards this little critter.

"I love you, Hector," I whispered. He looked at me for a moment, then lay back, his chest heaving. His labored breathing hurt me.

Chapter 27

Natasha said, "Hector, this is the lady who rescued you and brought you here." For a moment, he seemed to perk up, looked at me, and then fell back. I saw the light of life leave his eyes. I felt no movement or breathing. Tears ran down my face, and Natasha's.

Anna climbed onto my open palms, covering Hector's body with her wings. We sat there until we saw the rosy streaks of dawn through Natasha's French windows. The day brought dull light and relentless rain, perfect for mourning. I heard Natasha sob, but couldn't hug her because I held the birds.

Natasha wept ferociously, like a sudden storm.

"Shhh, there now," I said, trying to soothe her. My heart clenched in its casing — she was a therapist who couldn't help herself. After a time, she quieted down and took Anna and Hector's corpse out of my hands. She put Anna back in her cage and wrapped Hector's body in a fluffy pink face towel. She rocked him gently.

"I live with everyone's tragedy, so no room for self. But when I dance, I am my best self." For a moment, her eyes shone with happiness, then filled with tears.

"Poor Anna, twice in one year." We nodded to each other, unable to imagine such tragedy.

We buried Hector in one of the planters on Natasha's terrace. Anna sat on Natasha's shoulder.

"I guess we should go buy her a new friend."

Natasha said, "She needs day or so." She put Anna back in the cage and covered it. "Sleep's the best thing for grief, don't you think?"

I wasn't sure, so I kept quiet.

I went home. As soon as I got inside, I ran to the bathroom and barfed, but nothing came up. I took a shower and realized how tired my body was. I wrapped myself in the soft robe I'd worn with George, poured myself some wine and made a three-course meal out of a box of microwave popcorn. Since I hadn't thrown out all of the living-room furniture, I could stretch out on the couch.

Was I crying for Hector, or was it because it was the last connection to my father? Yes, that was the one. It was over, and here I was, unable to follow well because of my anger towards a dead man. Wasn't the point of living to experience love? What demon inside me talked me out of this choice over and over again? And what did that inner enemy actually look like?

Aha! I had a flash of insight: this was the ongoing inner monologue that the A.R. and Cassandra diverted me from hearing. This was the real soundtrack for the movie of my life.

My father never liked me unless I acted all sweet and girlie. If my grades were less than A's, he took it hard, like a personal insult to him. His voice had been gravelly, like Peter's, and I could still hear him saying to me: "Stand up straight, plumpie. You need every crumb of height you can get. You're so stupid, you'll need your looks." He took my being short personally and blamed it on my mother's genes. He would tell me that God gave me the bustline to make up for my lack of height.

When I thought of Hector, I felt good. Thanks to me, he'd had another life where he was loved. I hoped that God would send me something good since I had done something that, in the abstract, my father would have approved of. Norman called it "Going the extra mile," and he did it for everyone except my mother and me. He was a salesman, a big man, a charming buffoon, but when we were alone the mask came off and he became a tyrant who complained about everything, complained about the character of his customers, and told mean stories. When he was angry, he'd slam the table or the wall with enough force to terrify me. My mother would scurry around like a mouse trying to please him.

"Honey, would you like something to eat? A beer, a cocktail?"

"I'd like you to shut your fucking mouth."

Chapter 27

She would run off to the other room, crying.

I would always take the opportunity to disappear. I was never missed. My mother would come into my room and sleep in bed with me. I never liked the way she smelled, and it would be hard to sleep. I would make up stories about a princess who was tall, and I'd fall asleep describing the bedroom or the ball dresses. The stories concerned the princess becoming the queen, and they were not about men, except that there was always a ball where the princess had many partners, all of whom were interested in her, but not the other way around. Once I had to go to the bathroom and, on my way, crept past the kitchen door. I saw my father sitting alone at the kitchen table, a glass and a bottle of scotch in front of him. He looked like a big wilted balloon after a parade.

I always wondered why he was loved. Couldn't people see that this clown's mouth had sharp corners, not the friendly ones of Ronald McDonald or circus clowns? Perhaps that explained my lack of enthusiasm for people in general. You never know what they're really like until you see them at home in their skivvies.

I had a shock then, because while I'd always been proud that I had escaped the global conditioning of humanity, I'd unknowingly accepted Norman's personal condemnation! No wonder I often felt like throwing up. I was like a fish who'd swallowed a hook and was trying to get it out. The bait I'd taken was "I'll love you if you agree that you were born with Original Sin, not the Catholic kind, but a bigger, nondenominational one: the sin of being yourself, she who isn't good enough."

That's why I compared myself to others, and judged them: because I wanted to be accepted and wasn't. I knew that I had to separate feelings from facts in order to figure out what was right and wrong about myself on some empirical basis. I had to accurately access who and what was inside me, then decide if I wanted to make improvements. Maybe I was just fine. Maybe

I'd just given away my power at some point and could take it back now with the right perspective.

I was shocked at a vision of myself as an evil puppet master cackling as I controlled two tango dancers and made them dance badly. In the mental image, I wore a witch's hat and had long bony talons instead of hands. Control freak, much? Did Peter or any other man have a chance to succeed with me? It was the opposite of being pre-approved for a mortgage or a credit card. I was creating pre-rejection. There was always something wrong. Even if it was right, it wouldn't last because I couldn't take the risk of being rejected. I could never be enough.

Until I found some way to accept myself as a dancer, however flawed, as long as I experienced dancing through this cracked prism, there was no chance of mastery.

Bonnie called. She'd heard about Hector from Natasha. "Are you okay?"

"Fine, fine." I was so not fine.

"I can tell you aren't, but come over. We have a *milonga* with a surprise."

"Now?"

"Yes. It will be good for you to get out of the house." I looked at the clock and realized that twelve hours had passed, unnoticed. I was hungry. Bonnie always had great food, and her private *milongas* were always attended by the best dancers.

"Okay." I took a shower and put on a lilac wrap top and a drapey purple skirt, and took my silver shoes. I would dance in Hector's honor. I called Natasha, but she didn't want to leave Anna just yet, so I went solo.

Chapter 28

Bonnie had a large loft in Tribeca with a big bay window. I looked up as I pushed the bell and saw the silhouettes of dancers. I was buzzed in.

Entry was through the large open kitchen. A huge Mission-style wooden table was laden with bread, cheeses, salad, empanadas, and steaks. On one of the counters there was a zinc bar with wine and soft drinks.

The walls in the main room were covered with large colorful paintings of tango dancers. White twinkling Christmas lights made the room feel festive. The purple velvet couches and orange rug had been pushed back, so there was a lovely dance space.

This was a *milonga* with a bonus. After food and dancing, there were consultations with a psychic. Bonnie had gotten a bunch of her friends to sponsor a visit to New York for Gustavo, a famous tango teacher from Argentina, who was also a clairvoyant. We each got a session with Gustavo. Bonnie had put a screen in one corner so that there was privacy during the reading.

I hung my coat on the coatrack and sat down to change my shoes. But before I could, Bonnie hurried over, hugged me, and said, "He's waiting for you."

I walked behind the screen. Gustavo was an old man with erect posture, a full head of wavy silver hair, and dark eyes that had seen everything. He wore an elegant dark suit with a black shirt and lavender tie.

"Sit, sit," he said in almost unaccented English. I took a seat, and he sat facing me.

I was suddenly nervous. "Don't worry," he said. "This will help you move forward."

There was a deck of tarot cards on a round table covered with a black tablecloth.

He shuffled the cards then handed them to me. "Cut the cards three times, then pick five, like this." He demonstrated how to cut the cards. "Is there something you want to know?"

"Yes. Why haven't I found love?"

"Good. Now cut, pick five." I did and picked five cards. He laid the cards out and studied them.

"In your last life, you were a Jew in a concentration camp and survived by having an affair with the camp commander. But when you had the chance to shoot him with his own gun, you couldn't do it."

"But isn't murder a cardinal sin?"

Gustavo nodded and said, "Some sins are worse than others."

"Who decides that?"

"He does."

"Then why is 'Thou shalt not kill' at the top of the Ten Commandments?"

"If you kill the one to save the many, it's okay, as a soldier does in war."

"Just to be clear, murder is relative. Some murders are more murderous than others."

I felt the two sides of my brain twist into a pretzel. Was life like being in a casino, where no matter what is right, or consistent, the house always wins?

That made sense. "I thought God was all-forgiving."

"He is, but that doesn't mean there are no consequences."

"So, I'm being punished in this life for failing to commit murder in a previous one."

"Not punished, just being given a hard lesson. Something you failed to learn in that life is presented again and again until you learn it."

"What is that lesson? I will learn it pronto."

He smiled and collected the cards. "To lose your hubris, the arrogance that you can control things, when really all

Chapter 28

that anybody can control is the way you respond to what is happening around you. This is wisdom."

"So, if I'd been more 'accepting,'" — I made finger quotes with my hand — "I would have been able to shoot this creep, though I'm sure I would have been tortured and killed."

Gustavo shrugged. "I'm just a messenger."

"Okay, good. Can you talk to Him and get me in a time warp? Send me back? This time I won't screw it up, and maybe I can be taller when I re-do this lifetime." My head was literally spinning: in this karmic narrative, I was being punished for *not* killing somebody. If I'd already failed in a past life, what hope was there for me in this one? No wonder I didn't like myself much. I was a designated loser before I was born, and was stuck with myself, till death do us part, and beyond!

"So, I will never find love?"

Gustavo shook his head. "We cannot escape our karma."

"Isn't there someone bad I can kill in this lifetime and make things balance out? Maybe my ex-boyfriend?"

Gustavo laughed. "I wish it were so simple. What you can do is imagine how love would feel."

"Yes, isn't that why we dance the tango?"

Gustavo nodded. "Yes, and each time you dance, make the request that you find your love, and see what happens." He gathered up the cards. The session was over. I thanked him and left.

I went to the bathroom, splashed cold water on my wrists and forehead, and inspected my unsatisfactory face in the mirror. Blotchy, tired, pointy. Luckily, thanks to my dress, no one would be looking at my face.

I suddenly understood why I'd tried to commit suicide, and why that act of self-annihilation was futile. We could never get away from ourselves. If we snuck out of this life, we'd just have a do-over in another one until the debt was repaid, the lesson learned.

So, contrary to all the New Thought material I'd studied, I did not create my reality; I responded to what was there both in my past life and in the present one. Was that what was being passed off as free will? What a sucker I'd been. How was it free will if my damaged perceptions shaped my so-called choices?

If someone was going to create my future, I didn't intend to leave it up to some impersonal deity with his own agenda. Was there an alternative? Did I really believe that I was the one controlling my life, not some ethereal God force?

Ouch! I had found the splinter that festered in my heart and sent a thin stream of poison through my veins. I knew that being able to find the love that I was so desperate for required trust, but I didn't trust myself, and I didn't trust God. Aunt Cindy believed that love was trust.

If I didn't love myself, how could I know how to love someone else? But if you couldn't trust an inconsistent God who calibrated the act of murder based on a moving criterion, who could you trust? I would never find love.

I realized that someone was banging on the door. I exited to dirty looks from the line of needy *tangueras*. "Sorry, sorry, something I ate," I murmured as I headed for the dance floor.

The room was filled with dancers, the music a lilting waltz. Terence, my old friend, gave me the *cabaceo* and I nodded. He was as handsome as always, with his mane of white hair and noble features framed by a fedora. I noticed that he seemed frail.

"Hola, Dots, written any new books lately?"

Ouch. I smiled anyway. "I'm working on a new one."

"Is it about me?"

"Of course."

He smiled and offered his hand to begin the dance. When we got into the embrace, his hands shook slightly.

Chapter 28

I pretended not to notice, but he said, "Parkinson's. They're going to change my meds next week."

"I thought it was passion," I joked.

"Ha! I'm eighty years old, not sure if I can even spell that anymore."

"No, you're eighty years young."

He laughed with pleasure and said, "Young, I love it! Tango till you die! Which might be soon, so let's dance."

We danced a wonderful waltz, and I was relaxed and danced better than I had before. The feeling of connection was like a warm blanket surrounding me. I felt loved and loving, and in a state of bliss.

What a difference a word makes. Old versus young. It was humbling to see Terence transform from a gloomy old man trying to keep it together to an exuberant, confident ageless *tanguero*.

On my way home, I called Natasha, who'd been drinking vodka and slurred her words. She sent me a photo of Anna nestled in her hands. Natasha launched into a tirade against the ex, and I felt her pain. After ten blocks, I was at my doorway and out of breath.

"Natasha, it's okay. You'll find someone new and better. You found Hector, and you'll find your own lovebird."

There was a silence. Then I heard Anna chirp. Natasha laughed.

"She is hungry. I go feed her." She hung up, and I was happy she was snapping out of it. As for me, I knew grief was a physical reaction, that the body had to be respected, and it took time. My gloom lessened, and I reminded myself that death had taken Hector home.

Chapter 29

I was cloistered in my shaggy lilac bathrobe writing when Tomas called and asked me to assist him. It was good timing, because my attempts to relate tango to life were making me cringe with their cheesiness. Maybe some applied theory would help.

When I arrived at the studio, Zevi was putting on his shoes. I went to the ladies' changing room and found Maureen crying on the little faded rose velvet love seat. She looked up when I came in.

"What's wrong?" I asked as I ran water on a paper towel and brought it to her.

Maureen dabbed at her eyes.

"Zevi told me I was leaning too heavily on him." This brought on more sobs. Tango. I should have guessed.

"Staying on your axis is one of the hardest things to do. Has he always complained?"

"No, just after our last lesson."

"Sometimes when you improve one thing, something else gets thrown off. Do your feet hurt more?"

She nodded, surprised. "Why?"

"Because what's happening is that you started to lean more forward than you were before. You're off-balance."

"I don't know what to do." Her desperation matched what I had felt.

"Don't bend your knees so much. Lift your quads, and engage your hamstrings, then dance on your 'inside' arch, as Tomas says." I touched each spot, and she straightened her knees, lifted her thighs and shifted her weight back.

She stood up. "I'll try now," Maureen said. When I turned her, she was smooth and effortless. She hugged me. "Now I know what to do! You're a great teacher! Tell Zevi I'll be right out."

Chapter 29

On the dance floor, Tomas and Zevi practiced a step. Tomas was acting as a bad follower, holding himself stiffly, knees bent, butt pushed out. They did a turn. I saw Zevi pulling Tomas. Tomas clicked his tongue and gestured for me to join him.

"Don't pull your partner. She will lose her balance. Watch."

I smiled and got into the embrace. Tomas led me in the same turn. This time, I took my own advice and I followed him easily. I was excited. By helping Maureen, I'd helped myself. We went again, and I noticed that Maureen was quietly watching from the doorway.

Tomas looked at Zevi. "You must adjust the turn so that she has time to complete it. Otherwise, you will activate her primal fear of falling."

"But she's heavy and stiff," Zevi complained.

I saw Maureen wince and Tomas saw it, too. He gestured for Maureen to join us.

"If you don't give your follower time, she will cling onto you for dear life." He gestured to Maureen to join him, and she entered the embrace.

She looked at me, and I nodded and smiled. I watched her concentrate. Tomas led her in the turn. As she pivoted, he said to Zevi, "It's not just a turn. She has to pivot and then take a step. We need to give her time to execute." He gestured for Zevi to take his place.

Zevi led Maureen slowly in the turn. They both smiled happily, and Tomas applauded. "Now we have to practice. Consistency is the mark of good dancers."

After the song ended, Tomas asked me to dance with Zevi while he worked with Maureen.

Zevi went to the men's room. I heard Tomas say, "Look, Maureen, you're a powerful woman. That means you can let him lead you, you know? It doesn't mean you let him push you off your balance. It's your responsibility to stay on your own axis. You can be powerful and follow at the same time."

Wow, that was the solution expressed in a single sentence: *You can be powerful and follow at the same time.* I repeated it in my mind so I wouldn't forget to write it down after I danced with Zevi, who had returned.

Zevi held out his hand, and I stepped into the embrace. He stiffened as his chest touched mine. I've had these girls for a long time and know what they can do, but not in tango, until now. He clearly was excited by feeling my breasts against his chest, and turned beet red after I caught his eye. He was a short guy, so they hit him around the collarbone. Maureen was slim and athletic, my dream that would never be.

Zevi was sweating heavily, and his hands were slippery. He jerked my arm as he turned me, and it hurt my wrist, so I stopped dancing. Tomas came over.

"Ow," I said and shook it to make sure I was okay.

"What's wrong?" Tomas asked.

"He pulled my arm and hurt my wrist."

Zevi said, "No, I tried to pivot you, but you didn't turn."

I expected Tomas to defend me, but he said, "Let's try that turn again."

He held Maureen's hand. Zevi and I got into position and he began to turn me.

"Stop right where you are, both of you." He looked and saw that I'd been trying to keep my chest from touching Zevi. I saw a flicker of amusement in his eyes, then he frowned. "Tango is about the dance that the two partners create. It's not about how anyone feels about anything except the dance. Zevi, you must use your chest, not your arms, to lead, and Dots, you must allow yourself to pivot more on the standing leg by lifting the heel. If you don't collect your feet on the turn, you won't stop yourself. Collecting there throws off your balance and stiffens the left rib cage. Instead, thighs are together, let one knee follow each other, and let the hips be in sync with the knees."

Chapter 29

He demonstrated with Maureen, who was able to follow. I was upset at being corrected. Meanwhile, I'd assume a "silver lining" approach as I called it, and enjoy the rest of the lesson.

When it was over, I grabbed the computer and took notes. "You can be powerful and follow," safely captured on paper. I felt sick with rage at Tomas's betrayal.

"Good work, do you want to have a coffee?"

"No thank you, and goodbye."

"Is something wrong?"

"You humiliated me in front of a student. I'm supposed to be your assistant, not another student."

"The hardest person to tell the truth to is yourself."

"What the hell is that supposed to mean?"

"You embarrassed yourself."

"How was that? He pulled me off my axis and hurt my wrist."

"You showed no compassion. He didn't pull you off your axis; he responded to your physicality and you pulled away from him. You humiliated him."

"The hell I did. He was hurting me."

"It was a compliment to you. You hurt your own wrist. He did nothing inappropriate, yet you punished him by rejecting him."

"I don't know what you mean."

Tomas laughed. "You had me at 'hell.'"

I couldn't help it and laughed, too. "So, Tomas, what did you mean?"

"Dots, are you really completely unaware of your physical beauty?"

"Oh, are you hitting on me now? You remind me of my old boyfriend, first you correct me, like I'm your underling, and then you make a pass at me." I was furious. I snapped the computer shut. I was still wearing my tango shoes but didn't care. I grabbed my bag and walked to the door.

He watched me, and as I turned the handle, he said, "Tell yourself the truth, Dorothy. Just this once. Take ownership of your beauty, and your soul. Don't be a ghost haunting yourself. Accept it as part of yourself."

I stood in the doorway, considering. If I walked out, I was back to zero with no book for Suzanne to help me succeed with. If I stayed, I'd have to consider what he said. There was no reason for him to lie. I glanced back. He stood still and raised his hands as if surrendering at gunpoint.

"I'm not hitting on you, Dorothy. As the poet said, 'I don't shit where I eat.'"

That was it. I laughed. "You stole my line."

He looked puzzled. "Your line?"

"Yes, I don't date anyone I work or dance with."

"You're wise."

"You, too. Enough with the clichés." I opened the door.

"Is suggesting a drink too clichéd?"

"Yes. Let me finish the book."

Chapter 30

I went to feed the birds. They swarmed at me, obviously hungry. I'd only brought a little bread, so I left and hurried to the pet store to get some seeds. The other Dorothy, whose picture I had taken, was behind the counter, wearing a badge that identified her as the manager. I was beyond embarrassed. I had thought she was a homeless person. In the late-afternoon light, her creamy mocha skin and reddish curls looked cared for, and she wore expensive jeans and the signature T-shirt.

I turned to flee, but she called out, "Hey, namesake, five dollars off first purchase."

"I'm so sorry. I thought…"

"You thought I needed help, and you offered it. How rare is that?"

"Thank you." I showed her the screen saver on my phone — the photograph of her wearing the T-shirt that read, "Don't look back, you're not going that way."

"This has been my guiding thought, whenever I start to brood about the past."

She laughed. "I'm flattered. What do you need today?"

"Birdseed for pigeons and sparrows." She fetched a five-pound bag of mixed seeds. "I see you help other living things besides people." I handed her my credit card, and she handed it back.

"No charge. Next time, and you'll still get the five-dollar discount."

We were more than even, and to my delight, I'd made a friend. I nodded my thanks and left. As I walked back to the bench, Frank called me.

"Hi, Dots, I'm sorry but your dad made a later will."

"Okay, what changed?"

"You're not in it."

I asked Frank when it was dated, and sure enough, it was dated after my confrontation with Norman about Hector. Norman had been spiteful to the end, determined to win by cutting me out of the will. Did Frank know about it? Dad had died so soon after our fight.

"No, I didn't prepare it. He got some local guy to do it, but it's legit," he said.

"I'll take them to court."

"You could ask for some consideration for not contesting. It'll make the whole thing go faster and save money in lawyer fees."

"What was Dad worth?"

"The will's still in probate, so I don't have a total."

"Okay, but whatever it is, I think I'm owed a third." I heard him gasp, and felt a grim satisfaction.

"Dots, the new will is legit."

"Listen, Frank, you know how much of a nuisance the nuclear child can be. Silence and cooperation are expensive. Brad and Thad can afford it, however miserly they are. I just hope you're getting paid in advance."

Frank laughed an honest laugh. "You have a gift for understatement." He paused and confided, "Your father put a provision in the will that I get paid, and for what it's worth, I'm on your side. I've never been a big fan of the boys."

"Really? I never knew that."

It suddenly occurred to me that the evil twins could as easily be Frank's as Norman's. He had made a pass at me when I was a teenager. When you discover something bad about someone, it's never the first or the worst.

"Annette was your first cousin. You were very close. She was a wild girl. It was a shotgun wedding."

There was a long silence. I couldn't believe that I'd just said that!

Chapter 30

"How far do you want to take this?" He was another Suzanne! I was suddenly angry in a dry-ice sort of way. A coldness that would burn.

"As far as I need to. They should take a DNA test."

"Seriously?"

"They want to cheat me."

"Let me talk to them."

So, there was reason for concern. Ugh! They were all sleazy and how had I not seen this before? Had Annette gotten knocked up by her first cousin, and Norman had married her because she was pregnant with what he thought were his own kids? Had he known? It didn't make sense that he would have — what would have been in it for him? Then why had Frank invited me to the funeral? To keep me from sniffing around. Of course. Frank was Dad's lawyer, and that's how Annette was in the picture. She'd been Frank's office manager.

All of the money could be mine if I was right. My rage was running me as I gleefully imagined the look on Brad's and Thad's smug, entitled faces as Frank gave them the bad news. Then a sob filled my throat, choking me. I coughed to fight back the sudden overwhelming grief. All little girls love their daddies, and I had, too, however hateful he had been. I was grateful for the knife-sharp pain that stabbed me in the heart. It meant that I was accepting what had happened and was therefore moving forward.

Norman had been their father, too. I'd had my identity wiped away by Suzanne, and I didn't have the heart to do it to Brad or Thad. Either way, a paternity challenge would damage them. But money would get me out of Suzanne's clutches.

"I'd appreciate that, Uncle Frank, because I will insist if we don't come to an understanding. Now, what about Aunt Cindy? Is she included?"

"What about her? She was your mother's sister." The deprecating way he said "mother" spelled out worlds. I wondered if he'd made a pass at her, too, and been rejected less delicately. Maybe he'd also tried with Aunty Cindy, who would have verbally slapped him at the very least. I promised myself that I'd give Aunt Cindy twenty-five percent of whatever I got.

I stayed quiet, and after a long pause, Frank said, "I'll see what I can do. Is there anything else?"

"Yes. About protecting my book."

"Send it to me when it's done. I'll have it copyrighted, and let me look at any contracts."

"Thank you." I hung up. I was numb. Had Norman always been so vindictive? Did Aunt Cindy know if there had been any dirty business? No information would change the fact that my father had cut me out of his will because we fought over Hector. The first is not the worst, so what else had happened that I was ignoring? I'd thought that ignorance was bliss, but now seeing that it put me in hell, it was time to wise up. No more victim. Where else was I playing that role? How did the victim story manifest in tango? I still saw myself as a student, not a partner or a teacher. That's what had to change if I wanted to be happy. Being a student was being a victim, and for all of my brave talk to Babette about choice, I'd never chosen. I was choosing now. I had to find a new role, fast.

Chapter 31

I had a better chance of attracting a miracle if I had a manuscript. I did research and found a long-out-of-print tome about a famous dance couple from the fifties. The leader wrote the book about the follower's teaching methods. I was inspired by his perspective as the reporter of the techniques. I could be Watson to Tomas's Sherlock Holmes. Having found my voice and narrative point of view, I forged ahead.

Six weeks later, wearing Tomas's shoes, I completed a first draft. I called Uncle Frank. He gave me a nondisclosure agreement for Suzanne to sign. He agreed to copyright the book even though it could change a lot. He told me I could amend it, if I had to.

Aunt Cindy always said, regarding correcting a mistake, "First time, shame on them. Second time, shame on you." I knew it was unlikely that anyone would be desperate enough to steal a tango-book idea, but as Frank pointed out, that wasn't my business.

I now saw a pathway to a larger audience. Tango suggested romance and mystery, something everyone wanted in their relationship. Knowing how to lead and follow was a lost art in life, and the metaphor of dance was a way to demonstrate the best way to interact. I went back to sleep for forty-eight hours, and when I went outside to feed the pigeons, the season had changed from winter to spring.

Suzanne called and we met for dinner at La Vierge. Suzanne was all aglow, and for once she wasn't late.

She ordered a bottle of wine and poured us each a large glass. I waited. This time I'd had Frank copyright the book, and included the email notification in the attachment I'd sent her with the manuscript. I'd also included photos of Tomas, of Zevi and Maureen, of me dancing with Tomas, and of the studio.

Suzanne had printed everything out. She pulled the manuscript and photos out of her bag and handed them to me. I took them.

"What am I supposed to do with this, Suzanne?"

"Revise it."

The waiter arrived with our food. I was hungry and cut a piece.

"I love it," Suzanne said. "But I'm not sure how to sell it."

I chewed my salmon. It was perfectly cooked, the wine matched, and the background music was vaguely tango-ish. I wanted to remember this moment. I felt like a writer. In my mind's eye, the A.R. unzipped her costume, and from inside it, a version of me as a child stepped out, looking around anxiously. The frizzy writer hurried over, hugged the little me, and we blended into one being with a blinding flash. The Approval Rat vanished, hopefully forever.

Cassandra appeared. "It's about time," she sneered, but I didn't care. When she realized that, she disappeared, too.

Was I actually integrating? Woo-hoo. I knew better than to feel too happy, lest some axe fall. I came back to reality and realized that Suzanne had been talking at a furious rate. I held up my hand.

"Sorry, Suzanne, can you repeat that?"

"You weren't even listening, were you?"

"I'm a little overwhelmed, is all."

"Really?"

Her tone was accusing. I saw what an abusive stinker she could be — no, was being. When did I start making excuses for her behavior? When did she become the talent? I realized that she'd always been the talent. She, the chief, and I, the scared little Indian, as my mother had been to my father.

I waited to feel shame, but instead I got mad.

"No, I wasn't listening. Care to try again?" I took another sip of wine and didn't give her the apology she was expecting.

Chapter 31

"What I said was, I can get Rex, Gabriel's agent, to allow you to be at the training, maybe even be his partner during the lessons."

"Who's Gabriel?"

She looked at me aghast. "You wrote this book and don't even know what the trump card is?"

"No, I'm the writer. Publicity is your job." She didn't know how to respond to this different version of her former victim. I enjoyed her discomfort.

"I'm a very powerful agent."

"You are what you say you are."

"It was easy for me to find out who was going to use tango in an upcoming film. Do you want to know more?" I shrugged, and waited.

Suzanne blurted out, "It's Gabriel Ripley."

"I don't get it."

"That's all you have to say? Do you even know who he is?"

"I don't live under a rock, but I didn't know you were a starfucker, Suzanne. I should have guessed. As far as I'm concerned, he has no cred. He makes action movies."

"He's an A-list star who is going to dance a tango, being coached by a tango dancer who's almost as hot as he is."

"Who's that?"

"You do live under a rock! The teacher is your collaborator, Tomas Gardel."

"What? How did you…"

"I have my ways."

"Tomas hasn't said anything. Besides, he's the only teacher."

"No, you're now a teaching team, and you are the author of the forthcoming book. You're the top, he's the bottom. Every woman will want to read this and try to figure out how you nailed him."

"That's gross, and not true."

"That's show business."

I saw the light. That's why Tomas wanted me to assist him. He was teaching me to teach without actually telling me. He needed a front man or woman.

"Just to be clear, you're suggesting that my brand could be tango teacher to the stars."

She nodded. "Why not? We need to get you on the map somewhere."

I thought to myself, Oh, so now we're a "we" again. That means there must be money I don't know about somewhere.

"You have a contract with Tomas, I presume."

I nodded.

"Good, this can work if you were Gabriel's dance partner during the training."

"I'd have to ask Tomas."

She looked at me, narrowed her eyes. "You're shtupping him, aren't you? I approve. He's an upgrade over you-know-who." I had no idea what she was going after, but it felt good that no one had any sexual leverage over me.

"I don't eat where I dance. You know that about me."

"Okay, but you'd like to do him?"

"And your point is?"

"Every woman would."

Suzanne's phone rang and she answered, listened, then held up her hand to warn me not to talk. The call ended. Suzanne laughed, a loud cackle. The waiter brought champagne and popped the cork.

"Isn't this a little premature?"

She looked at me in disgust. "You know what your problem is, Dots?"

"I only have one? If so, then the champers is timely."

Suzanne actually rolled her eyes. I rolled mine back and outstared her.

Chapter 31

"The bubbly is to celebrate the book's completion. You always do this. You can't take a minute to appreciate any accomplishment."

She was right. I felt a rush of gratitude. "But you still want me to revise it."

Suzanne waved the point away. "Details, details. Just drink. That was the call that will sell the book. That was Gabriel's agent. He's willing to support our book and arrange to have Gabriel train in New York, at Tomas's studio."

"Hoo-ha!" We clinked glasses. "Let's toast to the new tango teacher to the stars. You should be jumping up and down for joy."

The last time I got this angry was when I took the rifle away from my father. I stuttered in fury.

"Really? Because, thanks to you, I'm not going to be the center of a diet revolution. I'm going to be a one-trick pony tango instructor to an unlikely celebrity. If I'm really lucky, I'll open my own dance studio and spend my days coaching clumsy beginners. In Queens! Of course, you, my noble friend, will direct the odd celebrity or two preparing for a movie, my way. Thank you so very much!"

There was quiet. Would she apologize? I bet myself a dollar she would ignore it, and I was right.

"Gabriel's divorced and I hear he's looking. And, drum roll, he's not a player." So now she was matchmaking. Would I owe her ten percent of any pre-nup?

"Does he like dwarves?"

"As long as they're stacked and have a sarcastic take on the world."

"You do realize that you are offering me crumbs."

"But Desiree wants you to write the workbook, and the sequel. That's $50,000 right there, if you're willing to sign the NDA."

"I need to have editorial approval. Send it to my lawyer."

"You've never asked for that before."

"More fool me."

"I don't know what's come over you, Dots, you seem so different."

I didn't want to tell her about the Oxycontin cocktail, so I just said, "For starters, you can now only call me Dorothy." I held my hand out for the MS, and she handed it to me. I was in control for once. Did I trust myself? Who cared.

Chapter 32

Why hadn't Tomas told me about Gabriel Ripley? Tomas didn't answer his phone or respond to my texts. After a couple of hours, I went out to Queens. The studio was closed when I got there. A handwritten sign read, "At lunch, back at 5:00pm." He wasn't downstairs in Tapas, so I walked around the corner to Paco's Place.

Tomas was at the bar, his back to me, the manuscript next to him. I walked over and touched him lightly on the shoulder. "Hola."

He shot me an angry look. "I hate it." He didn't offer me a seat.

"What?" Oh, I see he's just teasing me. I smiled at his joke. "Okay, I get the joke."

"No, you don't. You have made me into one."

I was shocked. "How have I?"

"You've reduced it to a dance instruction book."

"As opposed to what?" I said bluntly. "You are a tango teacher as far as I know, and a good one. You teach people to dance in person and on paper."

"Yes, to dance, not paint by numbers."

He had a point. "Okay, I dumbed it down a little because it has to appeal to a non-dancing audience to lure them to try it."

"Tango is so much more than just a dance. You didn't convey that. There's a philosophy, a mindset and a spiritual aspect."

"That, I think I did. Did you not read the intro?" I picked up the manuscript and read from the opening of my introduction.

"Tango is a unique dance that's full of mystery and paradox. It's steeped in history but also timeless. Unlike other dances, the follower interprets the leader's steps, although the foundation is eight basic steps. Tango is full of contradictions: the upper body is still, the ribs move, and the legs do the work, yet you must use your upper back to move those legs. It's these paradoxes and contradictions that give tango its endless mystery."

"Okay, but where is the philosophy we discussed? You put in diagrams with arrows."

He took the manuscript back and flipped through it to show me. Did he want to train Gabriel without me? Too bad. My teeth still hurt from where Suzanne kicked me.

"Yes, I did. Beginners need to know what the basic eight is and where to initiate the movements from. You have to make learning tango seem simple, which we both know is a lie."

He laughed bitterly. "You want to sell this book with a lie."

"I thought you were worldlier, Tomas. Let's call it an optimistic promise."

"You want to lie about lying."

"No. I want people to buy the book, fall in love with the tango, and hire you to teach them. What do you want?"

"I want to share tango, establish my credentials, and teach on a larger scale."

"So where is there a conflict?"

"Tango is mysterious, layered, and precise."

I laughed. "And that's your idea of an advertisement? People want sexy, easy, understandable. There's always a price tag, Tomas."

"You have a point."

"And on that note, are you sure that you're willing to give up your anonymity? You told me that you were ostracized from the Buenos Aires scene."

"Yes, it gives me pleasure imagining Cho-Cho's face when he sees a copy."

"What about the robber you sent to prison? You don't think he'll come after you?"

Tomas shrugged, but something dark passed over him and I shivered. Something wasn't right. Not my business.

Chapter 32

"Tomas, we're basically in agreement. Teaching is your expertise; writing persuasive books is mine."

"You wrote this like one of your cookbooks."

"What's wrong with that? No one cares about philosophy. They want concrete results, as in, what will dancing tango do for them? I intend to share your philosophical insights with our readers. They are brilliant, but must be slipped in during the revision work. For example, your obsession about how, when danced well, tango is a metaphor for a perfectly lived life will make readers feel that they can't succeed. No one's life is perfect, why rub it in? That's why I want the opening chapter to be modeled on another great insight, that if you can walk, you can dance." The A.R. was gone, but she'd left me her silver tongue!

"I'm not obsessed. I'm realistic."

"That's what Nostradamus would say."

"What is wrong with the truth?"

"People are lazy. They're looking for an easy fix. They want results, but don't want to do the work."

He sighed and nodded. "I get your point, but it's too simple, too elementary. Isn't there a middle ground? You mention mystery, but there isn't any discussion of it besides the introduction."

"I'll weave that into the manuscript once it's sold." I had a sudden thought — had he even read it? Could he read that well in English? I'd never seen him with a book.

"You can tease people with the mystery and talk about connection, but people need access, a way in. For example, when I first work on a book, I look to provide a context such as: What is the benefit they will receive by reading the book and taking the advice offered? In a diet or a cookbook, the context, the reason why they should add these new principles to their lives, is obvious. Eating is something we do for survival. People have been eating too much since whenever the age of agriculture started. Dancing is not like eating, although you and I both feel it's more like breathing. The goal is to make tango seem easy, not like something that will humiliate the reader who attempts to dance. We both know that really learning the tango often sends people into a tailspin of self-doubt and self-criticism."

"I didn't survive the siege of Sarajevo to end up just being a tango instructor."

"But that's what you are, boyo." Cassandra had stuck her nose in, but I covered my mouth with my hand. No point puncturing the balloon of his fragile ego.

"As portrayed by me, you aren't. You're a distinguished tango philosopher and mentor to the stars. I'm the narrator. Perhaps you should re-read the book. I'm Watson to your Sherlock Holmes."

But he had a point. And had caught me. I didn't have the perfect hook because there wasn't one. Tango was its own unicorn. I also knew that Suzanne would push a book on hemorrhoids to keep me in her orbit. Who else could write a book so fast? She didn't believe in me as a brand, but she wanted to keep me in her writing stable. Once I had my "fifteen minutes of fame," she reasoned, I would calm down and go back to ghostwriting, and she wasn't wrong. I didn't really expect success, as much as I tried to convince myself I did.

"The book title is 'Solving the Mystery of Tango: How Dancing Can Set You Free.'"

"What does that even mean? Sherlock Holmes solves mysteries, but every tango has its own story."

"You solve a mystery for each student: how they can dance well. Besides, Suzanne loves it and thinks she can get Gabriel to be featured in the book, and me to be his study partner."

He was surprised and suspicious. "How did you find out it was him?"

"I didn't. Suzanne told me. And why didn't you tell me? It's great news!"

"I don't want any part of it."

"The book or training Gabriel? Maybe you just don't want me to be a part of it."

Tomas banged his hand on the bar so hard his glass went flying. I caught it in mid-air and handed it back.

"Feel better now?"

"You make me feel cheap and shallow. That I'm a short-order cook, not an artist." He glared at me. Everyone is a critic. Ingrate. He was a tango instructor, not Pablo Picasso. I opened my mouth and closed it. I looked at him. I'd never noticed what a weak chin he had, or the mole on his cheek. I felt my heart clutch as if it were being squeezed by a fist. If Tomas squashed the book, would I really have the strength to start again?

"Is this a posture to cut me out of the book now that Gabriel is involved?" This direct question was me borrowing Cassandra's fearlessness, and I blessed her. He didn't answer.

"Please. Let's set up a meeting with Gabriel. And I could add more in the case study about Maureen and Zevi."

"You'd better go," he said, avoiding my gaze. "We'll just forget we ever met. I'll pay you when I can. By the way, Gabriel is my sensei, my friend, my pal, while there are dozens of writers who could work for me."

I was a ghost.

Chapter 33

I ended up at La Boca, after walking for miles. Fernando was happy to see me. "What did he think of the book?"

I shrugged. "He didn't like it."

Fernando put a glass of wine in front of me. "Really? That surprises me."

"Truth. He hated it. He said I made him into a mechanic."

"It doesn't matter. You don't need him, Dorothy."

"I thought you were his best friend? This was your idea. You paid for the contract."

"One of them, yes. But I am disappointed that he feels reduced rather than distilled into a book. Who would want that?"

"I would, I would!"

"You're a writer, that's natural. I thought he was a bigger man."

"Me, too."

"Can you see that for a little man with an ego, to have everything you know put between covers would make him angry?"

"I'm confused, Fernando. Whose side are you on?"

"I remember you had this problem with the one you called 'the Bellmore princess.' When word got out that she'd used a ghostwriter, she trashed your stuff. Your analysis of why she behaved that way was similar to what I just said."

I had to admit that he was right. I wrote her a cookbook-memoir that portrayed her as a heroic survivor of domestic abuse who'd cooked her way to happiness. Just like Tomas, she'd had a temper tantrum over it. She'd threatened a lawsuit and worse — she'd refused to pay me and tried to ruin my reputation. Suzanne had been my champion then, though she

Chapter 33

got me the assignment and it was in her best interest, convincing the princess to have a TV producer read it, and when he liked it, the princess turned on a dime. Suddenly I was a genius, somehow able to capture her soul, albeit a very shallow one. The reviews had been positive with comments to the effect of "Long Island never tasted this good! The princess bares her soul and pours it into her lobster bisque." After a brief stint on the Food Channel, she now owned a chain of seafood restaurants, and my book had helped open the pathway. Who said, "Hell is other people"? They were right.

Fernando reached over and wiped away the frown lines between my eyebrows. "He'll either come around or he won't. Tomas needs to feel more important than he is."

"Don't we all?"

"No, we don't. You are too humble, take no credit for how many people you've helped find a new identity and purpose, whereas I am content to have helped my friends, maintained my family's legacy, and will soon sing in public. Further, I have fed many people, educating them in the cuisine of my country, and I feel just fine about myself. You believe that if you don't make a name for yourself, you don't exist. That isn't true. You exist because you have helped others, made people happy with themselves, and now you're upgrading to help yourself. I wish you could see yourself through my eyes."

"Me, too. Thanks, but I need Tomas."

"Why?"

"There's no hook."

"Not true. You've written an excellent primer, and you dance well enough to teach."

I opened my mouth to protest, but Fernando put up his hand to stop me. "Listen to me, you don't need Tomas. You could easily teach Gabriel without him."

"That's impossible."

"I read it, remember? What could Tomas do? Sue you? Your agent would probably be thrilled not to have Tomas involved at all."

"Gabriel is Tomas's sensei. He'd never go for it."

"It's not up to Tomas. Gabriel is a star and needs to dance a good tango in an upcoming film. It's Tomas who needs you, Gabriel, and the book. Tomas should go break a few dozen blocks of wood with a karate chop and get real."

I wished any of that could have been true. My spirits fled, and dark angels hovered in my brain. I stood up and fumbled for money.

"Thanks for the pep talk, but you're wrong. Maybe a miracle will occur."

He pushed my money away. "Dorothy, listen to me, please. Your book makes me excited that there's something mysterious and sexy about tango!"

"But not enough to actually want to try it."

"Not at all. I'm an Argentinean that doesn't dance. I tried it a few times and gave up because it was too difficult. Your book makes me feel confident that I could learn enough of the dance so that I could actually do it, and make that magical connection with a partner!"

"That's pretty much what Suzanne said. And the opposite of what Tomas said. Which is it?"

Fernando rolled his eyes. "Consider the source: a thumbs-up from a successful agent versus so-called objective criticism from the lips of Mr. Insecure himself. You need to accept that you're a good enough writer to succeed on any level you want."

"Aw, shucks."

The last customer gestured for the bill. Fernando came out from behind the bar, took the money and made change, and the customer packed up and left. Fernando turned off the front lights and locked the door.

"Tomas will come around. Give him time."

Chapter 33

"I want more…"

Fernando cut me off. "Of course, we all think we do. I want it all! I want love! I want millions! I want immortality and youth." He laughed. "What about romance?"

"I'd like to add that, but I'm content because I know the truth."

"That makes no sense."

"The real problem is that what you expect is all that you will allow yourself to have. Our expectations are corrupted by religion and money. The bad news for everyone is that you already have what you want, and that is the problem."

"By that logic, I wanted to be in this mess because I can't see myself as a successful anything."

"Yes, but don't dismiss yourself. Like most people, you didn't realize how much control you have, until now. You're a writer, so make up a new story and tell it to yourself: Your book is a big success, it starts a new tango craze, the actor wins an Oscar for his role in the tango film. You and Tomas partner, etc."

"But it's not real."

"That's the point. Is it unreal or just not yet? I can't change my age, okay, but look around. I own this place, I make a living. I have status as the owner, and I have friends. I help by paying my employees well, donating my leftovers to a service that feeds the hungry, giving to my church. That doesn't mean I don't want more. It just means I can't imagine more."

Imagine more. That was it. I couldn't imagine what I would like to happen. I based things on words, remembered phrases, snippets of books and articles. The past. There was no freshness, nothing about the specifics of me, just a generalized expectation that I was always excluded from. Wow. If I couldn't see myself, who could? What I saw was failure to meet my own expectations, and I was punishing myself for not measuring up. Maybe that was the thing that was always wrong! Maybe it was my own inflated expectations that no one or nothing could measure up that created this.

"Does this mean I don't want Tomas to like the book?"

Fernando looked thoughtful. "No, I believe that you want him to. But this is his story — that tango is a spiritual practice, and his insights are too deep to be captured in a book, especially by a woman."

"So, there's no hope then?"

"Not at all. Opportunity creates possibility. Give him time."

"Okay. What about you finding love?"

Before Fernando could answer, there was a knock on the door, and Shane, the food-bank collector, entered. He was striking. White skin, gray eyes, and buff. One hundred percent actor. One hundred percent gay.

"Hi, Fernando. Hi, Dots. Good time?"

Fernando smiled and smoothed his hair down. "Yes, Shane, follow me." Shane followed him down the stairs to the kitchen, and the two men returned carrying two grocery boxes and several bags.

In the doorway, Shane turned to Fernando and said, "So I'll stop by for a coffee over the weekend."

Shane left. Fernando was glowing.

I teased, "I could imagine you imagining that."

"Hope springs eternal," he said, smiling. "You need to imagine that dancing can be just for fun. It'll cheer you up when everything else is bad, like now. Let's go. You can leave your computer in the safe but take your shoes."

"Where are we going?"

"It's a surprise. Let's go. My van's up the street."

Fernando drove an immaculate white minivan with gray upholstery. The name and address of the restaurant were inscribed on the sides of the truck in the same cheery red script as the restaurant awning. As he drove, he smoked a cigarette

Chapter 33

out of the window, and I napped. I awoke as we drove across the Brooklyn Bridge. He turned down a side street, and a big white box of a building came into view. He pulled into a small, crowded parking lot. Fernando came around to my side and helped me out. I was about to ask where we were, but he held a finger to his lips and said, "Just enjoy. No technique. No lessons. For you, just count 4-5-6 and take a quick step back with your left foot. All you do is keep the beat."

He pulled my chin up, rolled my shoulders back and pulled the ponytail holder out of my hair, tossing it with his fingers. He surveyed me. "Good. Do you have any lipstick?" I nodded. "And your nose is shiny." I fixed it.

We walked up to the entrance of the building. Two Hispanic men, obviously brothers, handsome with matching cleft chins, both squat but almost as wide as the building, greeted Fernando with familiarity and respect, and ogled me. They spoke in Spanish for a moment, money changed hands, and we walked inside. We walked down a flight of steps into a big room that reminded me of the old 70s movie *Saturday Night Fever*. A glittering disco ball created a time warp. The room was sultry, full of well-dressed men and women in showy, low-cut outfits.

I felt mousy in my New York black and yanked my V-neck top down an inch. The shoes would add three inches. Only then did I really tune into the music and watch how people danced. The music was Cuban salsa, which I'd never danced to. I'd always looked down on salsa as being "easy." Fernando led me to a banquette and went off to get drinks. I put on my shoes, and he returned. I sipped my drink, something with rum. The song was rhythmic with male vocals and fantastic drums. I could make out the words of the chorus: "Besame, Mama."

I watched the men turn the women in dizzying spins while Fernando changed his shoes. He finished his drink, stood, and held out his hand. I nervously took it and got up.

"Remember, step back on 1, count 4-5-6, and keep the beat." He put his hands lightly on my hips. "Oh, and in salsa, you move your hips and ribs." He demonstrated.

I stared at him, terrified.

"Drink up."

I gulped my drink.

"Keep your arm soft, lean forward and look at me."

I took his hand, and he led me onto the dance floor. He counted quietly for me as he moved me forward and back, then side to side. He twirled me, and I was able to turn efficiently, and got a nod and a smile. The rum hit me and I relaxed.

As we danced, Fernando seemed to grow taller and more confident. I noticed that the other men kept checking out his moves. As I danced, I counted 4-5-6. I felt a rush of pure joy, very different to the tango trance.

Fernando said, "Keep your eyes on me," and spun me expertly away from himself and then back. The song ended, and as we waited for the next one to begin, I looked around at the happy followers around me. What was their secret?

Shockingly, I realized that dancing for me was not about partnership, it was about me, and my performance. I was a totally selfish dancer! I wasn't even dancing with my partner! I was focused on evaluating my own performance. I was everything I sneered at! I was just like all of the other tango dancers I'd felt superior to. I was the one who needed this book! No wonder Tomas didn't like the tango book, and he was right. To me, feeling joy was irrelevant. It was a buzzword for feeling okay about my own performance. I had captured nothing of the dance, because I wasn't even truly concerned with how it felt. I was interested in showing people how to do it "right." I had fooled Fernando and Suzanne, but Tomas saw right through me.

A new song began. Fernando pivoted me, and spun me out away from him. I gritted my teeth, determined to enjoy the dance. I had to work hard to follow Fernando because I could only process his commands through the prism of my own negative self-judging statements, which filled my mind like rapid-fire radio announcers describing a natural disaster in progress. I focused on his smile and mentally recited t-a-n-g-o over and over until the self-attack receded. The song ended, and Fernando went off for refills.

I watched the dancers from the sidelines. The women wore relaxed smiles as they gracefully received the lead, not worrying, just remaining present. Was that because salsa was an easier dance than tango? Sure it was. I'd gotten the steps right away. But it wasn't the dance that gave those women their confidence, it was trust. If I got real, I wanted to be like one of those women.

Can you feel two things at once? Can you think two things at once? Fernando returned.

The beat changed and an intense song with pounding drums began. Fernando spiraled me in front of him, then expertly turned me so that I had no choice but to walk around him. I strutted like Carmen Miranda and caught a couple of the guys checking me out. I tossed my head and wiggled like I had never done in tango.

I kept my eyes on him the whole time, and that changed everything. Fernando led me in a side step, then grasped me around the waist and we danced chest to chest. He flashed me a smile of delight. 4-5-6 and 4-5-6. He let go and stepped back, and we improvised a bit. I used my tango embellishments and they worked. Then he grabbed my hand and pulled me toward him, and pushed me away.

Later, as we drove back and were crossing the Brooklyn Bridge, the beauty of the flashing stars against an indigo sky astonished me. On the van's sound system, a drum solo played, and then a flute jumped in and danced along with the drum beat. A miracle, a real one, happened: I stopped thinking. When I next became aware, we were pulling up in front of La Boca.

Fernando went inside, fetched my computer, and drove me home. As he opened the van door and hugged me, he said, "Don't let Tomas or any tango snob try to put you down. You are now a true dancer because you know how to have fun."

Chapter 34

Tomas agreed to meet me at Fernando's place. We sat at the bar. Fernando poured two glasses of Malbec and discreetly withdrew.

"Thank you for agreeing to meet me."

Tomas frowned at me and said, "This book holds my future."

"Mine, too. What is the actual problem?"

He shrugged. "Everything."

"Do you want to find a way to make this work?"

"I am here, no?"

"True. To meet you, I need specifics. Give me your copy so I can review your notes."

"I just want to expand my reputation as a tango teacher, with you as my partner. I would like to repay Gabriel for all of his teachings."

I realized what the real problem was.

"Tomas, can I ask you something, and not offend you?"

"Okay."

"Can you read this aloud for me? I just want to hear how it sounds."

I handed him a page from the book. He read, haltingly and mispronouncing words, but most importantly, he read flatly, without comprehension. I took the page back.

"Let me read it back to you." I read it with expression and nuance. We sat in silence.

He conceded, "Perhaps I need to re-read it."

Fernando arrived with three champagne flutes.

"You've been eavesdropping."

"Of course, it's part of my job." He poured sparkling wine into the glasses and placed one in front of each of us.

"What shall we drink to?" Tomas asked, raising his glass.

"I don't want to jinx this."

Fernando laughed. "Silly woman, we're drinking to the Creator who arranges coincidences so he doesn't have to take credit for miracles. The miracle in question is this book. Think of the series of events that needed to occur to create this moment. You had to find this bar, we had to become pals, I had to know Tomas, Tomas had to want to write a book, and you needed to be available to do so. And there had to be tango."

I saw his point. "I guess He is the greatest writer." Fernando nodded, and we all clinked and drank.

"Suzanne said we'd need a miracle to make a tango book a success." Fernando nodded. My phone pinged with a text from Suzanne.

"Gabriel is meeting us at Le Singe Bleu tomorrow at 6:30. Put on a dress!"

Chapter 35

We met at Le Singe Bleu, a world-famous five-star restaurant. I wore a low-cut black dress and heels. I put on a real push-up bra, not my usual sports one, and added jewelry and a gold watch. I wore my *Just Dessert* writing pumps — they gave me three and a half inches. I was early and went to sit at the bar. Gabriel was already there, a glass of red wine in front of him. Gabriel had recently won an Academy Award for his role as a detective in an indie remake of a nineties action movie set in the future, and wore a similar outfit to the one he did in the film. He was striking in a white button-down, black leather blazer and jeans. The snowy shirt contrasted with his ebony skin and close-cropped, graying hair. He smiled at me with his eyes.

"You must be Dorothy." His deep, mellifluous voice was unmistakable. In truth, I'd seen all of his films. I pinched myself. I, dreariest of Dotties, was sitting at the bar of a fancy restaurant with a movie star. I corrected my posture, smiled, and nodded.

"Yes. Nice to meet you, Gabriel."

"My friends call me Gabe."

"Okay, Gabe it is."

His smile sent the flash of male appreciation I was always hungry for and he said, "What're you drinking?"

"Malbec."

"Spoken like a true *tanguera*. I'll join you." He finished the glass in front of him and signaled the bartender, who refilled his glass and poured one for me. I was a *tanguera*. Woo-hoo!

"How long have you been teaching and is tango your only dance?"

"It's my dance. And you?"

"I'm a cowboy at heart," Gabe said with a smile. "Although I'm from Guyana, I feel as if I were born in the Old West from watching American Westerns as a boy. My first dance was the two-step."

"Is that why you picked that dance?"

"Yes. There was a bar in the city where you could dance and a couple of radio stations that played country music. I would listen to it as I drove my cab to the dojo."

"So, how did you get from country to tango?"

"I freelanced as a livery driver for extra money. I had a customer, an older man, who I drove to Dance Gotham on Monday nights. There was a free practice, and I would watch when I had time. The country place in the city closed, and I would've had to drive forty minutes to dance the two-step. I was already going to the tango studio, so I thought I'd try it."

"Sure. I know. Tango looked easy." We both laughed.

"I was about to give up, then luckily, I met Tomas. He was my student."

"When did you find the time to act?"

Gabe looked away. "I had to take a break. I was studying acting hard and getting nowhere. I was in despair. I took a year off and lived this other life."

"How did you get your break?"

"I was discovered by a fare! I met a guy while I was driving limos, and he was, and is, my agent, Rex. He said it was the way I made a U-turn when I picked him up on Third Avenue and 57th Street. I cut across three lanes as the light changed. And he got in. He said, 'Who's crazier? You for crossing like that, or me for getting in?' I told him he was the crazy one, I was just making a living. He laughed and asked me to audition. It just went from there. So, here I am. Do you give private lessons?"

I was saved from answering. Suzanne, Tomas, and Rex, Gabe's agent, arrived together. Rex was a tall, thin man with pockmarked skin and glittering green eyes behind glasses. He had large teeth and a red mouth. If a human could look like a shark, Rex fit the bill. The Creator loves his stereotypes!

We sat at a round table with a white tablecloth and elegant place settings. Rex and Suzanne sat next to each other, with Tomas on her other side. I sat between Tomas and Gabe. There was desultory conversation; food was ordered. It was interesting for me to see the effect that his stardom had on the room, on Tomas, Rex, and Suzanne. I wasn't the only one sitting up straighter and trying to look their best.

Halfway through the meal, Rex and Suzanne began to speak about me as if I weren't even there. Rex ripped the book apart in front of Gabe, and neither Suzanne nor Tomas defended me. I knew it was just Rex's attempt to get the cost down, but I felt sick to my stomach. It was a terrifying moment, because I knew that I was going to throw up.

I tried to wait until he finished, but there was no comma. I grabbed my purse, muttered, "Please excuse me," and just made it inside a stall. More projectile vomiting. I feared that my stomach lining would come out of my throat. I had to lean against the wall afterwards. Tears of shame poured down my face. I shook. I flushed the toilet, praying that my eyes wouldn't be too red.

I washed and put on lipstick, wondering what polite excuse I could offer. I'd had a delicious bouillabaisse. My hands smelled of garlic. I needed a lemon. I needed to disappear. I needed to go back to the table. I had no idea what I'd say. Luckily, I had breath mints and a bottle of hand sanitizer, and my hair didn't stink.

How long had I been gone? Ah, I had the perfect line. I'd received a phone call, which I had to take. I checked the mirror. My face was a little worse for wear even with fresh lipstick. I put on my reading glasses. There, much better. When I stepped out of the ladies' room, there was a little area with a mirror and a couple of chairs. A man was there, and he was on the phone. He turned, and I saw that it was Gabe. So much for my excuse; no, I could have had the phone call before I went into the bathroom.

Gabe put his phone in his pocket. "Are you okay?"

"I'm fine, I'm fine. I had to take a call."

"Your agent?"

"Ha. No."

"Your husband?"

"No."

"Your boyfriend?"

"No, nosy."

"Are you single?"

"Are you hitting on me?"

"Why not? I'm not a fool."

"Fair enough. But..."

"I know, you don't wash where you eat. Tomas told me." He laughed, showing his perfect teeth, and I laughed with him, not knowing why.

"We're not going to work together long. I have a couple of weeks to learn the routine."

"But I thought it was a month?"

"Budget cut. Maybe we can have dinner once we're no longer professionally acquainted." Okay. A movie star had asked me out even after his agent trashed the tango book, but that didn't make things right.

"And Rex can be a real prick. I liked it and was inspired by it." That made it right.

"Okay, we'll see. Why aren't you practicing with the actress in the film?"

"It's a *milonga*. The woman is not that familiar with me. In fact, we have never danced. It's part of the plot. She is not a *tanguera*. She has the basics, but that's all she needs to know. In the scene of the movie where we dance, I don't know her, I've never seen her before. I want to be totally comfortable. You are near her size and shape, so it's perfect."

My stomach flopped over again, but I remembered that I was going to give this project one hundred percent. Whatever it took. I nodded.

Back at the table, Rex, Tomas, and Suzanne were deep in planning, so my absence had been unnoticed. I was relieved. Suzanne said, "Tomas, I want to film Gabriel training."

Gabe looked at Rex, who shook his head. "Maybe on the last day, but the work is going to be trial and error, and I don't want Gabriel to look less than sure. On the last day, you can have Tomas show Gabriel things seemingly for the first time."

Suzanne looked relieved. "Great, we can arrange to have your dance partner in the film be there to practice with."

Gabe spoke up. "Not a chance. It has to be Dorothy."

Rex and Suzanne exchanged an unhappy look. I was as surprised as they were. She gave me a quick death stare.

Gabe spoke to Rex. "What happens in the scene is that I run into a *milonga* and grab a random partner. I want that to feel real. Raoul won't mind."

Rex said, "Lucky for you, you have his ear." His tone was bitter.

After dinner, Tomas offered to escort me home. In the cab, he was elated with how the dinner had gone. I'd thought his ego might have been bruised, and I learned something good about him: he was a team player. Very rare.

"It should make you feel very good that he wants to learn the routine with you."

"Routine? I thought he was dancing with the woman in the movie for the first time. I guess they don't improvise since it's a movie."

"No, he will improvise. What he wants is to develop a series of possible choices that he is letter-perfect on."

When I got home, Suzanne called. "What did you do, blow him in the bathroom?"

"No. Aren't you the one who told me he was divorced? And thanks for defending me."

"I'm so jealous," Suzanne bubbled, ignoring my comment. "You've got these two hotties buzzing around you."

"Don't be. What does one do with men once you've enjoyed them? They're not famous for their after-talk or their follow-through. And all of them want to be mothered. It's not worth it."

"Cranky, much? Peter really did a job on you. It's been a year. When do you get over it?"

"I'm not an extrovert like you. I'm suffering this to aid and assist you getting me a great deal on the book. Am I even going to get paid for this?"

"Of course you are. That's really why I called. Just got off with Rex. How's SAG minimum?"

"I guess I can count on you to lowball me every time."

"Did you barf when you went to the bathroom? You looked a little green after you came back from the loo."

"What do you care?"

"Okay, okay. Be like that. I'll speak to you in the morning. Oh, and by the way, be there by 10:00 a.m."

Chapter 36

I arrived to find a different Tomas. Here was the stern martial artist, serious and emotionally removed. He didn't kiss me hello as usual and said, "We don't have much time. I was planning to teach him and his partner, not you."

"Don't worry, I won't let you down."

"Not worried about you; it's about me." He held out his hands, palms down. He was shaking.

"I can only imagine how nerve-racking it must be to be teaching your sensei."

Tomas grinned and nodded. He kissed my cheek.

"Thank you for understanding."

When Gabe arrived, we got to work. For the first hour we did drills, and I saw how sloppy I'd gotten. When Tomas finally put us in the embrace, I was relieved to discover that Gabe was shorter than he looked, and we were a good fit.

We practiced the absolute basics: we walked backwards and forwards, replacing each other's steps until we were both comfortable "replacing" the other's foot. We practiced changing weight from foot to foot, in place and moving, then worked on the embrace.

By lunchtime, we still hadn't danced. I was tired, sat down, and pulled out my laptop. I quickly made a list of the basic drills we'd done.

I had already outlined a new section called "Training a Movie Star." The drills helped me to flesh it out. I enjoyed Tomas treating me as an equal. He frequently asked me to describe things from the follower's point of view.

"I guess men do want to know what women want," I joked, but neither of them got it, and instead nodded their heads earnestly and looked at me with doggy eyes.

We went to lunch at Paco's. Tomas produced a choreographed routine that Gabe had requested. I was confused.

"I thought we were improvising."

Tomas winked. "It's a relative term. There are three sections where improvisation can be done. For the sake of time, you and Gabriel will rehearse this routine until it's letter-perfect, and the improv sections have a good natural shape."

Back in the studio, Tomas put on music and said, "Okay, just dance for a couple of songs."

The first song was "El Aristocrata," by D'Agostino, a swoopy, romantic tango from the forties. The song was about an old-style *tanguero*, a dandy who conquered all hearts. I felt a nice connection and found it easy to remain focused on my tango recipe for perfect tango posture: chin up, sternum up, shoulders down, quads back, dance from the ribs, back and legs always in a spiral, elbows forward.

Gabe smelled of patchouli oil, and his hands were heavily calloused from martial arts. He sang along, and translated bits. We danced *milanguero*-style, close together with small steps.

Tomas stopped the music and showed us the routine. Tomas took the follower role with Gabe and I had a chance to sit and watch. The song used in the film would be "Recuerdo," by Pugliese, a classic tango that was both dramatic and lyrical with a strong beat.

I had to pinch myself: I was now a tango instructor preparing a movie star to dance in a Hollywood film.

Gabe and I rehearsed the middle portion of the tango, followed by the second improv section. The improv had to include a lift, multiple leg wraps, and *secadas*.

Eight hours later, my feet needed a soak in cold water and all of my joints hurt.

The days flew by.

Chapter 36

I arrived at the studio early on the final morning, Gabe and Tomas were practicing karate. I watched as I put on my shoes. I could see where Tomas got some of his cool tango moves.

Gabe seemed to have no bones as he moved effortlessly into position. In this role, he was clearly the sensei, and Tomas the Grasshopper. I watched their torsos and saw how their heads moved with their bodies. How their shoulders were relaxed and the eyes led the movement. I also watched how each figure was fully executed before the next was begun. I resolved to work on my weight changes. Tomas must have read my mind, because when Gabe went to change, we kissed hello, and he said, "I want you to focus on your weight changes today."

As we practiced, Gabe became more and more frustrated with himself. I was consistent, kept my shoulders down, my weight on my leg, and my arms in a connected embrace. We attempted a complicated series of steps that Gabe knew well, but he fumbled at the very last moment.

"Sorry," he said and walked away from me. I was calm. I didn't blame myself. I knew his misstep wasn't my fault. I'd successfully internalized the new idea that there wasn't anything wrong with me!

I went over to him in the reception area, where he was sitting with his head between his hands, lips moving in meditation. I'd worked with enough actors to know what the problem was. I waited until he opened his eyes. He looked at me, unsure. I smiled and put a hand on his arm. "Consider this a dress rehearsal. The worse things go, the better the performance will be."

Tomas chimed in. "Yes, she is right. Let's begin the sequence again."

Everything went wrong. Suddenly, Gabe couldn't remember any of his steps. He was off his balance, and we almost fell performing a leg wrap. I laughed it off and said to Tomas, "Let's end this dress rehearsal now."

Tomas insisted. "No, one more time, and do the lift."

This time we did fall. I landed on my butt and allowed myself to slide onto my side. Gabe and Tomas rushed to help me up. I looked up at Tomas. "I said it was time to stop. We're stopping."

I'd never spoken to Tomas with such authority and knew I had become a teacher. He didn't answer.

"Tomas, please give us a minute." This was a command. He heard it.

"Okay, Dorothy, I'll go make that call." He escaped.

I looked at Gabe. "What's wrong?"

"What do you think? I have to leave for LA in ten hours!"

"Relax. We'll get this."

"How can I relax? You won't even be there." Gabe paced, clearly upset. "I can't do this. I'll make a fool of myself."

"Just stop trying so hard."

"I can't. It's my default when I'm afraid."

"Do you want us to come with you?"

"That's a good idea." He pulled out his phone and left the studio, still wearing his dance shoes. He didn't return.

Tomas came back a few minutes later with two ice packs for me.

"Let's put one of these on the ankle, and the other on the hip where you landed."

"Did you see Gabriel outside?"

"Yes. You think you know somebody. I passed him outside and he wouldn't even look at me."

"It's embarrassing to make a mistake in front of a student."

"I know how that feels."

"So?"

"He blames me."

"No. He blames himself. And maybe he had the idea that he'd be able to just dance. Tango's harder than it looks. Also, it's always scary to have to perform."

Chapter 36

"He's an actor. That's what he does."

"But he doesn't think of himself as a dancer."

Tomas nodded. "True."

"He's not performing here, it's school. We're just his teachers."

My phone rang. It was Suzanne. I walked outside.

"Raoul's going to fly you and Tomas to LA to be his on-set coaches. Are you thrilled? You are getting the referred glory of teaching with Tomas. Now you have a brand. Please do your best to look good."

Ouch, could we not have one conversation without an attack? "As opposed to the way I usually look?"

"Don't be like that. You know what I meant."

"No, actually, I didn't. What's wrong with how I look?"

"I just meant, make an effort."

"Have you ever seen me at a party in sweats and no makeup?"

"No, but what I meant was…"

"I'm short and chunky."

"Dots, c'mon, that's not…"

"Oh, shut up, Suzanne. Yes, it was."

"Jesus, you dance with a movie star and your ego blows up like Mount Fuji."

"Is it ego not to want to be insulted? I promise not to take my flannel shirt and work boots. I'll take my false teeth and my tightest spandex. I'll even take a blow-dryer, just in case they run out of them at the hotel."

Suzanne was silent. Very rare.

My anger blazed like a tree hit by lightning. Was Suzanne always like this, or was I just hearing it for the first time? I told myself to calm down. Took a breath. My voice sounded almost normal.

"Look, Suzanne, I'm going to ask you for a favor."

"I can probably get you a first-class ticket."

"That would be great, but that wasn't the favor."

"What then?"

"Ready?"

"Yes."

"Do you realize that every time we talk, you make a nasty comment about me?"

"What're you talking about? My goal is to look out for my friend."

"Then why do you constantly make remarks about my lack of looks, for one thing?"

"I don't know what you're talking about. But maybe you're just having a little case of nerves, dancing with Gabriel and all."

"There you go again. Can't you hear the veiled insult in what you just said?"

"No, I can't."

"You implied that dancing with a movie star is too much for me."

"I don't get it."

"Okay. But hear this: in the future, be careful how you speak to me."

"Or else what?"

I should have expected this attack. I took a breath.

"I'm not threatening anything, Suzanne, just trying to create a level playing field."

"Okay, I'll try to get Tomas first class as well."

"Thank you."

She'd perceived the conversation as a maneuver to get Tomas a better seat, not as two friends having a dialogue. I felt a bitter heaviness in my heart, which in my visualization looked like an old shipwreck at the bottom of the sea, rotting and covered in green algae. Did friends insult each other? I'd accepted her treatment of me because I needed to see her as a friend. I'd sugarcoated the truth for a long time, but now, somehow, I no longer needed to. What or who else would I need to see differently to have a better life? Oh, duh. That would be myself.

Chapter 36

I remembered the advice I'd given Babette to stop seeing herself as a victim. To call this a relationship was inaccurate; it was a profitable association. Suzanne was a predator, and I, her victim, because I'd exchanged the fantasy of a friendship for the truth.

I felt queasy as I realized that I probably saw myself this way in every situation except when I was actually writing. Yikes! Even when dancing tango, I excused myself from taking responsibility by invoking my difficult family relationships as the reason why I struggled. Maybe it was the other way around: I struggled because I kept telling this story. What if there were a blank slate and I could reinvent myself? What would that look like?

This was a moment to be enjoyed and savored, but instead I was angry at Suzanne and felt crappy about myself.

The words we use shape our reality. How was I going to describe myself from now on? What was the difference between being a victim, a teacher and a practitioner? A victim was someone at the mercy of the tango, while a practitioner was someone engaged in the study, doing it rather than studying it.

Teaching was showing others how to dance. I wanted to share what I knew, not teach it, so therefore I was a tango practitioner. I was not studying it; I was practicing it. Improving and studying were part of practicing, but not all of it. I saw the situation clearly; being a victim kept you in the audience in the game of life. I was sitting on the sidelines at a *milonga*, not on the dance floor. How much courage did I really have?

Cassandra sneered. "Is that even a question?"

The Inner Voice answered, "Yes. Get on the dance floor."

I'm a seasoned traveler, but Suzanne's words soured my confidence. I reminded myself that if I let her infect me, it was my choice. If I wanted to find love, I had to take responsibility for seeing things as they were. I tried imagining myself confidently sitting in a director's chair on the movie set, flanked by Tomas and Gabe. I began to smile and felt myself relax. Suzanne pinged me, but I sent her a message saying I'd call her back. I didn't owe her anything.

I'd packed a copy of the manuscript, as I had much to adjust and wanted to create a blueprint for what I'd write about being on set in my new role. I took all the notes I'd made during the past week. I looked at my phone and was pleased to see that I'd taken lots of usable photos. I uploaded them onto my laptop. My task now was to document the process of putting the dance on film. I wanted a simple recipe that would cook up into a tasty dish.

Tomas called to say the car would be there in fifteen minutes.

Chapter 37

I sat next to Tomas and across the aisle from Gabe. He was in the opposite window seat with the shade down. Tomas had had a glass of champagne and was dozing.

Gabe wore a baseball cap, had headphones on, and was reading a script. He'd warned us that he would be working. But as the plane taxied for takeoff, I looked over and saw that he was sweating, and the script was upside down. His lips moved in prayer. I slid across and took his hand.

"Hey, teach, I'm fine."

"Of course you are, but just relax, and breathe."

He pulled his cap lower and muttered, "I said I'm fine," but his hand was slick with sweat.

"I never met a driver who liked being a passenger."

He looked at me and nodded.

"I won't tell anyone." He held my hand. I could feel his heart beating wildly.

I sang in his ear, "Somewhere over the rainbow, way up high," and he sang along. "There's a land that I heard of once in a lullaby." We hummed the rest as the plane lifted off. I enjoyed the rush of takeoff and closed my eyes to feel the power of the plane. When I opened them, Gabe kissed me on the cheek.

"Thank you."

I nodded okay and moved back to my seat. I worked on the new section about Gabe appreciating the cleverness of how Tomas had sequenced the drills for maximum familiarity with the counterintuitive movements of this maddening dance. I included a lot of Tomas's "philosophy," but something was still missing — a love letter to his grandparents. Tomas had taken off his sneakers, so I borrowed them. I wrote a new foreword in Tomas's voice, then dozed off. When I woke up again, the flight attendant advised us that we would be landing soon. Tomas was reading my stuff.

"This is so much better, more truthful! I like it! You're getting to the heart of tango. What else will you add?"

"A chapter on fear and anxiety."

He laughed. "That's in every chapter. Why not add a chapter on 'dancing on the one,' like I showed you?"

I smiled. I got it. I understood why the book wasn't good. I was still ghostwriting, avoiding taking responsibility. I laughed out loud and hugged him.

"What?"

"I've solved the mystery of tango."

"What is it?"

"Both the leader and the follower are one hundred percent responsible for their part in the dance." Tomas thought about it and smiled. "Now you've got it!"

The plane landed with a thud. I laughed and said, "Not on the one."

Chapter 38

We went directly to the set. It was not the blockbuster I'd imagined, but rather an indie, so it was on a smaller scale. They'd built a set that looked like a restaurant in Buenos Aires, with red walls, white tablecloths, and candles. Gilt mirrors and tango photos covered the walls. It reminded me of La Boca.

In the scene, Gabe's character was on the run and enters the dance. In order to escape being caught, he borrows a fedora and asks a woman to dance. The bad guys enter, look around, but can't find him. They leave, and the woman he's dancing with turns out to be a ringer for someone he loved long ago. He has a flashback and remembers dancing to the same song near the Buenos Aires waterfront back in the 1920s.

Five hours later, jet lag kicked in. I sat in a director's chair, not one with my name on it, snoozing, the script in my lap.

As Gabe did take after take with the actress, a pretty blonde woman, Tomas hovered, and there were huddles with the director, who I'd been told was shooting this as his passion piece after having a big win at the box office.

There was just one day budgeted for this section, so the shooting was fast and furious. The plan was to shoot the dance live with several cameras against a green screen.

I jumped when I heard my name being called. Tomas hurried up to me. "C'mon, put on your shoes, pronto."

He knelt down and buckled them for me, just like old times.

"What's going on?"

"You'll see." He grabbed my hand and walked me over to where the director, Raoul, a large, sloppy man wearing round glasses and a baseball cap with a patch that read, "Uck Fu takeout," and Gabriel sat in deep conversation. We stopped in front of them.

Bad Girl Pie

Tito, the assistant director, a tough-looking Latino with pockmarked skin and a ponytail, yelled for everyone to take lunch. The set quickly emptied, the cast and crew heading for the craft-services tent that had been set up in a corner of the set.

Raoul got up and walked around me with a frown. I took a deep breath and counted back from ten. He walked away, leaving me standing unsure of what to do next.

"Okay," Raoul said and left. Rex came over and handed me a contract and a pen. It was long and had very small print. I was surprised to see him on set, but he smiled and said, "Gabriel summoned me."

Gabe joined us. He smiled and said, "Please sign it, Dorothy."

"I have to read it first."

"No, there isn't time."

"Time for what? I don't even know what this contract is for."

"What do you think? You saw me trying to dance with that woman."

"Yes, I did."

"You didn't see how totally off it was? Nothing Tomas said worked."

I glanced at Tomas, who shrugged apologetically.

"You think I can offer better advice?"

"No, I think you should be my on-screen partner."

I laughed, but he was dead serious. My brain left my body. Was this a joke? Did he mean it? I looked at their faces, also dead serious. This would upgrade my profile and would give me a shot at getting a new agent, one whom I could train not to insult me every time I spoke to him or her. Rex handed me the contract. I shook my head. Not being legal-minded had cost me *Just Dessert*.

Rex took the contract from me.

"I'll read you the highlights: you'll be considered as having joined the union, and the paperwork for that can be retrofitted.

Chapter 38

This contract ensures that you'll be paid very well." He showed me the pleasing number on the page.

"What's the worst that can happen?"

"It could end up on the cutting-room floor, but you would still get paid."

"Sorry. I'll have to have my lawyer look at it." I gave Rex Frank's email. Rex took photos and sent them.

Raoul said, "I understand, but each minute we wait is costing thousands of dollars. We can't hold up shooting much longer."

I shook my head.

Gabe said, "Please let me talk to Dorothy."

He led me over to the craft-services table and poured me a coffee.

I took a sip.

Gabe leaned in. "Please do this for me?"

"You're not just flirting?"

"Maybe a little."

"Isn't this going a little far to get me to go on a date with you?"

He looked perplexed.

"That was a joke. Why do you want me to do this?"

"I told you. I'm blowing this big-time. I've got to nail this in the next two hours, and I know how to dance with you. Please, Dorothy, please. I know it will be good for your book, too."

He was right, and I got an inspiration. If they couldn't shoot it without the signed contract, they couldn't use the footage without a signature either.

"All right. You decide if you trust me enough to go ahead on the assumption that I will sign it. Whatever happens, remember that we rise or fall together."

Gabe took this idea in, smiled, and nodded. I gave him a thumbs-up. Gabe gestured for Rex, and they went off to talk.

Tomas came over and was about to reproach me, but I said, "Tomas, the last time I didn't check the contract my book was stolen."

Tomas nodded. "I understand. I just hope you just didn't kill your big chance."

My heart was heavy, and I watched Rex gesturing angrily with the contract. Gabe spoke to him intensely. Raoul returned and joined the huddle. I tried not to write a bad scenario, and forced myself to imagine having a successful dance and Tomas saying, "You did great, Dorothy. You've gotten the heart of the tango." I kept seeing this in my mind's eye.

The conference ended, and Gabe came over and offered his hand. Tomas and I were now on a different level. I was the talent, and it felt good. Rex came over with my phone. Frank had texted me. "This one's okay, break a leg!"

"Okay, Rex, I'll sign."

Tomas rehearsed us, then Raoul filmed.

Gabe relaxed when I hummed a few lines of "Over the Rainbow" and whispered, "Breathe." The command worked, and Gabe was able to concentrate. I enjoyed knowing what I was doing. Gabe and I danced the whole tango without a mistake. I didn't realize that there was a lot more to filming a dance. There were many takes from various angles.

We danced and danced. Raoul watched each shot live on a video monitor. Tito came to warn him that they were approaching overtime.

Raoul looked at his notes and asked if we would dance the whole song from beginning to end. This was for the dream sequence.

The set was changed so that we were alone in a dance studio with a wooden floor. Suddenly, there was a spotlight, and I felt like a starlet getting her big break in some 1940s B-movie. The music played, and we danced. It was almost as good as the tango I'd danced with George, and, in my mind, Gabe became George.

Chapter 38

We were dancing nude on that terrace in Cancún. The song ended. The set exploded with applause and cries of "Bravo." As we danced, the cast and crew had come to watch.

Raoul whispered to Tito, who shouted, "Okay, wrap it." The crew moved swiftly to dismantle the set.

Gabe hugged me and whispered, "Thank you."

He went to change.

Tomas hugged me and said, "Thank you. It was one heart and four legs when you danced." Tomas looked at me in a new way, with respect for me as a dancer, not just a writer. A practitioner, not a student. I remembered how he'd let Rex trash the book. I lost a little respect for him.

I went to change in the dressing room, which had a dressing table and a big lighted mirror. I felt as if I were still in an old classic movie. As I cleaned the makeup off my face, I felt calm and relieved. In my mind's eye, my father appeared and handed me my rifle.

"I'm sorry, can you forgive me?" he said and opened his arms for a hug. There was no question, and I felt something hard inside me melt.

My cell phone rang. I answered it. Concepción was crying so hard I could barely understand her, but finally I got that Aunt Cindy had died in her sleep. Did I want them to make the funeral arrangements? Yes, and I comforted Concepción by reminding her that death was a release from suffering. She calmed down and we hung up.

The Inner Voice spoke again. "Yes, Aunt Cindy's gone home, but let yourself grieve."

Chapter 39

Suzanne made good on her word to try to make the book a success. Tomas and I danced everywhere, promoting the book. I dedicated every dance to my beloved mentor, who I felt would be enjoying my success from wherever she now was.

Tomas was a natural star, and I didn't mind being Ginger Rogers to his Fred Astaire. It was hard to watch myself doing the tango with Tomas on TV and social media, but I felt Aunt Cindy's spirit with me, urging me on.

Frank called me to tell me about my father's will. My half-brothers had agreed to settle a fifteen percent portion, and I was happy. I planned to re-do my apartment, or maybe even move nearer to the studio in Queens.

A year after she passed, I wanted to celebrate the anniversary of Aunt Cindy's death, so I organized a memorial party for her at Tomas's studio. A catered event that would become a *milonga* after the non-dancers had left. Fernando would sing. I wore the dress I'd worn in the film.

Gabe and Rex arrived and came over together. "I'm so sorry for your loss." Gabe hugged me. Rex hugged me, too, and whispered, "The film got picked up, thank God. Maybe you can dance with Gabe at the premiere?" I realized that they were in love with each other, whether they knew it or not. I felt happy that Gabe might find his way to love after all.

Suzanne followed and reached to hug me, but I stepped back. She looked hurt.

"I have a surprise for you."

"What have you done?"

"I thought of the old TV show *This Is Your Life* and wanted you not to miss your life. I wanted to let you know that underneath I am still a real friend."

Chapter 39

"With friends like you, who needs enemies? This is Aunt Cindy's party, not mine." I was annoyed but understood that it's best to keep your friends close and your enemies closer. She was just giving me what any good narcissist would want for herself.

"And that's not all. I figured out how to make it up to you. A new book called *The Tango Diet: How to Be in Partnership with Your Food*. It's a natural."

It was a natural dud. It was hard enough to diet without having to learn a new and difficult dance. But I appreciated her intention. We hugged, all forgiven — but not forgotten. As Aunt Cindy would have said, "A truce? Huh. Not as long as everyone knows where the hatchets are buried."

The door opened, and Peter, looking solemn, entered carrying flowers.

I looked at him. "Thank you for coming." I felt nothing. Nothing! God was great! I was free at last.

"Suzanne called me. I'm sorry, I know you loved your Aunt Cindy. I also wanted to let you know that Grace finally moved out. If you ever want to try again…"

"No, but we can dance from time to time." I felt the release of forgiveness.

George entered wearing a cowboy hat, boots, and his signature belt. George without Tara. He removed his hat as he entered and looked around uncertainly. There was no ring on either hand. He broke into a wide smile when he saw me, picked me up and twirled me around.

"It's so great to finally see you again, darlin'."

"Please put me down." I don't like being handled. I smoothed my hair.

"How did Suzanne track you down? I never told anyone."

George drawled, "Who's Suzanne?"

"My agent."

"She didn't. I've followed you on social media since we met. I couldn't get you out of my mind. When Tara wanted to go to South America to dance with Carlos, it seemed like an opportunity for me to regain my balance, and here I am."

"Thank you."

"Are you free after the party?"

"No."

"Why not? I flew all the way from Houston to see you."

"I know, George, and I so appreciate it. However, you did cheat on your wife with me. If you did it once, you'll cheat again."

Aunt Cindy's friends from the home arrived, led by Concepción. I began the service.

"Aunt Cindy was a wonderful person, who helped everyone around her. There are several of her friends who'd like to share about her." Several of the oldsters spoke of how Aunt Cindy had been a friend. Concepción made a tearful farewell.

My eulogy was short. "I loved Aunt Cindy like a mother, and she taught me how to be a woman. Aunt Cindy loved a good party, and I hope we can honor her by having fun. Tomas?"

Tomas spoke and ended with, "Thank you all for coming. Now there will be a lesson and *practica*."

Natasha and all of her tango cronies arrived. They'd never been to the studio and had gotten lost. Among her crew was Cho-Cho, Tomas's nemesis. He reminded me of an older Carlos — still slimy beneath his heartthrob exterior. Tomas looked at me, ready to bolt. I grabbed his arm. "No," I said, "have it out. Aunt Cindy would want this."

The two men exchanged words, then left. They returned a few minutes later, both worse for wear, but clearly they'd worked something out. Tomas looked at Cho-Cho.

"Perhaps my mentor and esteemed friend would teach the lesson." Tomas played a waltz, and I watched as Cho-Cho taught.

Chapter 39

Tomas assisted as his follower, and I saw a happy future in front of me. I didn't feel my usual fear of impending disaster because this was a future that wasn't based on the past.

After everyone left, Tomas led me over to the mural and pulled aside the curtain that covered it. I looked at it and couldn't believe my eyes. Tomas's old partner had been replaced by me wearing the dress I'd worn in the film. I looked taller. Tomas pointed to himself and smiled and said, "I told the artist you were five-three. To me, you're a giantess!"

As the Bard said, "All's well that ends well," but no one could say it had been a breeze.

Chapter 40

It was a sad world without Aunt Cindy, but I knew she'd gone "home." I decided to move to Astoria, where I could afford to own something. Mr. Right wasn't showing up, so I had to make my life instead of waiting around, but I was very attached to Charles, Henry, and the other birds, so I stayed in my apartment in the city and became a landlord in Queens. My life was now completely different. I had a life with friends and a community. I was happy, mostly. I was finally a tango insider. Because I was surrounded by Argentineans, I tried to make myself want to learn Spanish, but my obsession with the English language blocked my attempts.

As predicted, the movie was a success and created new interest in the tango. Our book got a little traction, then died. Suzanne did her best.

We capitalized on our success by expanding Tomas's studio and hosting a series of *milongas*, *practicas*, and workshops. We found a venue to have a weekly *milonga*, which became very popular, fast, because when Gabe was in town, he would come to the *milonga* and we'd dance.

Tomas was proud of our success but needed to be top dog, and he'd interpreted Gabe's choice to dance with me on-screen as an insult to his own teaching, and there was a reserve between us that could not be crossed.

I wasn't built to be an employee, so I was relieved when Cho-Cho moved to New York with his wife, Nadia. She was the great office manager that Tomas wanted me to be. I was able to step away and just teach private classes.

When Gabe had panicked during the filming of the movie, he'd compensated by moving only on one level and dancing in a box, not a spiral. Tango requires circular momentum, which is gained by the leader varying the height of his partner! He was

Chapter 40

dancing so badly, and I saw why. I'd said, "C'mon, Gabe, we rise or fall together." There'd been an instant, almost magical change in his dance. I never told Tomas my insight, because it wasn't something that he taught.

Now I was surrounded by men who respected and enjoyed me. When I went to a *milonga*, I was sought-after, and all the men who used to snub me now lined up for a twirl. But I always went home alone, and the tango blues were as bittersweet as ever.

For six months, I enjoyed my "celebrity," and Suzanne did what she could to keep interest in the book, but the venues Tomas and I danced in got shabbier. I called a halt after being asked to be one of several dance acts in a dance-camp weekend showcase in the Catskills.

Once we were done with the dog-and-pony show, I wanted to write something new. I missed Suzanne's daily calls, and, to be honest, I was lonely.

One night as I was cleaning out my computer files, I came upon the recipe I'd created for "Babette's Bad Boy Pie." I'd never tested it. I went out and bought a ready-made graham-cracker crust, all kinds of sweets, a pint of bourbon and whipped cream. I carefully measured the ingredients, adding them until the crust was bursting, then poured in a half-cup of bourbon, sweetened with honey, and put the whole thing in a preheated oven for thirty minutes at 350 degrees. It came out bubbly, gooey, and smelling delicious. I sampled it and had to admit that it was tasty, but I'd given it the wrong name. It needed to be called Bad Girl Pie, because Babette was being "bad" when she ate it. I'd never turned it in to Suzanne, and when I checked the table of contents of Babette's book on Amazon, I saw that they'd added a pecan-marshmallow pie to fill in for the missing recipe. I sent the recipe to Suzanne with a note of apology and a photo. The next morning at 7:00 a.m. my phone rang.

"I'm downstairs. I have coffee."

"You don't want to see me at this hour."

"I don't care. I'll avert my eyes."

The phone went dead. I rushed into the bathroom, threw water on my face, and changed into sweats. She didn't need to know that I slept in jammies decorated with Yorkies. The doorbell rang. I opened it, and she marched past me into the kitchen.

"Where's the pie?"

I took it out of the fridge.

She looked at me. "It hasn't been touched. Did you even taste it?"

"A spoonful." In truth, I'd had a spoonful and spit it out.

"And?"

"You decide. I'll microwave you a piece." I cut a slice and put it in the microwave. She handed me a coffee. Silence until the oven dinged. I topped it off with whipped cream and handed her the plate and a fork.

"Watch out, it's hot."

Suzanne ignored me and took a bite. A sip of coffee, a bite. Silence reigned until she finished the last bite and wiped the plate clean with her forefinger.

"Mmm, mmm," she said, licking her fingers. "I'm a bad girl." She giggled. "What the ef, Dottie? This is effing great!"

"Glad you like the pie. Thank you."

"Not just the pie. The recipe, the concept."

"What're you talking about?"

"This is a great hook!"

"I don't get it."

"Remember those gals who had a company that sold bottled mixed alcoholic drinks without sugar back in the nineties?"

"Sure. They called them Badassho cocktails."

"Yes. Bad Girl Pies could be a total category sweep."

"So low-cal desserts as Bad Girl Pies, but this pie is not lo-cal."

Chapter 40

"But it could be. And not just pies — a whole line of naughty foods and drinks. A social phenomenon! Imagine Bad Girl Pie parties, where us ladies can get down with some sugar and no guilt."

I had to laugh. "Are you suggesting that you want me to write another book on desserts?"

She nodded and cut herself another slice. I put it in the microwave, dressed it and handed it to her.

"But you stole my book."

"So, we'll steal it back. Fair's fair."

"Two wrongs don't make a right."

"Why not?"

She had me there. "It took forever to come up with all those recipes."

"Oh, c'mon. Really? When did you turn into a pussy?"

"Ouch, that hits my feminist hackles."

"Whatever. Just refurbish the recipes from *Just Dessert*. Make 'em smaller, larger. I've got it! Smaller like pie cupcakes. Bad Girl Pie Cuties. BGPC! It's perfect, for now. Everything in cute, small portions, in pale-pink packages."

I laughed. I was going to plagiarize myself. With the blessing of the frenemy who'd stolen my book in the first place. Wow. The Creator had quite the sense of humor.

"Why should I trust you?"

"I made good with the tango book."

"Oh, Suzanne, that was a pity fuck and you know it."

Suzanne ate another bite of pie. She closed her eyes in pleasure. "Yum!"

"Well?"

"What if it was? If someone else had handled it, you would have gotten a lot less."

"Not really. If Gabe had put his name on toilet paper, everyone would be using it, but even he couldn't help create a tango craze. The dance is just too complicated. We both knew that the book was only intended for a limited audience beyond his fan base."

"What're you saying?"

"That it wasn't valuable enough for you to bother stealing."

"Wow." Suzanne put her hand to her cheek as if I'd slapped her.

"But this one might be. The book is a bestseller. I saw Desiree's face on the side of a bus yesterday advertising the *Just Dessert* home-delivery service. I'm getting mail inviting me to sign up for the yearlong program. Next week, Desiree's giving a TED Talk about the principles of eating dessert first. *Just Dessert* is the hot new show on the cooking channel. And you get a piece of everything. How was that book not worth stealing?"

"I told you then and I'll tell you again, I had to."

"What's worse is that you genuinely expected me to be satisfied with performing in a series of second-rate venues and giving dance lessons to toads."

"I got you on all of the big dance shows on TV."

"But you didn't get us a show. From a financial point of view, Suzanne, you failed me big-time."

This hit her where she lived. "Okay, I'm sorry! I'll make it up to you. Just write this new book, please. I can't do anything without something to sell."

"That's probably the only true thing you've said so far. No, I take that back — you did like the pie."

Suzanne teared up. "And I will make it up to you."

Anything to avoid the waterworks. I sighed. "Okay. Just send me a real contract this time."

"I will, bye!" She waved her fingers at me as she left.

Three hours later, she sent me a contract, but when I sent it to Uncle Frank, he called me and laughed.

"Are you kidding me? There's no licensing or merchandising in this contract. That's where you'd make your money. Have her call me."

Chapter 40

I could have been devastated by yet another betrayal, but instead I thought about Aunt Cindy. She'd told me the parable of the scorpion and the turtle when I was a kid. I smiled as I imagined her widening those sea-green eyes at Suzanne's latest moral lapse and shrugging as she said, "It's just her nature."

And I was finding mine — and maybe it was time to buy myself Toro II. I wondered if the other Dorothy's pet store sold Yorkies?

As I said, I don't like it easy.

The End

Tango Glossary

Boleo: A whip-like lash of one leg to the buttock that's opposite the free leg followed by a circular movement on the way back to the starting point.

Cabaceo: An "Argentine" method of asking someone to dance.

Gancho: A sharp move when a dancer hooks a leg around a partner's leg by bending the knee and then straightening.

Milonga: An event where Argentine tango is danced; also referred to as a dance that incorporates the same basic elements as Argentine tango but permits a greater relaxation of the legs and body.

Molinette: Translates as "mill" and is the part of the mill in the center, the axis. In tango, it is the leader's step, accompanying the follower's *giro* or "grapevine." In a *molinette*, the leader pivots on the ball of their foot so that the foot stays behind the body and the follower stays close. The leader may either pivot on one foot or two feet, or alternate feet in time to the music, while staying on the ball of the foot.

Ocho: A figure eight traced on the floor by the follower's feet.

Practica: An informal event where Argentine tango or salsa is danced.

Tanda: A turn of dancing in a *milonga* and, by association, a set of pieces of music, usually between three and five, that is played for one turn.

Tanguero or *Tanguera*: An aficionado who is passionate about any or all of the levels of tango, its history, music, lyrics, and dance.

Vals: A faster tango in 3/4 time with flowing movements.

Appendix: Outline of *Just Dessert*

CHAPTER 1: THE GOALS

1. You'll learn how to always eat what you want, when you want it, in just the right amount to be satisfied but not to add weight, and in the perfect combination with other foods and liquids.
2. Eating will become a source of pleasure because you will trust yourself.
3. You will be able to accept yourself and be at peace.
4. But first we have to look at what's preventing you from being in this place.

CHAPTER 2: FEAR

1. Recognize that we're all driven by fear, and learn how to overcome it.
2. Biological fear versus emotional fear.
3. On a biological level, humans fear two things: falling and loud noises.
4. On an emotional level, humans fear: greed and loss.

CHAPTER 3: WHY YOU DON'T WANT TO LOSE WEIGHT

1. WHAT??? The basic logic flaw in how we think about weight control.
2. Why you had to buy all of those other diet books.
3. No one wants to lose anything, even that which is unwanted. Why? Because there are different parts of your being at war for those extra rolls. Diets generally call for a restriction of food. The body sees this as if it's being starved or punished.

CHAPTER 4: THE FANTASY OF DENIAL

While the mind delights in the fantasy that denial will be effective, the body, which is more practical, tells each cell, "Now, look, we're in some kind of a famine. I need you to stretch those calories and make them count." So, the body finds a way to use fewer calories. Now, instead of the reduced calories creating weight loss, it just slows down the metabolism.

CHAPTER 5: CAN YOU LOSE WEIGHT WITHOUT DIETING?

1. Yes. You have to let go of the belief that food is the problem. (Whoa. Was I really willing to say that on paper? Yes. It was true.)
2. Food is a substitute for other things.
3. The body's main preoccupation is survival, and extra pounds aren't part of that plan unless you threaten your body with famine, also known as "willpower." (Include a list of medically supported health hazards to being overweight.)
4. Your body would never overeat!

CHAPTER 6: WHO'S EATING

We all have different aspects of ourselves, which are present at different times. Identifying which part of us craves all of this stuff that's not good for us will help you turn your struggle around.

CHAPTER 7: WHO'S IN CHARGE?

1. If your body would choose to eat to maintain health and the right weight, who or what part of you has an emotional relationship with food?

2. Before trying to answer that, can you, for the sake of this book, suspend disbelief and try on the idea that it's your emotions that drive your eating?
3. Comfortable? Stuffed? A little hungry? Eating is emotion-based, and you must take any judgment off the words we use to describe it.

CHAPTER 8: HOW EMOTIONS AND FOOD CONNECT

1. You are what you eat, mentally as well as physically.
2. If you have more body fat than you should, it's because the balance of nutrition is out of whack.
3. Thoughts are spiritual food – whatever you put into yourself has a consequence and a reaction. If you eat more than your body needs, it means you are not being nourished properly.
4. The real solution is to understand where you're not being nourished in other areas of your life.

CHAPTER 9: WHAT ARE YOU HUNGRY FOR?

1. To successfully create a healthy body, learn how to distinguish true hunger for food.
2. There are several types of hunger that have nothing to do with actually eating.
3. Try mindfulness, not self-criticism.
4. The next time you find yourself eating not in accordance with your plan, tune into the moment, and do research.
5. Ask yourself: Am I truly hungry? If so, eat until you feel satisfied. Ask yourself what "satisfied" means.

CHAPTER 10: THE MYTH OF SATISFACTION

1. The wisdom that you need to eat until satisfied is another error in reasoning revealed in language.
2. Human beings by their nature are never satisfied and have been conditioned to disrespect a feeling of satisfaction or contentment. So why would we want to attain something that we fundamentally disrespect? Satisfaction can cause anxiety.
3. What we need to do is have another goal: to nourish the body correctly and understand how that feels. Once accomplished, we can work from this baseline and see what the other elements are of eating and food.

CHAPTER 11: ARE YOU HUNGRY OR THIRSTY?

Half the battle to health is drinking enough plain water. We confuse thirst and hunger.

CHAPTER 12: THINK OF YOUR BODY AS IF IT WERE A CAR

1. The body is what gets "you" around the planet. Whether or not "you" are eternal, the body has a shelf life that can be improved by good self-care. Remember to think of your body as a car that gets you from place to place. If you take care of your car, you will never get a flat tire.
2. If you take care of your car, it will take care of you.
3. Your car has its own consciousness. It's like another person. Your feelings are part of the body. The brain is part of the body. Your mind is part of your soul but gets corrupted and sucked into the big collective mind. This is the part of you that can be influenced to make you feel bad and stop trusting yourself.

Appendix: Outline of *Just Dessert*

4. Try mindfulness, not self-criticism. The next time you find yourself eating not in accordance to your plan, tune into the moment, and do research. Ask yourself: Am I truly hungry? If so, eat until you feel satisfied. Ask yourself what satisfied means.

CHAPTER 13: DIET — WHY YOU HAVEN'T SUCCEEDED

Everyone is looking for the holy grail of weight control, and that's what the industry has done by catering to this fantasy and created a host of complicated diets, some of which are bad for your health.

CHAPTER 14: THE BASICS OF ANY WEIGHT-CONTROL PROGRAM

1. While it's important to manage the emotional aspects, the main problems are overcomplicating the mechanics and food-shaming. If you can separate emotion from food, and keep it simple, you will succeed and be free and healthy.
2. Sleep. Sleep will help you because you won't be using food to create false energy.

CHAPTER 15: EXERCISE, SELF-DISCIPLINE, AND SEX

1. Exercise promotes weight control by burning calories and adding muscle and self-esteem. Sex does the same and more.
2. Portion control — get in the habit of imagining your stomach, which can only hold so much food at one time. You can gauge this by making a fist, because that is roughly how big your stomach is. If you can look at what you're

about to eat and drink and imagine how it will fit inside your stomach, you will have a new level of control.

3. Drink water, one glass for every cup of tea or coffee, plus a quart a day.

4. Eat mostly vegetables, proteins, and fats. Fruit in moderation. Avoid processed food.

5. There is no magic except for consistency.

6. Most importantly, eat dessert first. Even if it's only a bite, rewards are a critical component of our happiness.

FOOD PLANS

A Week
Two Weeks
A Month
Maintenance

Dessert Recipes 1–11

1. Bad Girl Pie
2. Good Girl Pie
3. Maria's Flan
4. Dulce de Leche
5. Suzanne's Easy Apple Tart
6. Tres Leches Layer Cake with Blueberries and Raspberries
7. Liz's Bread Pudding
8. Elizabeth's Chocolate Coconut Pudding Pie
9. Good Girl Apple Tart (low-cal, low–carb, keto)
10. Good Girl Chocolate Coconut Pudding Pie
11. Norman's Hunting Cookies

Bad Girl Pie

Ingredients

- 3 to 4 cups of candy, such as miniature Reese's Peanut Butter Cups, Rolo Minis, chocolate bars, cookies, and M&Ms
- 1 ready-made graham-cracker pie crust
- ½ cup bourbon
- 4 tbsp. honey
- Ice cream
- Cool Whip or whipped cream
- Chocolate syrup and extra candy

Directions

1. Preheat oven to 350° F.
2. Coarsely chop candy with a stand mixer or food processor.
3. Fill pie crust with candy.
4. Mix bourbon with honey or sweetener and pour over filling.
5. Bake until everything is melted, approximately 30 minutes.
6. Remove pie, let cool.
7. Top with ice cream, Cool Whip or whipped cream, chocolate syrup, and the extra candy.

Good Girl Pie

Ingredients

- 3 to 4 cups of sugar-free candy
- 1 ready-made graham-cracker pie crust
- ½ cup bourbon
- Stevia or other sweetener
- Low-cal Cool Whip
- Sugar-free chocolate syrup

Directions

1. Preheat oven to 350° F.
2. Coarsely chop candy with stand mixer or food processor.
3. Fill pie crust with candy.
4. Mix bourbon with sweetener and pour over filling.
5. Bake until everything is melted, approximately 30 minutes.
6. Remove pie, let cool.
7. Top with Cool Whip and sugar-free chocolate syrup.

Maria's Flan

Ingredients

- 1 cup sugar
- 12 oz. whole milk
- 12 oz. heavy cream
- 3 large egg whites, one whole egg
- 1 vanilla pod, halved
- 1 tablespoon of orange zest
- 1 teaspoon salt
- Dulce de leche (recipe below)
- A strawberry or blueberries
- Low-cal Cool Whip

Directions

1. Preheat oven to 350° F.
2. Add sugar to a cast-iron frying pan over medium-low heat, stirring continuously for 4 to 6 minutes or until melted into a deep-brown caramel.
3. Pour into eight ramekins before caramel sets, swirling it around to coat the bottom of each dish.
4. Mix the milk, cream, eggs, vanilla, orange zest, and salt in a medium bowl.
5. Pour the mixture into ramekins and place them in a large roasting pan.
6. Fill the roasting pan with 1 to 2 inches of warm water.
7. Bake 30 to 40 minutes, or until a knife inserted in the center comes out clean.
8. Remove the flan from the roasting pan and let cool.

Maria's Flan

9. Run a spatula around the edge of each ramekin, then flip it upside down to release the flan onto a plate.

10. To serve, garnish with a dollop of dulce de leche, a strawberry or blueberries, and top with Cool Whip.

Dulce de Leche

Ingredients

- 2 tbsp. water
- 4 cups whole milk
- 1 pinch baking soda
- 1 ½ cups sugar
- 1 tsp. pure vanilla extract

Directions

1. Pour the 2 tbsp. of water into the bottom of a saucepan and thoroughly wet the bottom of the pan with the water.
2. Pour in the milk, baking soda, sugar, and vanilla.
3. Heat over medium heat while stirring to dissolve the sugar.
4. Once the preparation begins to boil, lower the heat and simmer, stirring occasionally for about 45 minutes. By this point, the preparation should have thickened.
5. Continue cooking, stirring very frequently until the mixture turns golden brown.
6. Stop cooking when the consistency suits you. However, make sure the mixture does not get too thick as it hardens a little while cooling.
7. Pour the mixture into a glass jar.
8. Dulce de leche can be kept in the refrigerator for up to two weeks.

Suzanne's Easy Apple Tart

Ingredients

For the filling:

- 5 apples, peeled, cored, and sliced
- ⅓ cup packed brown sugar
- Juice of ½ lemon
- 1 tsp. ground cinnamon
- 1 tsp. pure vanilla extract
- Pinch of salt
- 1 tbsp. granulated sugar
- 2 tbsp. butter, cut into small cubes
- Melted apricot preserves

For the crust:

- 1 ⅓ cups all-purpose flour
- ¼ cup packed brown sugar
- ½ tsp. kosher salt
- ¼ tsp. ground cinnamon
- 10 tbsp. butter, melted

Directions

1. Preheat oven to 350° F.
2. In a large bowl, toss apples, brown sugar, lemon juice, cinnamon, vanilla, and salt together.
3. In a large bowl, whisk together flour, brown sugar, salt, and cinnamon. Add melted butter and stir until dough forms. Press mixture into a 10-inch or 11-inch tart pan with a removable bottom, pressing until dough is smooth.

Bad Girl Pie

4. Arrange apples over crust. Stack a dozen or so slices together tightly, then place them into the crust cut side down, shingled slightly. Sprinkle with granulated sugar and dot top with butter. Bake until crust is golden and apples are tender, about 1 hour.
5. Brush with melted apricot preserves and let cool slightly before slicing and serving.

Tres Leches Layer Cake with Blueberries and Raspberries

Ingredients

- 1 cup (2 sticks) unsalted butter, softened
- 2 cups white granulated sugar
- 10 eggs
- 2 tsp. vanilla extract
- 3 cups all-purpose flour
- 2 tsp. baking powder
- 2 cups whole milk
- 1 12 oz. can evaporated milk
- 1 14 oz. can sweetened condensed milk
- 1 pint heavy whipping cream
- 2 tbsp. powdered sugar
- 1 tbsp. powdered milk
- 1 tsp. vanilla extract

Directions

1. Preheat oven to 350° F, and butter and flour three 8-inch round pans.
2. In the bowl of a standing mixer fitted with the paddle attachment, beat together the butter and sugar until light and fluffy.
3. Add in the eggs, one at a time, until all incorporated. Stir in the vanilla.
4. Beat in the flour and baking powder a bit at a time until a smooth batter forms. Divide the batter between the three pans and bake for 25 to 30 minutes, until a toothpick inserted in the center comes out clean.

5. Let cakes cool to room temperature, then take out of the pans and use a large knife to level out the tops.
6. Place the cakes on cooling racks, and place the racks on top of cookie sheets. These will work to pick up any stray soaking liquid that might come out!
7. In a medium bowl, whisk together the whole milk, evaporated milk and sweetened condensed milk. Prick the cakes all over with a fork and, using a ladle or large spoon, pour the milk mixture onto each cake a bit at a time. I suggest pouring on 1 to 2 ladlefuls, giving it a couple of minutes, and then adding more. This minimizes the spilling and dripping from the cakes! Repeat until all of the mixture has been used up.
8. Place the cakes in the refrigerator overnight.
9. The next day, when ready to assemble, make the whipped cream. In the bowl of a stand mixer fitted with the whisk, beat the heavy cream to soft peaks. Add in the powdered sugar, powdered milk, and vanilla, and beat until stiff.
10. Grab one of your cakes, place on a cake stand or platter and spread one-third of the whipped cream on top. Repeat with the other two cakes, and finish the cake with the remaining whipped cream and berries. Serve immediately and store leftovers in the refrigerator.

Liz's Bread Pudding

Ingredients

- 2 cups half-and-half
- ¼ cup butter
- 2 eggs, lightly beaten
- ½ cup brown sugar
- 1 tsp. ground cinnamon
- 1 tsp. vanilla extract
- 1 tsp. ground nutmeg
- ¼ tsp. salt
- 6 cups soft bread cubes (about 6 slices of bread)
- ½ cup raisins
- ½ cup chopped walnuts
- Whipping (heavy) cream, if desired

Directions

1. Heat oven to 350° F. In a two-quart saucepan, heat half-and-half and butter over medium heat until butter is melted and half-and-half is hot.
2. In a large bowl, mix eggs, brown sugar, cinnamon, vanilla, nutmeg, and salt. Stir in bread cubes, raisins, and walnuts. Stir in milk mixture. Pour into ungreased 1.5-quart casserole.
3. Bake uncovered 40 to 45 minutes or until knife inserted one inch from edge comes out clean. Serve warm with whipped cream.

Elizabeth's Chocolate Coconut Pudding Pie

Ingredients

- 1 package Oreos
- ½ stick butter
- 1 cup shredded coconut, divided
- 2 packages instant chocolate pudding mix
- 2 ¾ cups heavy cream
- 1 container Cool Whip, divided
- Chocolate syrup

Directions
For the crust:

1. Blend Oreos into crumbs.
2. Add butter.
3. Add ½ cup shredded coconut.
4. Press into a pie pan.

For the filling:

1. Beat the pudding mix and heavy cream together.
2. Add Cool Whip.
3. Spread filling over crust.

For the topping:

1. Spread Cool Whip over pie.
2. Sprinkle remaining coconut.
3. Drizzle on chocolate syrup.

Good Girl Apple Tart
(low-cal, low-carb, keto)

Ingredients
For the crust:

- 6 tbsp. butter, melted
- 2 cups superfine blanched almond flour
- ⅓ cup erythritol / monk fruit / stevia sweetener
- 1 tsp. ground cinnamon

For the filling:

- 3 cups thinly sliced Granny Smith apples (peeled and cored)
- ½ tsp. lemon juice
- ¼ cup butter
- ½ tsp. ground cinnamon
- Pinch of nutmeg
- ¼ cup erythritol / monk fruit / stevia sweetener

For the topping:

- 1 tsp. sugar-free apple or apricot jelly
- ¼ teaspoon ground cinnamon

Directions
For the crust:

1. Preheat the oven to 350° F.
2. Combine the melted butter, almond flour, sweetener, and cinnamon in a medium-size bowl.
3. Stir with a fork until well combined and crumbly.

4. Press the crust dough firmly into a 10-inch springform pan. Create a rim about one-half inches high up the sides of the pan, using your fingers or the back of a metal teaspoon to measure.
5. Pre-bake the crust for 5 minutes.

For the tart:

1. Combine the sliced apples and lemon juice in a medium bowl.
2. Place the sliced apples evenly across the top of the crust in a circular pattern. Press the apples down lightly when done.
3. Combine the butter, cinnamon, nutmeg, and sweetener in a small bowl and microwave for one minute. Whisk until smooth and brush or spoon evenly over the top of the apples.
4. Bake the tart for 30 minutes.
5. Remove the tart and gently press the apples down flat with the back of a spoon or spatula.
6. Return to the oven and bake for another 20 minutes.
7. Remove from the oven.

For the topping:

1. Combine the cinnamon and jelly. Microwave until liquid.
2. Brush lightly over the top of the tart.
3. Serve warm or chilled.

Good Girl Chocolate Coconut Pudding Pie

Ingredients

- 1 ½ cups cold 1 percent low-fat milk
- 1 (1 oz.) package sugar-free instant chocolate pudding mix
- 6 oz. Oreo-cookie prepared pie crusts or graham-cracker crust (your choice)
- 1 8 oz. container fat-free Cool Whip
- ¼ cup coconut flakes

Directions

1. Pour milk into a large mixing bowl.
2. Add dry pudding mix.
3. Beat with wire whisk for 2 minutes.
4. Spoon half of pudding mix into crust.
5. Gently stir 1 cup of Cool Whip into remaining pudding mix still in the bowl.
6. Spoon over pudding layer in the crust.
7. Top with the remaining Cool Whip and sprinkle with coconut flakes.
8. Refrigerate at least 3 hours.
9. Store in refrigerator.

Norman's Hunting Cookies

Ingredients

- 1 cup salted butter (2 sticks)
- 1 cup packed brown sugar
- ½ cup granulated sugar
- 2 large eggs
- 2 tsp. vanilla extract
- 2 cups all-purpose flour
- 1 tsp. baking soda
- ½ tsp. ground cinnamon
- 1 ½ cups old-fashioned rolled oats
- ½ cup chopped walnuts
- ½ chopped pecans
- 1 cup coconut flakes
- 2 cups dark chocolate chips

Directions

1. Brown 1 stick of butter by melting it in a medium saucepan over medium heat, then let it cook and bubble for an additional 3 to 5 minutes or until the foam and butter underneath is golden brown.
2. Immediately transfer it to a large, heatproof mixing bowl and swirl a few times to help it stop browning. Let cool to room temperature, about 30 minutes. Meanwhile, allow the remaining stick of butter to soften.
3. Preheat the oven to 350° F.
4. Add the softened stick of butter, brown sugar, and granulated sugar to the mixing bowl with the browned butter. Beat with a stand or hand mixer on medium-high speed until lightened in color and texture, 2 to 3 minutes.

Norman's Hunting Cookies

5. Reduce the mixer speed to low. Add the eggs and vanilla, then beat until smooth, scraping the sides and bottom of the bowl as needed.

6. Whisk to combine the flour, baking soda, and cinnamon in another medium bowl. Add it to the butter mixture in three increments, mixing on low speed in between, until fully incorporated. Scrape the sides and bottom of the bowl as needed. Add the oats, walnuts, pecans, coconut flakes, and chocolate chips, and mix on low speed or stir with a spatula to combine.

7. Line two large baking sheets with parchment paper. Using a 2-tablespoon-size cookie scoop, place cookie dough onto the baking sheet, leaving about two inches of space in between each. Bake for 12 to 14 minutes, or until golden brown and dry-looking on top. Let the cookies cool for two minutes on the baking sheet, then transfer to a cooling rack to cool completely. Sprinkle with flaky salt to finish, if you like.

About the Author

Marilyn Horowitz is an award-winning author, retired New York University professor, TV-show creator, and writing coach, working with successful novelists, produced screenwriters, and award-winning filmmakers. Two of her students have been nominated for an Emmy®, and a third won a Peabody. Horowitz received the coveted New York University Award for Teaching Excellence in 2004 and has an active online audience, including 2500 readers of her weekly blog. Since 1998, she has taught hundreds of aspiring writers to complete their feature-length screenplays, novels, and TV pilots using her trademarked writing method, The Horowitz System®. Horowitz has also written five books on screenwriting, two of which are used as textbooks at New York University. Recently, she served as associate producer of *Hunter Is F**cked*, an award-winning comedy short based on the life of gonzo journalist Hunter S. Thompson, and as associate producer of *The Heart Stays*, a Native American drama that will be released in April 2024. Her latest book, *Word of the Day: Transform Your Writing in 15 Minutes a Day*, will be available in bookstores in April of 2024. In addition, she has written two novels, *The Book of Zev*, published in 2016, and *Bad Girl Pie*, to be released in 2025. She's an active member of New York Women in Film & Television (NYWIFT), serves on the board of the Florence Belsky Charitable Foundation, and co-chairs their monthly writers'-group meetings.

ROUNDFIRE
BOOKS

FICTION

Put simply, we publish great stories. Whether it's literary or popular, a gentle tale or a pulsating thriller, the connecting theme in all Roundfire fiction titles is that once you pick them up you won't want to put them down.
If you have enjoyed this book, why not tell other readers by posting a review on your preferred book site.

Recent bestsellers from Roundfire are:

The Bookseller's Sonnets
Andi Rosenthal

The Bookseller's Sonnets intertwines three love stories
with a tale of religious identity and mystery spanning
five hundred years and three countries.

Paperback: 978-1-84694-342-3 ebook: 978-184694-626-4

Birds of the Nile
An Egyptian Adventure

N.E. David

Ex-diplomat Michael Blake wanted a quiet birding trip
up the Nile – he wasn't expecting a revolution.

Paperback: 978-1-78279-158-4 ebook: 978-1-78279-157-7

Blood Profit$
The Lithium Conspiracy

J. Victor Tomaszek, James N. Patrick, Sr.

The blood of the many for the profits of the few... *Blood Profit$*
will take you into the cigar-smoke-filled room where American
policy and laws are really made.

Paperback: 978-1-78279-483-7 ebook: 978-1-78279-277-2

The Burden
A Family Saga

N.E. David

Frank will do anything to keep his mother and father
apart. But he's carrying baggage – and it might
just weigh him down ...

Paperback: 978-1-78279-936-8 ebook: 978-1-78279-937-5

The Cause
Roderick Vincent
The second American Revolution will be a
fire lit from an internal spark.
Paperback: 978-1-78279-763-0 ebook: 978-1-78279-762-3

Don't Drink and Fly
The Story of Bernice O'Hanlon: Part One
Cathie Devitt
Bernice is a witch living in Glasgow. She loses her way
in her life and wanders off the beaten track looking for the
garden of enlightenment.
Paperback: 978-1-78279-016-7 ebook: 978-1-78279-015-0

Gag
Melissa Unger
One rainy afternoon in a Brooklyn diner, Peter Howland
punctures an egg with his fork. Repulsed, Peter pushes
the plate away and never eats again.
Paperback: 978-1-78279-564-3 ebook: 978-1-78279-563-6

The Master Yeshua
The Undiscovered Gospel of Joseph
Joyce Luck
Jesus is not who you think he is. The year is 75 CE. Joseph
ben Jude is frail and ailing, but he has a prophecy to fulfil …
Paperback: 978-1-78279-974-0 ebook: 978-1-78279-975-7

On the Far Side, There's a Boy
Paula Coston
Martine Haslett, a thirty-something 1980s woman, plays hard
on the fringes of the London drag club scene until one night
which prompts her to sign up to a charity. She writes to a
young Sri Lankan boy, with consequences far and long.
Paperback: 978-1-78279-574-2 ebook: 978-1-78279-573-5

Tuareg
Alberto Vazquez-Figueroa
With over 5 million copies sold worldwide, *Tuareg* is a classic
adventure story from best-selling author Alberto Vazquez-
Figueroa, about honour, revenge and a clash of cultures.
Paperback: 978-1-84694-192-4

Readers of ebooks can buy or view any of these bestsellers by
clicking on the live link in the title. Most titles are published
in paperback and as an ebook. Paperbacks are available in
traditional bookshops. Both print and ebook formats are
available online.

Find more titles and sign up to our readers' newsletter at
www.collectiveinkbooks.com/fiction